WELCOME TO SEABREEZE FARM

JO BARTLETT

Boldwood

First published in Great Britain in 2021 by Boldwood Books Ltd.

Copyright © Jo Bartlett, 2022

Cover Design by Debbie Clement Design

Cover photography: Shutterstock

A CIP catalogue record for this book is available from the British Library.

Paperback ISBN 978-1-80162-015-4

Hardback ISBN 978-1-80162-014-7

Ebook ISBN 978-1-80162-017-8

Kindle ISBN 978-1-80162-016-1

Boldwood Books Ltd
23 Bowerdean Street
London SW6 3TN
www.boldwoodbooks.com

For the Joneses, how every family should be.

xx

1

'Come on Barry, just keep it together for two more miles and I promise to give you the total overhaul you deserve. It's pay day tomorrow and I'll take you straight down to the garage to see if they can patch you up again.' Ellie gave the steering wheel a gentle tap of encouragement as she spoke to the old Beetle, which was emitting what sounded like a strangled cry in response.

'I know I've been neglecting you, but it's not because I don't love you, just please don't break down in the tunnel.' As much as Ellie was terrified of the car finally spluttering to a halt amid the frantic flow of traffic in the Blackwall Tunnel, the thought that whatever was making Barry scream the way he was might do so much damage to the old car that he'd have to be scrapped made her want to cry. He'd been hers for more than ten years, since her great-aunt Hilary had finally decided that she needed a sensible car – one she could get in and out of more easily. Hilary had owned Barry from new and every time Ellie had visited the donkey sanctuary her aunt owned, as a little girl, she'd sat in the driving seat of the stationary car and pretended to go on big adventures behind the wheel.

They'd had some real-life adventures too, over the last decade or so, but the running repairs an old car like Barry needed were expensive. Ellie's fiancé, Rupert, had said more times than she could count that the price of properly repairing Barry didn't make sense and that it would be more cost effective to scrap him, but the little car had held on – with patch up repairs done on the cheap – at least until now. He deserved TLC after all those years of faithful service and she'd let him down. Maybe with the promotion she was about to get, she'd finally be able to persuade Rupert that Barry was worth the investment. There were some things you couldn't put a price on.

'Come on sweetheart, nearly there I promise.' Ellie could see a chink of daylight up ahead, where the tunnel would open up and she'd only be minutes away from her office at Canary Wharf and the coveted underground parking space she'd practically had to sell a kidney to secure. She normally got the train to work, but with the biggest meeting of her life scheduled for an hour's time, and Rupert taking her out for dinner to celebrate her promotion afterwards, there was no way she wanted to risk arriving looking like a crumpled mess; always a risk with the joys of public transport to contend with. But as Barry started to judder and kangaroo hop towards the end of the tunnel, Ellie was getting hotter and sweatier than she would have in even the most packed of tube trains. Barry was dying and no amount of begging him to just hang on was going to help.

'Come on Barry, *please* don't!' Her plea was drowned out by a final sputter from the old Beetle as he came to a halt just a few metres from the end of the tunnel, earning Ellie a chorus of honks from the cars that had thankfully managed to skid to a halt behind her. Putting her hazard lights on, she dropped her head to the steering wheel. The decision to cancel roadside recovery had seemed like a good choice when she was looking at every possible way to save money, but right now it felt like one of the stupidest things she'd ever done. Rupert was working in Canary Wharf too, and the obvious thing to do would have been to ring her fiancé, but he didn't appreciate interruptions at work. After the last time, she'd agreed not to do it again unless it was literally life or death.

Ellie's head shot up in response to aggressive knocking on the passenger window and she leant over and wound it down just a fraction.

'What the hell are you doing? I nearly smashed my van straight into you.' The man standing with his back against the tunnel wall crouched down and peered through the gap in the window. He had a neck tattoo of a wolf's head and the sort of heavy set physique that would have made Ellie quicken her pace if she'd bumped into him on a dark night.

'My car's died.' She hated herself for the tears that sprung to her eyes, but she couldn't help it. The thought that not getting Barry to the garage earlier might mean he could never be fixed was just too much. He was her last link to Great-aunt Hilary, now that she was gone. The donkey sanctuary she'd run for years – where all of Ellie's best childhood memories had been made – had been passed on to a charity, just as Hilary had always said it would.

'Don't cry love, I know it's scary breaking down in traffic like this. The same thing happened to my daughter last week, but me and Jim can give you a push to safety. I'll just go and get him out of the van.' The man's face had transformed from a sneer to a gentle smile. 'We'll have you somewhere safe in minutes, don't worry.'

'Thank you.' The man's kindness just made Ellie cry even harder for having judged him straight away just from the way he looked.

'Right okay, love, we've got the hazard lights on our van and so have the two cars behind us, so that should hold the traffic in this lane back until we can get you out of the tunnel. There's a hotel just past the end and you'll be safe there until you can get the car sorted.'

'Thank you so much.' It was all Ellie seemed capable of saying, but it didn't even come close to expressing how grateful she was. Pushing her wavy blonde hair away from her face, she attempted a wobbly smile.

'It's no problem at all; someone did the same for my daughter and I'm sure your dad would want someone to help you.'

Ellie had to bite her lip to stop the tears from flowing even faster. Even if he had been alive, her father wouldn't have recognised her if he'd been sitting in the van behind her.

'What do I need to do?'

'Just put the car in neutral and steer towards the slip road on the left when you see the hotel, me and Jim will take care of the rest.'

'Okay.' Ellie did as she was told, trying not to let thoughts of her father crowd into her head; she had enough to worry about for one day already. Not only was her beloved car limping towards the end of quite possibly the final time she'd ever drive it, but she was going to be late for the most important meeting of her life too. It was a big part of the five-year plan that Rupert had outlined when they'd got engaged and the start of a life that would guarantee never having to choose between eating and heating again – the way she and her mother had so many times over the years. Rupert had promised her they could have anything they wanted in life, if they hit every target on their plan, and the one thing she wanted most was to make sure her mother never had to go without again. She'd do almost anything to make sure that didn't happen.

'Me and Jim are going to have to get back to our van now, love, but are you sure you're going to be okay from here?' Ellie's rescuer, whose name she still didn't know, raised a questioning eyebrow as she got out of the car, once it was safely off the road.

'I'll be fine, thanks to you. Have you got a card? I'd love to send you something to say thank you.'

'Save your money for sorting out that lovely old car; it's a classic but it looks like it needs a bit of work. Look after yourself too, love.' Ellie noticed for the first time that he had the name Clive printed on the front of his shirt and, as he turned away, she realised the name of the plumbing firm he worked for was printed on the back. It was one thing saving every penny she could to fit in with Rupert's plan, but she'd been brought up too well not to make sure that Clive and Jim's kindness was repaid.

'Thanks again!' Ellie called out and then glanced at her watch. She was going to have to beg for more kindness from the hotel's receptionist and hope she'd be allowed to leave Barry in the car park until she could sort something out. Then she was going to have to run to the meeting, even if it meant she ended up looking as though she'd been dragged through a hedge backwards after all.

'You're late Ellie; you've missed the meeting.' Will Naysmith, Ellie's boss, was Director of Acquisitions and Lending at the investment bank where she worked and had a tone as tense as a tightly wound coil. 'Can I see you in my office?'

It was a command rather than a request, and she nodded, her heart rate quickening at the prospect that she might just have blown her big promotion. Even worse than that was the thought of telling Rupert. Will shook his head and glanced up and down at her dishevelled appearance, as he took a seat behind his desk.

Even at the best of times, he had a way of looking at her that left her wondering whether he was trying to imagine what she looked like without clothes on, or whether he was planning to read her the riot act. Today was almost certainly going to be the latter, but, either way, it made Ellie's skin crawl.

'Take a seat and get your breath back. By the look of you you've clearly had quite the morning.' Will smiled frequently, but they never quite reached his eyes, which were shark-like, as though he was always on the lookout for the next opportunity. His office was a status symbol, all dark furniture, with black leather and shiny chrome, and the other chairs were much lower than his, so that anyone sitting in them would be at an immediate disadvantage. 'So what happened this morning?'

'My car broke down in the Blackwall Tunnel and luckily two really nice strangers pushed me off the road, but then I had to run to get here and I didn't expect the meeting to be over so quickly. I'm really sorry.'

'These things happen and usually for a good reason I've come to find. You're okay are you, and the car's all sorted?' Although Will asked the question, she knew he wasn't really interested, so she just nodded and returned his smile. 'Good, good, because I've got some news for you.'

'Oh?' Ellie tried to hold down the surge of hope that had fluttered in her chest. Maybe this was it, the moment where she'd sign off another bullet point in Rupert's plan. The idea of being second in command to Will, heading up the team assessing struggling businesses, which helped Will and the other directors decide which to buy up as part of the investment bank's strategy and which to cease lending to, definitely didn't make her heart sing, but the assistant director's salary would change everything.

Ellie tried not to think about how many more businesses she might contribute to closing down when their credit was withdrawn, or how many would get taken over when the bank bought their debts at a discount and then asset stripped them to pay off the reduced debt and make a profit on top. She'd already been involved in supporting the team's work after moving departments to get a higher salary, but as Assistant Director she'd be directly contributing to the decisions about which businesses to target.

Rupert worked in a similar role for a firm of venture capitalists at the other end of the spectrum, buying majority stakes in thriving small businesses to grow them into franchises or turn them into much bigger businesses, which often ended up looking almost unrecognisable from what they'd started out as. Rupert's firm had been involved in an exposé from one of their investments: a woman who'd set up a childcare business which had ended up being franchised and which she claimed had lost every principle she'd created the business to uphold. Rupert had written her off as bitter but reading the article had made Ellie uncomfortable and she'd shoved the newspaper into the recycling, pushing her doubts about the jobs they both did to the back of her mind.

'We're letting you go.' The smile was still plastered on Will's face, even as the realisation hit Ellie that he was telling her she was about to lose her job.

'I don't understand. I know I was late but—'

'It's not just about being late, it's about really wanting this enough.'

'You said I was up for a promotion?' Ellie was determined not to cry again, she'd already shed enough tears for one day, but she could picture the look on Rupert's face when she told him all too clearly. It was like a game of snakes and ladders, where she'd almost reached the top of the longest ladder and now Will was sending her hurtling back down to the bottom. There was no room for error in Rupert's five-year plan, not to mention the fact that it was down to her to pay all the bills at home until her mother was fully recovered from her knee replacement. Getting her mother back on her feet in both senses of the phrase had been part of Ellie's own plan, something that Rupert didn't need to know about, and it was why she'd refused to move in with him so far. She wasn't prepared to do that until she was certain her mum would be okay and it was only in the last week or so that her mother had been able to stop using the stick she'd relied on since her operation. Looking into Will's eyes, worries about her mum knocked even Rupert's reaction way down on her list of concerns.

'You *were* up for a promotion. You and Rich Hind. Like I said, it was down to who wanted it more.' Will shrugged. 'He was at the meeting on time, ready with a list of businesses we should look at. Even if you'd been on time, you wouldn't have had that, would you, Ellie?'

'No, but that's only because—'

He cut her off again before she could finish. 'It's because you're not really cut out for this Ellie, are you? We both know that, but the board are under pressure to promote more women.' Will pulled a face, as if the idea was absurd. 'But you being late was a sign that I should stick to my guns and promote the person who I really think is best for this job. Like I said, things happen for a reason.'

'So I was only ever going to be some token tick box?' Heat rushed up Ellie's neck.

'Something like that.' Will shrugged again. 'It's nothing personal. Rich just has the drive we're looking for and he's got a plan for restructuring the whole team.'

'Oh and I suppose I'm not part of that plan?'

'Rich doesn't think it would be a good idea. We don't want anything compromising our goals.' Will suddenly sounded so much like Rupert that it made her stomach turn. 'Bad blood in the team is the last thing we need, so we both think a transfer to another department would be for the best. Somewhere like corporate services, organising events and the like would probably be far more up your street. Rich says you've got a degree in events management – it's listed on your LinkedIn apparently.'

'He's clearly done his homework.' Ellie clenched her jaw, determined not to give Will the satisfaction of seeing her cry. He and Rich had probably cooked up this whole plan between them and, if she hadn't known better, she wouldn't have put it past them sabotaging Barry too. 'And what if I don't want to move to an events management role?'

'Redundancy I suppose, but we're probably looking at a compromise agreement, seeing as your old role will still technically exist. You just won't be in it.'

'But I'd get the usual redundancy rate, even with a compromise agreement?' Ellie had never been a maths whizz, but she was doing sums in her head to work out just how much of a cushion a pay-out from the bank might give her. She'd been there for almost ten years, working her way up from a customer services role she'd enjoyed far more than the past three years in Will's department, but then she'd only ever made the move at Rupert's suggestion. She might finally have been earning a decent salary, but the truth was she'd hated every moment, and with most of the money going to pay off her father's legacy of debt, and what was left being set aside in savings to fulfil Rupert's plan, there'd been almost nothing in the way of fun for a very long time. Ellie's whole life for the past few years had been so focussed on trying to wipe clean the slate of the past and to prepare for a future that always seemed just out of reach, that she'd forgotten to live in the present.

'Yes, but you should think this through. Events management

is a good fit for you, you've got the people skills, you just don't have the sort of business head needed to be my deputy.'

'Or a pair of testicles?'

'It's got nothing to do with—' This time it was Ellie's turn to cut Will off.

'I don't care what your story for making this decision is going to be, we both know the truth and I think taking the compromise agreement is best all round, don't you?' She was already getting up from her seat and heading towards where his PA sat, just outside the glass wall of his office. She wanted it put in motion, before Will had the chance to somehow take away the option. 'I'll get Janey to give HR a call and sort out the details, but I know the bank's policy, I've seen enough people paid off over the years to get straight out. Let's face it, profits always come first and we wouldn't want anyone hanging around who might cause trouble, would we? I can have my desk cleared by lunchtime.'

With shaking legs, Ellie pushed open Will's office door, taking the first steps towards a new life that there wasn't even a five-minute plan for, let alone a five-year one.

2

Ellie had attempted to invoke the life or death phone call to Rupert, but it had just gone straight to voice mail. By the time she'd got out of the building after her meeting with Will, she'd begun to think it might actually be life or death, because she'd barely been able to catch her breath since leaving Will's office.

Whenever Ellie felt overwhelmed there was only one option – to do something about it. Discovering by accident the amount of debt her father had offset against the tiny cottage she shared with her mother, Karen, after he walked out, had almost floored her. But instead she'd gone straight out and got her first job, at the tender age of fourteen. It hadn't made a lot of difference in the end, but it had helped Ellie feel as though she was taking some sort of control.

Karen had spent years working every hour that God sent to try and stop them losing the house. There were countless hours on her feet, working as a cook and sometimes waiting tables after she'd already done a ten hour shift in the kitchen, but in the end it hadn't been enough and they'd had to concede defeat. There was a tiny bit of luck on their side, when the couple who'd bought their cottage turned out to be investors looking for tenants. So, to the outside world, nothing much had changed when ownership of the cottage had transferred to them. But it was another little bit of security that Ellie had lost from her life; the knowledge that at any point their landlords could serve them notice to move on and suddenly home wasn't the safety net it had always seemed.

Even with the proceeds from the sale of the house, they hadn't been able to wipe out all of debts her father had accrued from years of gambling and Karen had continued working two jobs, insisting that Ellie went to university like she'd always dreamed of her doing. Ellie had stayed local to keep the costs down, but she'd still racked up new debts, and sometimes it felt as if they were never going to get their heads above water again. When she'd met Rupert, she'd seen a glimpse of another life. With his ambition, and a whole route planned out to get where he wanted to go, anything had seemed possible and he'd swept her off her feet.

They'd had things in common too; Rupert might have been born with a silver spoon in his mouth, but he'd known what it was like to have all of that taken away from him. His father had blown the family fortune on bad investments and a resulting reliance on cocaine. In the grip of his addiction, Rupert had been booted out of his boarding school for non-payment of fees and his life of privilege had evaporated almost overnight. He'd told Ellie, not long after they first met, that getting back that lifestyle was what drove him to work as hard as he did and that he'd do whatever it took to make sure he never felt like that again.

Ellie's idea of a comfortable life might have been a million miles away from Rupert's, but it was as though she'd found a kindred spirit the night they'd had that conversation. She'd found herself dreaming of being in a position where she could make sure Karen had whatever she wanted. So when Rupert had proposed, just six months into their relationship, it had been easy to accept. He represented a future free from worrying about money and she'd found herself clinging to that, despite the unease she'd sometimes felt about the rigidity of his plans and how long their engagement had turned out to be as a result. It was just because she was so unfamiliar with having a plan all set out, when she'd spent her whole life lurching from one crisis to another, plugging up holes along the way.

After her engagement, Ellie's mother had finally been able to reduce her hours enough to start up the catering business she'd always wanted to have, but then the years of spending all day on her feet had caught up with her and the doctors had said she'd needed both knees replacing. She was still recovering from the second operation and able to spend a bit more time on her feet every day. Ellie couldn't lose sight of making that dream come true and making sure that the future was brighter for both of them, which meant she needed to get another job as soon as possible.

When Rupert hadn't picked up her call, she'd gone from recruitment agency to recruitment agency registering her interest, before sitting in a coffee shop, searching online for jobs, and nursing the same latte until the barista started giving her a death stare. Rupert would be finishing work soon and she was supposed to be meeting him at his flat in an hour's time before heading out to dinner, but she needed to see him now.

'What are you doing here?' Rupert put his arms around her, enveloping her in a cloud of expensive aftershave that she could taste on her tongue, as she struggled to keep hold of the heavy bag she was holding. But she felt better just for seeing him. Her imagination had run wild all day about how he might react to her news and he'd become almost a shadowy figure in her mind, as if she might somehow have dreamed him up. She'd decided to wait outside his office for him to finish work, so she could get the reassurance she needed that little bit sooner.

'I just wanted to see you.' Tears were sliding out of the corners of her eyes again, but Rupert didn't seem to notice.

'Because you couldn't wait to start celebrating your success?' He planted a kiss on top of her head. 'My little superstar, Assistant Director at J D Merlon.'

'I—' Ellie couldn't seem to form the right shape with her mouth to enable her to say the words out loud. 'Barry broke down in the Blackwall Tunnel.'

'It's about time you scrapped that old car anyway. With a job like you've got now you can definitely afford to get something more suited to your position, without compromising our savings plan by throwing away a fortune on an old banger like that. We should easily be able to afford to buy the first property to flip before the end of the year.' Rupert had that faraway look in his eye, the one he always seemed to get when he talked about their plans. It was as if he was actually seeing them come to life, somewhere in the distance, just beyond where they were standing now.

Property development was a key part of his plan – buying one outright at first and then doing it up, selling it for a profit, before buying the next two, with a goal to keep multiplying until they made serious money. It was the same business model that Rupert's grandfather had built a fortune on, the fortune his father had flushed away, but they needed well-paid day jobs to support them financially in the meantime. Suddenly telling Rupert that they were about to take a massive step backwards was more daunting than ever. Talking about Barry's fate seemed like the lesser of two evils.

'I can't scrap the car. Aunt Hilary gave him to me.'

'I wish you'd stop talking about that rust bucket like it's living and breathing, instead of an inanimate object.'

'He's the last part of Aunt Hilary I've got.'

'Mores the pity. I'd have thought after all the time you and your mother spent visiting her, that she'd have left the farm to you and not some donkey charity. God knows she must have realised you could do with the money.'

'Her animals were what made her happiest after she lost her fiancé and she wanted to make sure they were okay when she was gone. We always knew that was going to happen and going to see her wasn't about what we might get out of it.' Ellie sniffed back the renewed threat of tears. It had been three months since Aunt Hilary's death, but because Ellie hadn't been back to Seabreeze Farm for more than two years, she could almost imagine her aunt was still there. It made it easier to cope with, but she couldn't keep up that pretence with the way Rupert was talking, and she couldn't keep up the rest of her pretence for any longer either. 'The reason I'm here is because I didn't get the promotion.'

'Oh very funny, El, you really got me going there.' Rupert feigned a look of shock and then rolled his eyes. 'You're going to have to do better than that to catch me out!'

'I'm not joking. Barry breaking down made me late for the meeting and, by the time I got to work, Will had already promoted someone else.'

'They can't do that. You should appeal. Giles Merlon told me himself that the board wanted more women in senior management. You were a shoo-in for that job.'

'Apparently not.' Ellie had to pick her fight for now. Rupert had clearly had a conversation with the chair of the board of directors at the bank about her, but she'd have to pick him up on that some other time. She'd known that Giles was an old school friend of Rupert's fathers, but the idea that he might have been trying to orchestrate her promotion, and yet she'd still failed, just made things even worse. It wasn't the time to have that out with him, though, because the fallout from telling him she'd left the bank was going to be enough to deal with for now.

'We'll put a rock solid case together for why this promotion should have gone to you, they won't have a leg to stand on.'

'I've already left.'

'What do you mean you've already left?'

'I've told them I'll accept a compromise agreement. I don't want to go back there, Rupert, not even if they change their mind and give me the promotion. I don't want to be given a job because they've been forced to do it and the truth is, I think Will was right, my heart's not in it and he was spot on when he said I'm not right for the job.'

'Now you're just being stupid. You can't afford to throw away all of our plans because of stubborn pride. Sometimes you just have to play the game.'

'Aren't you listening to what I'm saying?' Ellie was aware that her voice had got a lot louder, but Rupert's attempts to shoosh her were just making it worse. 'I don't want that job or anything else similar. I've been miserable for ages doing what I've been doing and, even though I felt like hyperventilating when I was walking out of Will's office, I felt freer than I have for years too.'

'Life isn't about feeling free, though, is it Ellie? At least not the life we want. We could sit on some hippy commune somewhere, foraging for food, but we've got a plan.'

'And where does how we feel figure in that bloody plan of yours? Or doesn't any of that matter?'

'We knew things were going to be tough sometimes.' Rupert reached out and tried to take hold of her hand, but she clamped it to her side. 'Come on El, we've talked about this, but we can't lose sight of our goals, otherwise what's it all for?'

'Do you know what, I'm not even sure any more. Sometimes I think it's the plan you're in love with and not me at all.'

'Don't be stupid.'

'Stop calling me stupid!' She was shouting now and there were people turning to look at them, but she couldn't help it.

'Let's go back to the flat and talk things through there. It might mean a few tweaks to the plan, but if you really want to try something else for a bit, I'm sure we can make it work, as long as the salary is up where it needs to be.'

'I just wanted you to tell me that it doesn't matter to you what I do for a job, that Will is an idiot who's going to regret not realising what I'm capable of and that you'll be right behind me whatever I decide to do next. Is that really too much to ask?'

'Ellie, you're obviously upset; let's go back to my place and we can talk about this properly when you calm down.'

'Calm down?' There was a nerve throbbing in Ellie's temple. 'Okay, I'll calm down, but I won't be doing it around you.'

'Come on, stop being stu—' Rupert caught himself half a second too late and Ellie was too quick for him when he tried to grab her wrist. 'Where are you going?'

'To the station.'

'What about your car?'

'I might be stupid in your eyes, but I'm perfectly capable of sorting someone out to pick up the car and I'm even more capable of getting the train home alone.' Not waiting for a reply, Ellie marched off towards the station as fast as she could. She was suddenly more desperate than she'd ever been to get home and she knew without a shadow of a doubt that home would always be where her mother was, whatever other plans she might try and make.

* * *

'Are you planning to push that button, or just stop everyone else getting off?'

The gruffness of the man's voice brought Ellie back to the present, and she dragged her gaze away from the poster advertising holidays on the south coast to look at him. The image had started to swim before her eyes anyway. After the day she'd had, there were only two people she wanted to talk to. One of them was her mother and the other was her great-aunt Hilary, who'd been able to help Ellie make sense of any situation and see a way through to the other side.

It was Hilary she'd confided in when she'd needed to persuade her mother to stop working so hard to try and save a house that would mean nothing if she killed herself in the process. Aunt Hilary had helped them both to realise it was just bricks and mortar, and as much as it had never felt quite the same living there after selling it, Hilary had been right. They needed each other far more than they needed a deed that said they owned the roof over their heads.

'Sorry?' It took a moment for her vision to adjust, but as the man who'd spoken to her finally came into sharp focus, there was no doubt his impatience was directed at her. His face was blotchy, and there was a muscle clenched in his cheek. Maybe he'd had a day from hell, like she had. That would have been enough to make anyone miserable.

'I asked if you're going to press that button when the train stops, because some of us have homes to go to, and I don't want to be stuck on here for any longer than I have to.' As he spoke, the train lurched to a halt and yellow lights illuminated the *open door* button.

'Yes, of course, sorry.' Mumbling a second apology as the

doors slid open, Ellie offered a smile, but the man had already pushed past her, snagging his briefcase on her tights as he did so. Fighting the urge to tell him what she thought of him, she made a silent wish instead that the next time he was in such a hurry, he'd catch a vital appendage in the sliding doors.

She stepped out after him onto the platform and caught her breath, forgetting all about him. Even the days' events seemed to lift off her shoulders, as if the breeze that had suddenly gathered pace on the platform had taken them with it, for a moment at least. In front of her was that same holiday advertisement she'd seen on the train – a meadow alive with wild flowers, perched high on the cliffs with a view across the English Channel – plastered across one of the station billboards.

'It could almost be Aunt Hilary's place.' She said the words out loud – the same thought that had been running through her head on the train – but she must've spoken much louder than she'd realised, because a couple of teenage girls turned round and sniggered, probably writing her off as just one more 'crazy' on the station platform. Staring down at her feet, Ellie waited until she was sure the girls had gone before looking back up at the poster. She needed to pretend for a little while that she was back at Seabreeze Farm and that at any moment her great-aunt would march across the meadow towards her, in a way that always belied her age.

Since Hilary had died, Ellie couldn't get the memories of Seabreeze Farm out of her head. Ellie hadn't been there – at least not to the house – for a couple of years. The funeral had been held half an hour away from the farm, in the town where Hilary had met her beloved fiancé, so they could finally be buried side by side. Now the realisation that she'd never get the chance to make one last to visit the farm, or Aunt Hilary, was hitting her all over again. Even the pain of the straps on the unwieldy bag digging into her shoulder couldn't detract from the burning sensation in her throat. One of the girls in the office had given her a spare bag when she'd been clearing her desk. Ten years at the same firm, and everything she'd had there could be stuffed into a bag for life.

As she left the station, Ellie's stomach gave a loud grumble in protest at the fact she hadn't eaten all day. The latte she'd stretched out for far longer than was fair to the coffee shop owner was the only thing she'd had. Not that it would do her any harm. Living with someone like Karen, who Ellie was convinced could win *The Great British Bake Off*, had one major downside. Just lately the waistbands of Ellie's work suits had started to leave angry red marks on her skin, and Rupert had made a comment about her getting *cuddly,* which almost certainly wasn't a compliment. Then there was the wedding, of course. At least there had been until today. Now she didn't know if she still had a fiancé. Worse than that, she wasn't even sure how she felt about the idea that it might all be over. It was just the shock of the day's events, it had to be.

Ellie's feet moved more swiftly along the pavement the closer she got to the place she called home – the place she'd called home for every one of her twenty-eight years – number twelve, The Copse. Of course, the neighbourhood had changed over the years, almost beyond recognition. The small patch of woodland that had once abutted their modest garden and given the road its name – where Ellie and the neighbours' children had passed hours swinging on an old tyre, strung up by one of the dads, or building dens between the closely woven trees – had long been flattened. In its place was a smart new estate shoe-horned into the plot, with houses that looked out across their own postage stamp-sized gardens and straight into the garden of number twelve.

Since a somewhat paunchy new neighbour had moved into the house that backed onto theirs, who insisted on mowing the lawn wearing only his underpants and a pair of trainers, Ellie had taken to averting her eyes when she pulled back her bedroom curtains, just in case. The patch of woodland and Aunt Hilary's farm had been the two mainstays of her childhood, and they'd seemed almost enchanted back then – only now they were both gone for good.

* * *

'What's wrong?' Ellie knew immediately that *something* was troubling her mother, before she even had a chance to blurt out her own news.

Karen was gripping a good quality, cream envelope in one hand, her brow furrowed in the distinctive way that had only meant one thing over the years – *official* news. In the past, it had always come from solicitors working for her father, detailing why he couldn't meet his financial obligations or dealing with the debt that he'd racked up against the house, without her mother's knowledge, until it was too late. Less frequently there'd be letters asking if he could see Ellie – in the years before she'd turned eighteen and been allowed to answer for herself. Not that her mother had ever stood in her way; she'd always encouraged the visits, but Ellie hadn't missed Karen crossing her fingers when she said that maybe he'd changed this time. He never had, though. He always let Ellie down in the end. Sometimes, it was after a week – but more often a month, or so, would pass with him visiting regularly, before something better would inevitably come along and he'd disappear again.

Ellie's grandmother would mutter about her father being a waste of space, her lips disappearing into a thin line of disapproval, but her mother had just smiled and squeezed Ellie's hand, saying they were lucky not to have to share her with anyone else. She'd been parent enough for both of them, and Ellie had never really missed her dad. She'd been surrounded by love, strong women, and her gentle grandfather, who was all the male role model she'd ever needed. Up until her latest operation, Karen had been working all hours, making fancy cakes for weddings, birthdays and every other type of special occasion, from their neat little two-up, two-down, with a downstairs bathroom extension, which was probably the only major change since the house had been built. Even now, with her mother being able to manage far less of the work she usually did, there was always some marvellous creation on the go, with delicate flowers made from icing that looked so real you could almost smell their scent.

When her grandparents had moved to Spain – the warmer weather being kinder to her grandfather's asthma – Ellie and her mother had kept an extra special eye on Great-Aunt Hilary. Not that she'd needed it. Right up until the end, and at the age of ninety-six, she'd still been driving and living alone at Seabreeze Farm. She'd insisted on meeting them in the town for the last couple of years, instead of at the farm. She'd drive down to her favourite tearoom in Kelsea Bay, declaring to anyone who'd listen that if meeting your family wasn't reason enough to indulge in a cream tea then nothing was. Ellie had lost count of the number of times she'd offered to pick Aunt Hilary up or take her back to the farm afterwards, but there'd always been some excuse or other why they couldn't do that. Ellie and Karen had suspected it was down to Hilary's pride at not being able to keep on top of the maintenance at the farm, in the way she had done when the donkey sanctuary had been open to the public. But any offers of help were vehemently rebuffed and Aunt Hilary always looked well in herself – clean and smart. So they'd decided to let her continue calling the shots, the way she always had done.

'Mum, did you hear me? What's wrong?' Ellie repeated the question, knowing that the official letter couldn't be from her father – he'd been dead for years.

'I think it must be about the house.' Karen had the same cornflower blue eyes as her daughter and right now they were wide with concern.

'What about the house?'

'I've known for a while, but I didn't want to say anything until I knew there was no chance of things changing.' Karen ran a hand through her hair, making it stick up like she'd been out in the wind. 'But I had an email from the landlord a while back, saying he'd agreed to sell the house to the developers who want to extend the new estate, if the rest of the homeowners in The Copse agree too. I knew that some of the neighbours were holding out, but if they got a good enough offer they might be able to be persuaded too. This must be the official notice to end the tenancy.'

'Why didn't you tell me?' Even as she asked the question, Ellie already knew the answer.

'Because you've shared far too many worries with me over the years that I wish you hadn't and I thought this time that maybe I wouldn't have to tell you, because you and Rupert would be married and living in your own place by then.'

'Oh Mum, I don't ever want you not to share your worries with me. We're a team, we'll *always* be a team.' Ellie slid her arm around her mother's waist. Whatever the letter said, they'd get through it, together, like they always did. Her job news could wait for now because she wasn't the only one who didn't always think a problem shared was a problem halved. 'I think we should just open it and get it over with, at least then we'll know what we're dealing with, instead of trying to imagine what it says. It might not even be what you think.'

'I suppose it could always be worse.' Karen laughed. 'It's probably telling me I've underpaid tax for the last ten years and that I owe them thousands.'

'Those sorts of letters come in brown envelopes. Go on then, open it.' Ellie waited as her mother pulled out the letter, tracking her gaze as it moved from side to side across the page and immediately spotting the tears that filled her eyes. 'Oh Mum, don't, it's going to be okay, I promise. We'll find somewhere else to live and I'm not going anywhere until you're all settled and properly back up on your feet.'

'Don't worry, love, it's not about the house.' Her mother finally looked up and gave her a wobbly smile. 'Only I can't get my head around it. Here, you have a look.' She passed Ellie the letter. 'See if I'm reading this all wrong.'

Ellie read the first few lines. 'It says that Aunt Hilary's left the farm jointly between the two of us.' Pulling out one of the pine chairs from the kitchen table, she sat down opposite her mother; her legs seemed to have lost the ability to hold her up. As she scanned the rest of the solicitor's letter, she shook her head. 'But it can't be right, it was supposed to go to charity. She always made that perfectly clear. Do you think Grandma might have known about it?'

'I'm going to try to call her now. After all, if the farm is going to family, by rights it should go to her – she's Hilary's closest relative, but she never mentioned anything about the farm when she came over for the funeral.' Karen mirrored her daughter and shook her head. 'Like you said, it just doesn't make sense.'

Karen picked up her mobile and pulled a face as the call to Ellie's grandmother went straight to voicemail. 'Hi Mum, it's only me. Can you give me a call when you get a minute please? We've had a letter about Seabreeze Farm and I wanted to know if Aunt Hilary had said anything to you. Okay, speak to you soon. Love you, bye.'

'Was there anything else in with the letter?' Ellie reached inside the envelope. There *was* something else in there and she hoped against hope it would be a letter from her great-aunt. Not just because it might explain things, but because it would be like hearing Hilary speak one last time, and that would be worth more to her than anything.

She swallowed her disappointment as she pulled it out. It wasn't a letter, it was a leaflet – the really old fashioned sort that looked as though it had been homemade using a typewriter. It was an advert for Seabreeze Farm Donkey Sanctuary, and, as she began to read the leaflet, complete with a stuck-on photograph of Gerald the III, it blurred in front of Ellie's eyes. 'It's one of Aunt Hilary's flyers.' Just as she spoke, the landline started to ring, making both of them jump.

'Sorry, love, I'll have to get that in case it's Grandma and she can shed some light on all of this.' Her mother disappeared into the other room to take the call, and Ellie turned the leaflet over, so that Gerald the III's kind old face looked back at her.

For a donkey, he'd mastered the sort of lofty expression that befitted her great-aunt's favourite. She'd often wondered what had happened to him, when Hilary had finally decided to close down the donkey sanctuary, two months after her ninetieth birthday. All she'd said was that he'd gone to a loving home, and, if the place was good enough for Hilary to send her beloved Gerald to, it was likely to be fit for a king. The donkey had followed her aunt around like a puppy. Everywhere she went on the farm, he went, too.

Ellie had accompanied Hilary on many a walk to check the perimeter fence, where the wooden stakes and surprisingly thin strands of wire were all that stood between the borders of her great-aunt's land, the crumbling cliff face just beyond it and the English Channel. The farm had never been a *real* working farm, at least not in Ellie's lifetime. Ten acres of grassland formed a triangle, which ran from the cliff face at one edge, to the borders of a more traditional arable farm on the other, with a small stretch of road frontage on its remaining side.

Most of the fields had been home to the occupants of the donkey sanctuary, who happily shared the space with an assortment of other rescue animals, including sheep, pigs, and several goats. Aunt Hilary had opened the farm to visitors, in an attempt to help meet the rising cost of keeping Gerald and his friends well fed.

It was on one of these trips down to check the fencing that Ellie had finally come to understand why both the farm and the donkeys were so important to her great-aunt. She'd always assumed Hilary had chosen not to marry, preferring the company of her animals, but it wasn't quite as simple as that.

'I never get tired of that view, you know?' Hilary had turned to look at Ellie, as they'd moved along the fence, pushing against the wooden stakes to ensure they were still secure.

Ellie was spending as much of her last summer before university at the farm as she could, knowing that her life was about to change. Study would be followed by work, and idyllic weeks spent at the farm wouldn't be as easy to fit in. 'It's beautiful.'

There was a cooling summer breeze, and the wildflowers which dotted the cliff edge, just beyond a hungry donkey's reach, swayed in unison with the waves washing on the pebbled beach, just visible below. White horses danced along the water, and Ellie could clearly see the cliffs of France across the expanse. She braced herself for what she was about to suggest.

'Have you ever thought about going somewhere a bit more...

manageable? If you have to stop driving, it will be a really long walk down the hill to the bus stop and, more importantly, back up again, just to get into town.'

'Ah, but you're forgetting that I'm Hils by name and hills by nature.' She grinned, taking Ellie by surprise and suddenly looking at least twenty years younger. 'And as to your question, the answer is no. They'd have to carry me off this cliff kicking and screaming, all the time I've breath in my lungs. I'm living the dream that Gerry and I had. I've had to live it for two all these years, so I'm not about to give up just because I'm an octogenarian.'

'Who's Gerry?' Ellie pushed against another of the wooden stakes as she spoke. It was as firmly set into the clay clifftop, as if it had been dipped in concrete. The name Gerry meant nothing to her. There were lots of black and white photos dotted around the farmhouse, and, as a child, she'd been curious about who they were, but the names of long past relatives had slipped from her memory like grains of sand, so she couldn't be sure if her great-aunt had mentioned him before.

'He was my fiancé.' Hilary smiled again, possibly at the look of surprise which must have crossed Ellie's face, although it suddenly made sense why her favourite donkeys were always named Gerald. 'We got engaged just before he was called up to war and we planned to get married as soon as he came home. He was going to take over his father's business, giving donkey rides to the tourists on the beaches, just around the coast from here, where it's sandier and flat. His dad made a good living at Margate; the tourists used to flock in their thousands back then. It would have been too pebbly here, of course. It was a simple enough dream, but we didn't even get that.'

'What happened?' Ellie could guess, but with Aunt Hilary finally telling her story, she didn't want her to stop.

'He was killed in the D-Day landings; I was eighteen and he'd just turned twenty. He died about two hundred miles along the French coast from the cliffs you can see across the water. I sometimes stand here and imagine he didn't die at all, that he's just on a cliff top somewhere, facing me from the other side of the Channel.' Hilary rubbed her eyes with the back of her hand. 'But then I can be a daft old bat at times.'

'It's not daft at all, it's a lovely way to think about him.' Ellie linked arms with her great-aunt, as they walked towards the next row of fencing that needed to be checked. 'And what about the farm, how did you end up here?'

'I never wanted to go out with anyone else after Gerry.' She turned her cornflower blue eyes toward Ellie; so much was written within their depths. 'So I took a job as a housekeeper for the couple who lived here. I thought they were ancient at the time.' She laughed. 'They were probably barely in their fifties and they were lovely to me, treated me like the daughter they'd never had. I ended up looking after the wife after her husband died, when I'd been working for them for more than twenty years. And then, ten years after that, Doris went, too, and they left all this to me.' She swept her hands in a circular motion.

'And did you start the donkey rides then?' Her great-aunt had been nearly seventy by the time Ellie was born, so it was perfectly possible she'd had a business giving donkey rides on the beach before that.

'No. Starting that up was something I couldn't face doing without Gerry, but I could offer the donkeys somewhere to retire to when they weren't of use to their owners any more.' Hilary pushed against a wooden stake, which barely moved. 'The farm had been wound down over the years, anyway. I had a few sheep and goats, but it wasn't really making enough money to keep going, so I hit on the idea of opening a donkey sanctuary, and having a few other animals, as well. Petting zoos seemed to be all the rage. I started it just after my fifty-fifth birthday, and here we are thirty years later and we're still... surviving.'

'So, is that why you won't retire? Are you worried about who would look after the animals?' Ellie loved the motley collection of donkeys who grazed on the plentiful supply of lush, green grass at Seabreeze Farm, but she knew her great-aunt made do with charity shop hand-me-downs so they'd be well fed in winter, and she hadn't had a day off from the farm in forever. Petting zoos had given way to rollercoasters over the years, and kids wanted more from a day out than the sanctuary could offer, so making ends meet had become harder and harder.

'I'm under no illusions about what might happen to the place when I'm gone, which is why I'm thinking of leaving it to a donkey charity. If there won't be donkeys here, at least it will do some other animals elsewhere a bit of good, and they've always been more loyal than most people I know.' Aunt Hilary had squeezed her arm as she'd spoken, as if to say that present company was excepted – but she didn't need to say the words out loud. 'No one else would have wanted this life, but me and Gerry, and I never wanted anyone else to share it. You only get one life, and I had to live my dreams the best way I could, without Gerry in them, but it didn't mean anyone else could take his place. After all, why settle for second best?'

Brought back to the present by the sound of her mother opening the kitchen door, Ellie put the photo down. 'Was it Grandma?' She glanced up to see her mother's nod. 'Did she know about Aunt Hilary's will?'

'She did.' Karen sat down with a thud, and the cake sitting on the dresser behind her jumped ever so slightly to the right. 'Apparently, it was always her intention to leave us the farm. She just told everyone it was going to charity to test a theory, to see if the rest of the cousins and their children stopped what she called their *duty visits.*'

'And did they?' Ellie sighed, not needing an answer.

'We were her only visitors once Mum and Dad left for Spain.'

'And does she mind? Grandma, I mean. After all, like you said, she was Hilary's favourite sister.' Ellie felt her stomach turn over at the thought of her grandparents being upset. Without Aunt Hilary to fill the void a little, she missed them more than ever.

'Not a bit. She and Hilary discussed it all, apparently, but she didn't want to tell us until the official documents came through. As she said on the phone, what on earth would they want with an ex-donkey sanctuary?' Karen's eyebrows almost disappeared beneath her blonde fringe. 'And what about us, do *we* want it?'

'The strange thing is, I think I do.' The words were out of Ellie's mouth before she had a chance to really think it through. 'I wasn't going to say anything until I'd worked out what to do, but I was offered redundancy from my job today. I've been getting more and more disillusioned with it anyway. I hate the commute and I think I'd have left a long time ago if it wasn't for Rupert.'

Karen reached across the table and took hold of Ellie's hand. 'Oh, I'm sorry love, that must have come as quite a surprise.'

But the truth was, Ellie wasn't sorry. Not at all. She felt a twinge of guilt at the excitement that was beginning to bubble in her stomach. She already knew what Rupert's reaction would be to her inheriting the farm. He'd see it as the perfect project, a chance to buy Karen out and do it up with the money they'd saved so far, propped up by her redundancy pay, using the profit when they sold the farm on to fast track his business plan. He might even accept that version of events as a solution to her not having a job, for a little while at least. But the last thing she wanted to do was to sell the farm. And it was the realisation that the farm meant more to her than what Rupert wanted that was making her feel so guilty

'What do you think Rupert will make of all this?' Her mother grimaced slightly.

'I don't think he's going to understand why it feels like what I've been waiting for – a new life in the country and a new job somewhere local to the farm, but just lately I'm not sure we understand much about each other at all. When I told him about taking redundancy, all he could say was that it was going to ruin our five-year plan.'

'He was probably just shocked; it's come out of the blue after all.' Her mother squeezed her hand. 'Rupert and I might not exactly be each other's cup of tea, but I knew when you got together that his ambition would mean you'd never have to worry about money again, the way we did when you were growing up. Give him a chance to get used to the idea of everything that's happened, because if we do decide to take on the farm, it's going to be an even bigger change to his plans.'

'I know you're right.' Karen was always so fair to everyone and it really must have been a huge shock to Rupert to hear that she hadn't only missed out on a promotion but had walked out on her job too.

'Just take things slowly with Rupert when it comes to the farm.'

'I will, but you only get one life, and Rupert will be happy as long as I am.' Ellie picked up the leaflet for the donkey sanctuary again, her great-aunt's words from ten years earlier ringing in her ears, as she crossed her fingers under the table for luck. 'I'm almost sure he will.'

3

It was ten o'clock in the evening before Ellie had the chance to think about calling Rupert. Her mother was right, she'd overreacted to the way he'd taken the news and she should have known him well enough to know that he couldn't just roll with the sudden change of plans. She hadn't given him a chance to even try to talk things through, when she'd stomped off to the station, and the truth was she probably owed him an apology.

When she finally picked up her phone there were three missed calls and a text from him.

Rupert
Stop sulking El and pick up the phone! You can't just run off like that, we're supposed to be partners in everything. Call me when you're ready to talk, but don't leave it too long.

It wasn't the most loving of messages, with none of the usual kisses, and there was a touch of the 'or else' about the last line, but Ellie had to admit she'd probably have been just as annoyed if he'd walked away from her without a backward glance. But it seemed as though she wasn't the only one who could sulk and, after trying to return his call four times, she gave up and sent a text instead.

Ellie

I'm sorry about earlier. I'd had the day from hell and I suppose I just wanted you to tell me that it was all going to be okay. Call me when you can and we can talk properly xx

Her fingers hovered over the keys as she deliberated whether to tell him the news about Aunt Hilary's farm, but text messages were too easily misconstrued and it was going to be a tense conversation, even face to face. She put her phone on the bedside table while she tried to decide what to do, and eventually drifted off to sleep.

When she woke up at six, there was a reply from him.

Rupert

Sorry I didn't pick up. I had a call from Seb asking me to fly to St Andrews first thing this morning to check out a hotel we're thinking of investing in, so I turned off my phone to try and get a decent night's sleep. I'm going to be in back-to-back meetings, so why don't you come for dinner at the flat when I get back on Friday night and we can talk properly then. I'll see you at seven thirty xx

He might have posed the suggestion to come to dinner as a question, but the confirmation of the time meant there was no real room for negotiation. Although he must have thawed a bit after her apology, because at least the kisses were back.

Ellie

Okay. See you then. Hope the trip goes well, love you xx

There was no reply from Rupert after that, but she hadn't expected there to be. He was probably on a flight to Scotland and she knew what he was like when he was in the process of brokering a deal, it was business all the way. Rupert had this way of compartmentalising the different aspects of his life and it was probably what made him as successful as he was. Sometimes it annoyed the hell out of Ellie, but right now she was glad Rupert would be completely absorbed by his work, because she had enough to think about without having to worry about what his reaction to her inheriting the farm would be. She needed to talk things through with Karen and work out a detailed plan of exactly what they wanted to do, before she even thought about telling Rupert. If she was going to make a decision and not give him any chance of persuading her she was wrong, she had to have it completely clear in her head first.

By the time they pulled up into the yard of Seabreeze Farm, later that day, Ellie was feeling more uncertain than ever about whether moving there could really work out. It had been years since they'd been up to the farm itself, not since Aunt Hilary had shut the sanctuary and rehomed the animals. She'd said it had given her reason to get out and about, and that there were far too few of those. Once Ellie was out of the car and looking around at the state of the place, she couldn't help but think her great-aunt had been driven by an ulterior motive for keeping them away. The yard looked as though it could feature on one of those reality shows about extreme hoarders, with bits of broken farming equipment and rotting straw bales stacked against the outbuildings.

'I can't believe it's the same place.' Ellie jumped as an ear-splitting *hee-haw* cut across the yard and literally rattled the wooden window frames of the farmhouse, which itself looked far more run-down than she remembered.

The *hee-hawing* reached an ear-splitting crescendo, like a hundred rusty old gates being opened in unison, and Karen shot Ellie a look of alarm. 'I should have known better when Hilary insisted on meeting us in town.'

'And if that's not Gerald, who she claimed was rehomed years ago, then I'll eat the straw hat he used to wear giving donkey rides before he retired to the farm.' Ellie led the way around the back of the farmhouse and down the shingle path toward the largest of the paddocks, where she spotted a moth-eaten looking Gerald staring mournfully over a fence that didn't look as though it would have held up if the donkey had given it a good push.

'Oh my God! Do you think anyone's been looking after him since the funeral?' All the colour had drained from Karen's face, and Ellie's throat tightened at the thought of her great-aunt's beloved donkey being half-starved without her to care for him. Although, if anything, Gerald looked a bit on the hefty side.

'There's a bucket of grain in the corner, so someone's been looking after him.' The words were hardly out of Karen's mouth, before a deep voice behind them made them both jump again.

'Someone's been looking after him, all right, and the rest of the menagerie, and *someone* still is. The question is, who the hell are you?'

Ellie took in the man's appearance. He was probably in his late fifties, wearing wellies that had seen better days, a jacket that looked as if he'd taken it off a scarecrow, and an expression bordering on contempt.

'We might ask you the same question, since it's you who's trespassing on our land.' Her mother bristled as she spoke, and Ellie placed a hand on her arm.

'Sorry, you just took us by surprise, that's all.' Ellie held out her other hand and tried not to notice how filthy the mystery man's rough, red hands appeared. 'This is my mother, Karen Chapman, Hilary's niece, and I'm Ellie.'

'Oh, I see.' She might have been insulted that Mr Angry ignored her outstretched hand, but she couldn't help feeling a little bit relieved. 'The vultures are closing in now, then? No one's been near, or by, for years, but you're here now there are goods and chattels to price up. Typical of your generation.'

'Not that it's any of your business, Mr...?' Karen paused, and eventually the man grumbled his name. 'Not that it's any of your business, Mr Crabtree, but I met with my aunt at least once a week, and I always asked to meet her here, but since she shut the sanctuary, she insisted on meeting me in town.'

'And a half-wit could have worked out the reason for that.' Mr Crabtree was not going to be easily thawed, and Ellie wondered, for the first time, if it wouldn't just be easier to sell the farm and walk away. 'Your aunt was a proud woman; she wouldn't want to ask for help. It nearly killed her to take it off me, and *we've* been friends and neighbours my whole life. I remember you coming here when you were younger, but you clearly had better things to do until there was an inheritance in the offing. I did what I could for Hilary because no one else was, but I didn't have the time or money to help her properly and the place has gone to ruin. But I suppose you'll sell it now, to some God-awful weekenders from the city who just want somewhere for their spoilt kids to roar around on their quad bikes. Then what will happen to Gerald and the others? Dog food, I'll bet.'

'Look, I'm sorry, we've got off on the wrong foot,' Ellie interjected before her mother could speak. Karen's cheeks had turned bright red, and she looked on the edge of tears. 'But we've got no intention of selling to weekenders, or anyone, for that matter.' If she'd been wavering about their decision to move to the farm, another glance at Gerald's mournful face was enough to convince her, and she wasn't about to prove Mr Crabtree right, if she could help it.

'Hmm, I'll believe it when I see it.' Mr Crabtree shrugged his shoulders as if he couldn't care less, but his face told an entirely different story. 'When you've finished working out how much money you can wring out of the farm, you might want to get Gerald looked at by a vet. Animals aren't my forte, and I could only do my best. He's been lame these last couple of days, and I've been meaning to call Ben, but like I said, I'm not made of money. He might be my godson, but I can't expect him to treat other people's animals for free.' With another shrug, he disappeared back up the track, and Ellie let out a long breath.

'Well, he was charming! Do you remember him from when you were younger? If he was such a good friend of Aunt Hilary's, how come I've never met him, in all the years I've been coming to the farm?'

'The Crabtree family owned the farm next door and I used to play with their son, Alan, when we were kids, but that can't be him.' The colour in Karen's cheeks was gradually returning to normal and she was shaking her head. 'He was always such a kind boy though, offering to help Aunt Hilary out with jobs that might be too much for her on her own. I know he went overseas at one point and Hilary said he kept himself to himself a lot more when he came back to the farm. I never saw him again on any of my visits after that. But I still can't believe that's Alan, maybe it's a cousin of his or something... He does look vaguely familiar, but that must be a family resemblance, because I can't believe anyone could change that much!'

'He said he recognised you, though, so doesn't that mean he has to be Alan?'

'There were lots of kids from Kelsea Bay who used to come up and hang out on both farms, right into our teens. If he is a cousin of Alan's, maybe that's when we met. I hope so, because it would make me really sad if I found out that's how Alan turned out – a miserable old git.'

'Either way, the more he keeps himself to himself, the better, as far as I'm concerned.' Ellie shivered at the thought of encountering their grumpy new neighbour again. It almost made her miss Jimmy Summers and his penchant for mowing the lawn in his pants. Living next to someone as miserable as Crabtree was nearly as bad as the thought of breaking the news of their planned move to Rupert. 'Come on, let's go and find out what sort of state the house is in, and I'll try and track down that vet's number. If the sound Gerald is making is any indication of how much pain he's in, we'd better get him seen to as quickly as possible.'

The house was just as Ellie had feared it might be, when she'd seen the state of disrepair of the rest of the farm. The kitchen, front room, her great-aunt's old bedroom and upstairs bathroom weren't too bad. She'd obviously kept on top of the areas she used the most, but Hilary had never been one to spend much on herself, and that included the furniture. Nothing matched and her bedspread had been patched more than a dozen times, but at least those rooms were fairly clean and things had been repaired. There was dust, from a lack of use over the past few months, but they were liveable – just about. At some point, her aunt had obviously started closing up the other rooms, which had locks built into the old fashioned, heavy, oak doors. Ellie found a set of keys in the kitchen, each one with a luggage label attached in her great-aunt's loopy writing. Some rooms were bare, but the peeling wall paper, and the windows that had begun to leak over the years, left a distinctive scent of neglect. Other rooms were stuffed with bric-a-brac and furniture – everything from broken vases, to a stool with two of its three legs missing. They had their work cut out, all right.

She could imagine only too well Rupert's expression when he saw the place: like he'd stepped in something that smelt even worse than the unoccupied rooms did. As much as she could see why he might feel that way, the spark of excitement Ellie had felt the moment she'd discovered they were inheriting the farm was growing. It was something she hadn't experienced in a very long while. Being at the farm without Hilary could have been really sad, but it was as if her great-aunt was somehow imprinted into every room and Ellie could almost hear her urging them on to make the farm a home again.

When she closed her eyes, she could see the farm as it could be, but what she couldn't do was put Rupert in that picture. Maybe she was overthinking it, but she had a horrible feeling she might end up having to choose between her fiancé and the farm, and what worried her most was that she didn't know which she'd pick. It was just because everything was happening so fast, that was all. Her mum had been right before when she'd said that Ellie needed to give both herself and Rupert time to process it all. But that was a problem for later, because right now there might still be something lurking behind one of the doors that could change everything – like irreparable subsidence or black mould.

Thankfully there was nothing too drastic behind any of the remaining doors and after opening up the last of the rooms, Ellie headed back into the kitchen to find her mother peering out of the window. 'Is he here, already?' She'd found the number for Ben, the vet, on the corkboard above the kitchen table when they'd first gone into the farmhouse. There were still ten minutes before he was due to arrive, but Ellie crossed her fingers that it *was* the vet, rather than the unwelcome return of Mr Crabtree, and that his godson wouldn't turn out to be anything like him either.

'Not yet.' Karen turned away from the window to face her daughter. 'I was just looking out at the yard, thinking how much there is to put right. Do you think we're biting off more than we can chew?'

Her mother had been busy scrubbing the kitchen, whilst Ellie had checked out the rest of the house. She was wearing one of Aunt Hilary's pinnies and it already looked like a different place – somewhere she could imagine her mum baking for hours on end and having the life she'd more than earned over the years. If Ellie had to make some sacrifices for that to happen, it was only a bit of payback for everything that Karen had done for her.

'It'll be fine.' Ellie wrapped an arm around her mother's waist, deliberately making her voice as bright as she could. 'We'll make Aunt Hilary proud.'

'I texted the landlord and he's just replied to say we can move out as soon as we're ready. He doesn't even want a month's notice.' For the first time since meeting Mr Crabtree, there was a smile on her mum's face and it suddenly all felt very real to Ellie. If they left The Copse there'd be no going back, however life on the farm turned out. It was exciting and terrifying all at the same time. 'I just feel guilty that he's probably already been on the phone to the developers to agree to the sale of the house and the neighbours will probably follow suit. The new estate will creep further out and it will be like we were never there.'

'Oh Mum, despite how hard it's been at times, we've made so many good memories at The Copse and no one can take them away.' Ellie gave her Mum a quick hug, trying to work out what to say to ease her guilt without sounding as though she was quoting what Rupert had told her hundreds of times, when she'd felt uneasy about a deal he'd brokered or what had happened to one of the businesses the bank had taken over. Especially when deep down she'd never been convinced by the words anyway. 'And as for the house sale, that's not your responsibility to feel guilty about. Everyone at The Copse has a choice, but more often than not people will choose the money. It's just the way it is.'

Another of Gerald's ear-splitting *hee-haws* crossed the yard, and Karen smiled again. 'I know, you're right, and at least I feel better knowing that we'd be giving Gerald the retirement he deserves. Hilary loved him so much and she'd want him to be looked after properly.'

'Talking of which, it looks like the vet's arrived,' Ellie said at the sound of tyres on gravel, a welcome reassurance that help was at hand. 'We'll get the old boy and this place sorted out, Mum. It'll be all right, it really will.'

Ellie returned her mum's smile and pushed down the thought she'd been trying to suppress all day. Rupert would be back from his business trip soon, and she couldn't put off the news for much longer. For all her bravado that, somehow, he'd see past the dodgy décor and the smell of damp, and be happy for her, she couldn't quite convince herself that her fiancé really would see things in the same light. Closing her eyes, she tried again to picture him at the farmhouse, but she just couldn't do it.

'I've got a good mind to report you to the RSPCA.' Ben Hastings shot her a look that made Mr Crabtree's introduction from earlier seem positively welcoming. 'This donkey's got laminitis. He's been gorging himself on all the spring grass he's got access to, because your paddocks aren't properly fenced, and he's got all this grain here, too.' He jabbed a finger towards the bucket.

'Is he going to be okay?' Ellie bit her lip. It hadn't been the easiest of days and she already felt terrible that Gerald and the few remaining animals at the farm were in such a bad state. What was it with the men around here, anyway? Whatever it was, there didn't seem to be a right side of the bed for them to get out of.

'Can't you see this?' Ben pointed to the donkey's pendulous belly. His dark eyes fixed on her face, giving her nowhere to hide. She was determined not to cry; she knew Ben was only angry because he cared so much about animals. He'd been perfectly friendly until he'd set eyes on Gerald, and the crinkles around the corners of his eyes betrayed him. He did know how to smile.

'I've only been here three hours!' Ellie's voice went at least an octave higher, and she dug her nails into her hand. 'It's your miserable godfather you want to take this up with.' She'd had enough of being pushed around and criticised for one day. She didn't even care if Ben was offended by her description of her new neighbour, because miserable definitely summed him up.

'Alan?' Ben ran a hand through his black hair, and, when he looked at her again, there was far less narrowing of the eyes. 'He's a rough diamond, but he's got a heart of gold if you can get past all the gruffness.'

'That's one description of him, but I can think of a few others that are far more appropriate.' Ellie could have sworn she saw a hint of a smile twitching at the corners of his mouth. He had lovely eyes too and he was the sort of person she might have gone for before she'd met Rupert, but she barely even recognised the girl she'd been back then any more.

'I'm sorry. I should have found out more about what's been going on before I had a go at you. I just hate seeing animals end up like this.' Ben patted the old donkey on his rump, and a cloud of dust rose up from Gerald's coat, making them both cough. 'You've got your work cut out getting the animals back to their best, never mind the rest of the place. What's the plan for the farm?'

'My great-aunt left it to us, but she hadn't let us visit her here for a couple of years before she died. Now we know why. She told us she'd got rid of all the animals, but I think she was scared that if she sent them somewhere else, they might end up...' Gerald began nuzzling her pocket, and Ellie felt choked up for an entirely different reason, as she remembered the way Hilary had always kept some pony nuts in her pocket for her best boy. She'd be horrified to see him in such a state.

'Well, if you're going to sell up, the kindest thing to do might be just that – to let the old boy go.' Although Ben said the words, he didn't sound very convinced, and there was no way Ellie would let that happen.

'Absolutely not!' Just because the donkey had teeth the colour of mustard, and a bray that could strip paint, it didn't mean he was ready to end up in a dog food tin. Gerald was still nuzzling at her pocket. If she was going to have to put him on a diet, it wouldn't be easy. 'We're not selling the farm and we're not going to let anything happen to Gerald either. There must be something you can do for him?'

'The first step would be an anti-inflammatory injection, then you'll have to treat him with painkillers and hose his legs down every few hours.' Ben was already opening his leather treatment bag. 'After that, you'll have to get the farrier out to do some remedial work to his feet, and I'd suggest keeping him in a stable with a deep bed of wood shavings. I also think he'd benefit from having a relief boot on his front right hoof.'

'That seems doable...' It was Ellie's turn to sound less than convinced. It was as if Ben was speaking a foreign language. What the hell was a relief boot, anyway? She stared down at her own feet. She was wearing what could only be described as sensible shoes. She'd bought them for commuting, but after Rupert had seen them and laughed his head off, asking her if she'd got them on prescription, they'd been assigned to the back of the cupboard. They were coming into their own now, though.

'It won't be cheap, and it's a lot of work.' Ben unwrapped the syringe he'd taken from the case.

'Gerald's worth it.' Ellie watched as Ben loaded the syringe with anti-inflammatory medication. The donkey barely even seemed to notice the needle going in; the poor old thing must have already been in so much pain.

'I'll have to come up and see him every couple of days, to make sure the treatment's working.' He took a long plastic tube of painkilling paste out of his bag and handed it to her. 'You'll need to limit his food to a pad of hay a day, and syringe a dose of the painkiller into the corner of his mouth, as well as keep up the hosing. Do you need me to write it down for you?' He looked up at her, and this time the smile moved more than the corners of his mouth. He had even, white teeth and a deep dimple in his right cheek when he smiled properly. Suddenly, the thought of seeing him every couple of days was strangely cheering.

'I think I'll be all right, but is it okay for me to call you if I'm worried about him?' Ellie felt pure relief when he nodded. Maybe the locals wouldn't be entirely hostile after all, but then again, who needed to watch *Game of Thrones*, with so much conflict on your doorstep?

Running through in her head everything she needed to do before she could sit down for the night, Ellie had a feeling that, like wearing shoes without a high-grip, rubber sole, her days of binge-watching must-see TV were long gone.

4

After Ben's visit to the farm, Ellie had decided it was best to stay overnight to keep an eye on Gerald. Waking with a start, she reached around on the unfamiliar dressing table for her watch, trying to make out the time in the dark. It was no good, it was still pitch black in the room. Knocking her legs on some of her aunt's furniture collection, she felt her way around the walls until she found a light switch.

Three thirty-five a.m. was the verdict when she eventually found the switch. The room was immediately bathed in a weak glow from the ancient light fitting in the centre of the ceiling, which definitely wouldn't have passed any kind of safety inspection. Perhaps she should have gone to bed in those rubber soled shoes.

She wouldn't get back to sleep, not now. Her mind raced with everything that had happened, and she needed to get things straight in her head, work out exactly how wide-ranging the implications of it all were, before she spoke to Rupert. It was always best to speak to him when her standpoint on something was fully formed. It made the inevitable cross-examination that bit easier to handle.

She rummaged in her bag for her iPhone and held it up. Whilst sitting on the bed, she had one bar of signal, but when she moved over to the window she was amazed to see she actually had three. She'd bank that there was a better signal here than at The Copse, where she sometimes had to walk up the garden waving her phone towards the sky like a mad woman, to get a text to send.

There was only one person to call at a time like this and, luckily, given the time difference, she wouldn't be disturbing her oldest friend in the dead of night. It was lunchtime in Australia, and, with any luck, Olivia would be at her desk in the office that had come with her recent promotion to head of house, about to wade her way through a mountain of marking of seven-year-olds' spelling tests, and would be more than happy for the distraction of a call from Ellie.

Ellie had texted Olivia as soon as she'd found out about inheriting the farm, and her friend had been almost as excited as she was in her responses during the frantic exchange that ensued. She knew all about the farm, having spent several holidays there with Ellie as a child, when the two of them had been inseparable and hadn't been able to bear the thought of not seeing each other for a couple of weeks. The games they played transferred easily from The Copse to the farm, and the bond of shared experiences had maintained a best friendship that sustained through separate universities, and even Olivia's eventual move to the other side of the world. Olivia's family had long since moved away from The Copse, but their friendship hadn't dimmed, and Olivia had always spent at least part of any trip home in the company of Ellie and Karen. In turn, Ellie had been out to Brisbane twice.

'Ellie!' Olivia's greeting was as enthusiastic as she had known it would be. 'It must be the middle of the night there. What's going on, an all-night rave?' Olivia had picked up the slight twang of an Aussie accent in the five years she'd been there, and Ellie could almost feel the sun on her skin whenever she heard it.

'Nope no party, just some sort of rave going on in my head.'

'Is everything okay? It's not your mum, is it?'

'Nothing like that.' Ellie could hear the concern in her friend's voice across the thousands of miles. Olivia really was like the sister she'd never had, the one person who knew her family almost as well as she did. As an only child, that sort of friendship was priceless.

'Something's wrong, El. What's he said this time?' Even if Olivia hadn't expressed her reservations about Rupert so freely after meeting him on her trips home, the tone of her voice would have given it away. Perhaps if their friendship hadn't been so strong, her feelings about Rupert would have threatened it, but they never had. The truth was that the things Olivia found difficult about Rupert weren't that hard for Ellie to agree with. Olivia had asked if she could be honest with Ellie, when she'd wanted to know what her oldest friend thought of her new fiancé, just after they'd got engaged. Ellie had given her the go ahead and she'd said some positive things at first, about how driven and ambitious he was, but then she'd looked at Ellie and shaken her head from side to side. *'I just can't see you making a life with him El; all he talks about is money and how to make even more of it.'*

Rupert's single-mindedness was what had kept Ellie awake for most of the night on the day she'd accepted his proposal, but she'd been able to rationalise it in the end. He might not be perfect and she might understand why Olivia had her doubts about him, but she just kept coming back to the security of the life they could have together if they followed his plan. No more having to lie on the floor to try and fool debt collectors that they weren't home, like she and her mother had been forced to do more than once, and no more being at the mercy of a landlord who could sell the house out from under them at any point. Most of all she'd be able to help her mum, and stop Karen having to wonder how her measly state pension might stretch far enough when the time came. She wanted her mother to have what she deserved – the best of everything – and the life she'd been building with Rupert could provide that.

'He hasn't said anything yet. He still doesn't know.'

'Right. So, you texted me the minute you found out, and I could feel your excitement literally jumping off the screen when I read your messages, but you haven't told the man you're supposed to be marrying?'

'I know, it's stupid.' Ellie automatically glanced down at her engagement ring. 'But it was easier with you. I knew you'd understand what the farm means to me and Mum, and that you'd be happy for us.'

'El, you can't marry a man who doesn't know the real you. All that corporate bullshit just isn't you.' Olivia had always been a straight talker when it came to giving advice. It was just a shame she couldn't take her own advice, sometimes.

'You know that, and so do I *now*, but when I met Rupert, I thought it was the career I wanted, and it's not his fault I've changed.' Had she really changed that much, though? Or was it the feeling that she'd never quite lived up to Rupert's perception of her that made her feel that way?

'If he loves you, then he'll embrace whatever changes you make. Seeing you happy should be all that matters to him. It's all that matters to me.'

'Oh, Liv, I wish you lived back home. I know you love it there, but I miss you.'

'Me, too, and who knows, maybe one of these days I'll get bored of the sunshine and dating sun-bronzed surfer types and want to come home.' Olivia laughed, and they both knew the irony of her words. There hadn't been much dating of any type, and she lived in Brisbane city centre, a world away from the rolling surf. She was in love with a man she could never have, but couldn't leave Australia because of him, and guilt washed over Ellie at the thought. There she was unburdening problems that she had some control over, whilst her friend patched up her own broken heart every day.

'How are things with you and Josh?'

'Still the same. He's still married, and I'm still working with him every day, knowing that he lied to me and let me fall in love with him before he let me in on that little fact. I wish I could hate him for it, El, I really do.'

'Me, too.' Ellie certainly did. 'Are you coming home this year? I really want to see you.'

'I'll be back for Christmas. Maybe a New Year's Eve spent at the farm will finally help me to stick to that resolution I make every year.' Olivia laughed again. 'After all, your aunt Hilary would have given it to me straight.'

'She would. She'd have told us both what to do.' Ellie found herself smiling. Aunt Hilary wouldn't have pussy-footed around Rupert, either. She'd have told him to like it or lump it, and it was what Ellie was going to have to do. Maybe not in those exact words, but this was her life now, and he was either in, or out.

Like Olivia said, if he really loved her, he'd embrace the change, and, if he didn't then she really was going to have to choose between Rupert and the farm. Either way, she had to find out.

* * *

Ellie had taken the train up to meet Rupert. The tube journey from Victoria was stifling, and it reminded her of all the things she'd started to hate about commuting to London for work every day. Since she'd returned to Seabreeze Farm, her every waking thought had become filled with the place, and even the prospect of bumping into Alan Crabtree or getting another telling off from Ben, was a thousand times more appealing than going back to her old job and the commuting that went with it.

'I thought you'd already be waiting at the flat for me, when I got back.' The tone of Rupert's voice was somewhere between husky and sulky, probably closer to the latter, when Ellie called to say that she was on her way but she was running a bit late. She'd managed to get on the slow train to Victoria, stopping at every station on the line between the coast and London, something that would have driven Rupert absolutely mad if he'd been with her.

Rupert didn't like things not going the way he wanted and she'd always fallen in line with his plans before. That was the way it went, when you were with someone you felt was way out of your league. Rupert was super bright, that much had been obvious from the moment they'd met, but sometimes he used it to make her feel she couldn't possibly understand things the way he did. When she'd pushed him about some of the decisions he made in his job, he'd told her she'd never understand the complexity of the business he was in. He'd said more than once that all she needed to know was that he was working towards financial freedom for them both and all she had to do was follow his plan. Whenever doubts crept in about whether he was really right for her, he'd seemed to have this innate ability to pull off a grand gesture that convinced her all over again that he just wanted the best for her. The most recent had been when he'd booked and paid for a flight for her mother to visit her grandparents just before she'd had her second knee replacement and arranged for her to be chauffeured door-to-door to make things a bit easier for her.

While Ellie was in London, Karen would be starting the process of packing up the house at The Copse. They'd paid one of the veterinary nurses to go up and bathe Gerald's legs in their absence, but just a night of one-to-one donkey nursing was costing a small fortune – Karen had to bake enough cupcakes to feed a small country to earn that sort of money – and it wasn't something they could sustain for long. Ellie tried not to ponder the financial side of things too much. When she thought about the farm, she preferred the romantic to the practical. It would all work out one way or another.

She might have metaphorically been putting her fingers in her ears, to drown out the voice of caution in her head, but she had to believe it. Her mother could expand the business, once they'd updated the kitchen and she'd established herself – maybe even get her cakes into some of the local shops. Ellie would get a job closer to the farm at some point. Everything would be okay. It was the mantra she repeated to herself when she woke up at night in a panic, and she was sticking to it.

'Why are you so late, anyway?'

'I've been really busy. A few unexpected things came up.' She didn't elaborate; it wasn't a conversation she wanted to have over the phone and if she told Rupert she'd got on a slow train up from the coast she'd have to explain it all. He clearly wasn't interested enough to ask anyway. Maybe it was just dread at how he might react, or some of the things Olivia had said, but she felt like she was slipping out of the spell Rupert had held her under for far too long. Had he always been like that? Only interested in himself?

'So, what time will you be here, then?' He paused for a moment, and when she didn't immediately answer, he added, almost as an afterthought, 'I missed you.'

'That's nice.' She wanted to ask him if he meant it, and what it was exactly he'd missed about her. She knew she should probably reciprocate and tell him she'd missed him, too, but she didn't. The truth was, she wasn't sure she had. She'd been busy, and Gerald had been one demanding male too many, as it was.

'I got you a little something whilst I was away, to let you know just how much I was thinking of you.' Rupert had bit of a track record for buying her what you might call *self-improvement* presents – everything from lip-plumping solutions to high-top control pants – so she wasn't exactly gripped with excitement at the thought of his latest gift.

'I should be there by six. Love you.' She said the words automatically, but they felt different than they had a week before. If he couldn't prove Olivia wrong and put Ellie's happiness first, she had a feeling that Aunt Hilary's bequest might be about to change far more than just her postcode.

* * *

Rupert's apartment was in a converted warehouse, overlooking the Thames. He worked hard and had all the material things to prove it – from his beloved red BMW to a set of veneer that wouldn't have looked out of place on a Hollywood movie star, and a bachelor pad that Ellie had always known she could never call home. It was loft-style, airy and open plan, with little more than an assortment of high-tech gadgets and large sofas to sully its perfect simplicity. There were no family photographs, ornaments or holiday souvenirs to clutter it up; it was the very opposite to Aunt Hilary's place, or even the house in The Copse, where her mother had covered every inch of shelf space with photographs and mementos of their family life. After spending the last couple of days at the farm, Rupert's flat felt cold, and it had nothing to do with the temperature.

'I've missed you.' Rupert repeated his earlier words as he kissed her, and she desperately wanted to feel that frisson of excitement, which had always come so easily in the past, only it wasn't there. It was probably just nerves, but all she felt like doing was turning around and heading straight back to the farm. The physical attraction she'd felt to Rupert the first time they'd met could still take her breath away, but right now it was like looking at a stranger. She could still acknowledge he was a very good-looking man, but suddenly it felt as if there was something missing – that recognition that you'd connected with someone on a deeper level. For a moment her thoughts flitted towards Ben and their conversation about saving Gerald; they'd shared an understanding with just a look and she wasn't sure that was something she'd ever had with Rupert.

'I missed you too.' The words tripped off her tongue without any of the feeling that should have gone with them, making it feel all the more as though she was on auto-pilot, and she picked up a glossy estate agent's brochure from the coffee table, to save her making eye contact with him. 'How was your business trip?'

'It was good. We bought an old castle that's been run by same family for years, but they need to double the number of bedrooms to turn a decent profit. It needs gutting, to bring it up to the standard of the rest of our hotels, but it should be a good addition to the portfolio in the end. They were desperate, so I got a very good price.' Rupert was already pouring her a drink, choosing what she'd have without even asking. She could just imagine his view of the revamped castle, original features chucked in the skips lined up outside, until it looked like almost any other hotel on the inside. Depressing and outdated was usually the way he described old things. A dilapidated Grade II listed farmhouse deep in the Kent countryside was unlikely to illicit much enthusiasm from Rupert, unless he could see a way of making money out of it. 'It'll make a great luxury wedding venue when it's finished, though. All that's big business these days and people seem to be willing to pay ridiculous amounts just to have a castle in the background of their photos.'

'Using the castle for a wedding venue sounds lovely.' She meant it. Organising weddings was a million times closer to what she'd hoped she'd be doing when she'd studied for her events management degree. That or music festivals, although, even at only twenty-eight, she was already past wanting to spend a week in a tent and queue for a toilet she was sharing with four thousand other people – even if Ed Sheeran was rocking the main stage.

'That reminds me, I've got that present for you.' Rupert handed her a glass of red wine, which was no doubt good quality but tasted like metal in her mouth as a nagging voice inside her head told her to just get on with it and tell him about the farm. Putting it off wouldn't change anything, but even the prospect of one of Rupert's self-improvement presents seemed preferable. He disappeared into his bedroom for a moment, before re-emerging with a large brown bag with rope handles.

Ellie looked up from the La Creuset pans in the bag at Rupert and back down again. 'Saucepans?'

'Only the best for you, my darling.' He seemed absolutely delighted with his choice of gift, but for once, she didn't feel the need to force a smile. Something like this didn't deserve the effort of pretending. 'After all, I think it's about time that you extended your repertoire from bacon sandwiches and pot noodles. They're great for cooking stir-fries in, too, and let's face it, there's always scope to cut your calorie intake a bit.'

'Never mind stir-fries, bacon sandwiches will taste all the better made in these.' She wanted to laugh, ask him if he was joking, only she knew he wasn't. The promises he'd made to her about always taking care of her had been so powerful when they'd first met, because for years she'd longed for someone to offer that security, that strength. She hated the thought that not having a father around might have made her seek out someone who took on that whole outdated head-of-the-household, bread-winner's role, but the truth was it probably had. Only somewhere along the way, 'taking care of her' seemed to have morphed into deciding what was best for her and now it was bordering on control. Suddenly a new life on the farm felt like more of a life-line than ever, whether Rupert liked it or not. 'The pans will be great in the farmhouse, and Mum will love them.'

'Farmhouse?' Rupert's voice had already taken on an edge of suspicion, but she ploughed on.

'Turns out Aunt Hilary left the farm to Mum and me.' She didn't pause for breath; it was too risky to give him a chance to interrupt. 'And our landlords agreed to let us out of our tenancy immediately, so there's nothing stopping us going for it.'

'Nothing?' He arched an eyebrow. 'What about your job? What about *me*?'

'I quit, remember?' Rupert's mouth was opening and closing, but no words were coming out, so she kept going. 'I thought you'd be pleased; you always said she should have left the farm to family. It's a great place, and we'd never have moved in together until after the wedding, when we bought our own place. I couldn't live here, you know that, and being away so much, you could base yourself anywhere.'

'Are you seriously expecting me to move to a farmhouse in the middle of nowhere with you... and your mum?' Rupert looked incredulous.

'I suppose I didn't think it would matter to you if Mum was there or not.'

'No, you didn't think. That much is clear.' He drained his glass in one and set it down on the table.

His reaction wasn't entirely unexpected, but a part of her had wanted him to surprise her. If he'd said that being with her was the important thing and it didn't matter where, the doubts she'd had about their relationship might have dissolved. But there was a muscle going in his cheek and her heart was hammering against her chest, as if it was almost as desperate to escape as she was.

Taking a deep breath, she tried to put herself in his shoes. This was big news and she'd be asking him to make a huge change, when she knew how much he loved his life in the city. She wasn't even sure how she'd feel if he suddenly said he was willing to move to Kent with her, or whether she wanted him to. But she had Karen's words ringing in her ears; she couldn't just make a snap decision. She had to give them both time to adjust, even if that took them in different directions. Even if they couldn't find a way to make it work, she didn't want things to end badly between them, because Rupert hadn't done anything wrong. He was still exactly the same person he'd always been, it was Ellie who was turning into someone completely different and that person didn't come with a five-year plan that would fit in with Rupert's.

'I know it's a lot to think about, but if you just saw the farm-house you might feel differently. It needs a lot of work, but that shouldn't worry you.' Ellie tried to shake off the feeling that had suddenly washed over her at the thought of Rupert taking over with the plans to renovate the farmhouse. The only person she wanted to share responsibility for that with was her mum.

'How much land did you say it has?'

'I didn't, but there's ten acres and there's still a collection of Aunt Hilary's rescue animals living on the farm.'

'I'm sure there'll be an easy way to fix that.' Rupert picked up his phone. 'The land has sea views, doesn't it?'

'To the right of the farmhouse, yes, the land on the left backs on to another farm.'

'If you could get planning permission on that land, you'd never have to worry about money again and your mum would have a nice little nest egg too, if we bought her out of her half of the farm straight away. I'm sure I could raise enough capital for that.'

'We're not selling the farm.' Ellie's tone was firm and she crossed her arms over her chest. Rupert was like an express train when he got an idea into his head and she'd been carried along like this before, but not this time. The farm was too important, it was Aunt Hilary's legacy and it was never going to be about the money, however hard Rupert might try and push. She might have forgotten how to stand up for herself lately, but standing up for the farm was easy.

'Don't be ridiculous. What are you going to do with it? An old farmhouse like that will just haemorrhage money and there's not enough land to run it as proper farm. There are a million glamping sites around, so if that's what you've got in mind, you'll never stand out from the crowd enough. Everyone wants Cornwall, not Kent.'

'I'll get a job locally to pay the bills and feed the animals. I won't have rent any more and Mum is almost back to normal now, so she can get her catering business up and running properly down there. We'll be fine.'

'Do you know how much running a place like that costs?'
Rupert's laugh was hollow. 'And I thought that was exactly what
you didn't want, a life of living payday to payday, earning just
enough to get by? Being *fine* isn't what we've been working so
hard for.'

'The moment I found out about the farm, none of those plans
seemed to matter.'

'How can you say that, when it's all we've thought about?
You're caught up in some ridiculous fantasy.' Rupert's tone was
incredibly patronising, but all that did was make Ellie more
determined. Maybe it was ridiculous to think she could find a
way of earning enough money to restore the farmhouse and keep
it running, but she'd rather kiss a toilet seat than admit that.

'How do you know it's a ridiculous fantasy when you haven't
even seen the place?'

'Because I know what I'm talking about.' Rupert stared at her
for a moment, the muscle still pulsing in his cheek, but then his
face suddenly seemed to relax and he reached out for her hand.
'I'm sorry El, it was just a huge shock to come home and discover
you were serious about quitting your job and life in London, and
that you're moving to the middle of nowhere. If you really want to
keep the farm, we'll find a way to make it work. You know I only
want the best for you – for us – but I just need you to keep an
open mind too. This could change everything if we handle it
right.'

'So you'll come and look at the farm?' Ellie tried to smile as he
nodded, but it was as if she was wearing a mask that was far too
tight. The farm had already changed everything and the last
thing she wanted was for Rupert to start trying to turn it into
something that Aunt Hilary would have hated. She'd been in his
shadow for so long and she'd let him carry her along for the ride,
because his certainty about their future had been such a contrast

to the instability of her past. But now Ellie was the one who felt certain about something and that meant she wasn't the person Rupert had fallen in love with any more. Guilt mingled with another emotion she couldn't quite pin down, but one thing she knew for sure now was that, if it came to a choice between Rupert and the farm, there was absolutely no contest.

5

One of the many charms of the farmhouse was that there were no double-glazed UPVC windows to spoil the character or keep out the sound of Gerald and the farm's resident cockerel, trying their best to out-sing each other. It was like being caught between Alfie Boe and Katherine Jenkins in full voice, only a lot less tuneful.

Ellie looked at her watch: 6 a.m. She peered out of the window; it was already a beautiful sunny morning and she could just make out Karen walking down towards the bottom paddock with a bucket. Her mother had certainly taken to country life and best of all there was barely even a trace of a limp any more. They'd shared a Chinese takeaway the night before, after she'd got back from London and Karen had come home to Seabreeze Farm with her car loaded up with stuff from their old place. The verdict from the garage about Barry hadn't been good and Ellie had been forced to let the old Beetle go to auction. All she could hope was that he'd find someone to take care of him the way Aunt Hilary had.

It meant that Ellie would be hiring a van when packing up the rest of their stuff on one final visit before bringing it all down to the farm. She'd thought about asking Rupert to help out, but she doubted he'd have the time and just getting through the night at his flat, after telling him about the farmhouse, had been tense enough. If they talked about her plans for the farm, they were bound to clash again. The subject seemed best avoided and she couldn't wait to leave Rupert's place in the morning, slipping out as soon as it got light.

Sleep had eluded Ellie until the early hours of the morning, her mind whirring with a mixture of excitement about all the possibilities the farm could bring and fear that Rupert might be right about them having no idea what they were getting into. But if her mother could be up – looking remarkably energetic – then Ellie could too.

Karen was filling up the water trough in the donkey's paddock when Ellie came up behind her, making her drop the hose. 'Morning.'

'You nearly gave me a heart attack!'

'Sorry. Maybe I should have whistled so you knew I was coming.'

'I just wasn't expecting to see you up so early. I got up in the night to go to the loo and I saw your light was still on. What time did you get to sleep in the end?'

'The last time I looked at the clock was about 2 a.m.'

'You should have slept in, love.' Karen patted the donkey nearest her, who lifted his head for a moment and then returned to eating the pad of hay in front of him. 'Although I'm guessing that Gerald's morning sing-song from up in the stables, calling out to the other donkeys down here and trying to out-sing the cockerel, might have had something to do with it.'

'It didn't help!'

'But it wasn't what kept you awake was it? Anything you want to talk about?'

'I've just got so many ideas about what we could do. I can't seem to quieten my mind down enough to get to sleep.' It wasn't a lie, but it wasn't the whole truth either. She didn't want to worry her mum, though. Rupert had known what he was doing when her tried to sow the seeds of doubt in her mind, but she was keeping those doubts to herself, until she had a solution for every single one of them.

'What you need is a good breakfast to give you some energy. Give me a minute and we can head back to the house, so I can whip us some up.'

'You don't need to wait on me, Mum. I haven't got to rush out of the door to commute to work any more. I can make breakfast for you, or we can do it together, after we've made sure this lot have had their food first.'

'Team work.' Karen smiled. 'So which jobs do you want?'

'Shall I start by letting the chickens out into their run?' Ellie tried not to shudder as she thought about it. Those beady eyes and that pecking at the ground, with the beaks that might be turned in her direction at any point. But she was going to have to get over her fear of birds at some point and now seemed as good a time as any.

'Are you sure? I know what you're like with birds.'

'I'll start with the chickens and then build up to the geese. I'm not quite ready to handle them just yet!'

'You'll get there sweetheart, I've got every faith in you. It's no wonder you're not all that keen on birds after what happened, but I'm really glad you're facing your fears head on. It's what we'll both be doing a lot of over the next few months, I think.' Karen squeezed her daughter's hand and Ellie had a feeling she wasn't just talking about the incident at the Tower or London, where one of the ravens had decided to attack Ellie, and Karen had virtually thrown herself over her daughter to stop her getting badly hurt. 'There's a bucket of feed and a basket by the side of the run, you can put any eggs they've laid in there. I just need to check on the fencing in the paddock the donkeys are in. I keep thinking about what would happen if it comes loose and they end up toppling over the cliff! It's become a bit of an obsession of mine already and I need to check on the fence every day.'

'Shall I feed Dolly or something whilst you're doing that?' Worrying about the pregnant goat was another thing that had kept Ellie awake in the night. Ben had told them she was expecting, when he'd examined some of the other animals after seeing Gerald. He was due to come up and check both the donkey and the goat over again later that day, and thinking about Ben being at the farm instantly made her feel better. She just had to put the thought of the resulting bills mounting up out of her mind. Some prices were worth paying.

'That would be great. Did you have a chance to check on whether we need to order more feed?'

'There's a couple of sacks in the store room next to the stable she's in. I'll put some new bedding down too, but we're going to need to order more of that. I thought I might ask Ben if he knows where the best place to get it from is.'

'I'm sure he does, he must know everything there is to know about looking after the animals and all the local suppliers around here. Maybe we should invite him for dinner one night to pick his brains, or you could invite him out for a drink?' Karen raised her eyebrows.

'Mum! I know what you're up to, you know.'

'I'm not up to anything, but this is going to be a steep learning curve for us and we could use all the help we can get.' Karen wrinkled her nose. 'After all, I don't think we can rely on Alan Crabtree for any support.'

'Probably not and it's definitely going to take a while to get to grips with this country life, but I remember everything Aunt Hilary taught me and I think I can handle the chickens and Dolly. Although I'll be keeping a firm grip on her, given how good she's always been at escaping.' There'd been an article cut out from the local paper pinned to Aunt Hilary's corkboard in the kitchen, about the goat escaping from the farm for the third time in one summer. Apparently she was famous around Kelsea Bay, but Ellie and Karen were planning to put an end to her escapades. Especially now she was pregnant.

'She usually just follows the food.' Karen grinned. 'She and I have got a lot in common, including the size of our bellies, but she's got the excuse of being pregnant.'

'You look perfect as you are, Mum, and there's no one in the world I'd rather have on my team than you.' Ellie gave her a quick hug, before leaving her to finish feeding the donkeys. She was determined to get over her decade old fear and she strode purposefully towards the chicken coop. Even after the raven incident, she had absolutely no problem with birds if they stayed where they belonged – up in the sky or perched high on a branch – it was just when she had to deal with them at close proximity that she could feel her pulse quicken and the desire to run in the opposite direction kick in.

'Out you go girls.' Ellie opened a door in the chicken coop, so that the chickens could wander down the slope to the run. The cockerel was in his own run next door and he was strutting around the place and ruffling his feathers, trying to impress the girls living next door. A couple of the chickens weren't too keen to leave their beds and Ellie closed her eyes as she gently put her hands underneath them to lift them up and shoo them out. She was okay if she didn't see their beady eyes. She could still remember how much it hurt when the raven had attacked her, but her mum had been there for her the way she always had been. So there was no way she was going to wimp out about helping with anything on the farm. Karen had been right about them being a team and she'd meant it when she'd said there was no one she'd rather do this with. It said a lot about her relationship with Rupert that she hadn't even considered the two of them buying her mother out. The prospect of him joining their team seemed less and less likely too. Three was a crowd after all.

Ellie's local job search hadn't thrown many possibilities up and so she'd decided to take an old-fashioned approach and pop into some of the local businesses in Kelsea Bay with her CV to see if they had any work. She didn't mind what she did, she just wanted to keep some money rolling in to pay the day-to-day bills, so that they could use the money she'd saved, and her pay off from the bank, to prioritise renovations to the farm and maybe even get some sort of business up and running sooner rather than later.

She'd visited all the local shops and cafes, the doctor's surgery and even dropped off a CV at Ben's veterinary practice, in case there was some reception work going. She told herself that the extra spritz of perfume she'd applied before going into the building had nothing to do with the prospect of bumping into Ben, but she hadn't felt the need to do it for any of the other businesses. As it turned out, she didn't see him anyway, which was probably just as well. She needed to sort things out with Rupert and an unrequited attraction to Ben was just a distraction technique, but sorting things out with her fiancé wasn't something she'd be able to avoid for long. Rupert would be coming down the following weekend and one way or another they'd both have to come to a decision about where they went from there.

She hadn't taken her mum's car down into town, anticipating

that the walk might be a good opportunity to clear her head and she was glad, even though the walk back up to Seabreeze Farm – perched as it was on the clifftops – was pretty steep. The sun was warm and the spring weather was living up to its promise of the summer to come. The winters on the farm could be tough, when the wind came off the sea, making it a much harsher environment for the animals and pushing the cost of caring for them up a lot too. She needed to be earning decent money by then and if she didn't find work quickly they'd soon have to start eating into her savings.

She wasn't concentrating when the car came past her and she barely noticed it until she heard the squeal of brakes and someone shouting.

'Casper!' The car had stopped about thirty feet in front of her and a woman, still wearing her slippers, had come out of a driveway and was peering under the front of the car.

Please don't let it be a child. Ellie's legs didn't seem to be moving and it felt forever before she got level with the car. An elderly man was sitting in the driver's seat, his knuckles white as they gripped the steering wheel.

'He's hit the dog!' The woman was cradling a small curly-coated black dog, which was whining. Although it didn't look to Ellie like it had sustained any serious injury.

'Shall I call the vet?' It was funny, she'd have known exactly what to do if it had been a person who'd been injured. But was there such a thing as an animal ambulance? At least she could phone Ben and ask him.

'Thank you.' The woman managed a wobbly smile. 'Is Bert all right?'

'Bert?' She'd been sure the woman had called the dog Casper.

'My husband – he was the one driving.'

'He's your husband?' Ellie pulled up the handle and opened

the door of the car slowly, not wanting to frighten the man who still hadn't even turned his head. 'Are you okay, Bert?'

'I didn't see him; I'd almost stopped to back into the drive and he just shot out in front of me. Is he... is he *dead*?' Bert's voice cracked on the word and Ellie placed her hand gently on his shoulder.

'No, he doesn't look badly hurt from what I can see. Your wife's looking after him.'

'Hetty will kill me if anything happens to Casper and I couldn't live with myself either.' Bert was still gripping the steering wheel and Ellie was starting to wonder if she was going to have to prise his hands off to get him to move.

'I'm sure it wasn't your fault. I'm just going to phone the vet and then we can get you indoors; I think you could use a nice cup of tea to settle your nerves.' She sounded just like her mother. Karen was of the school of thought that there was no problem that couldn't be solved with a cup of tea.

Just as Ellie got her phone out of her pocket, another car pulled up in front of Bert's and, for once, luck seemed to be on her side, as Ben got out.

'Has the dog been hit?' He moved to crouch next to the woman who was still holding the dog in her arms, although it seemed to be struggling to get free. The shock Bert had suffered meant he'd almost certainly come off worse.

'I thought I'd shut the front door after the man from the catalogue delivered my new duvet covers, but I can't have done it properly. And when Casper heard Bert's car pulling up, he ran out before I could stop him.' She held out the dog towards him. 'Please tell me he's going to be okay!'

'Don't worry, we'll get him sorted out. I think you've brought Casper into the veterinary surgery to see me before. It's Mrs

Sanders, isn't it?' Ben had the sort of soothing tone that a lot of doctors could learn something from.

'Yes, that's right, but he's never had anything seriously wrong with him before.'

'He doesn't look hurt; he's not whimpering and I think he'd jump down if I let him. But we can get him into my car and take him down to the surgery to take a better look and see if we need to get any x-rays done.' Ben looked up at Ellie.

'Is everyone else okay?' He looked straight at Ellie and for a moment she was almost envious of the little dog he was holding in his arms. 'You weren't caught up in the accident were you?'

'No, I was just walking home, but I think Bert's a bit shaken up.'

'Are you okay Bert?' Ben leant into the open car door, still holding the dog in his arms, and Bert finally turned his head.

'My legs feel like jelly.'

'It's just a bit of shock, but Casper's going to be fine, so perhaps we can get you inside first?'

'I'm not sure my legs will hold me up. I really thought I'd killed him when I heard that bump.' Bert's hands were shaking when he finally took them off the steering wheel.

'He's going to be fine I promise.' Ben turned towards Bert's wife and gave her another reassuring look that made Ellie want him to smile at her like that. 'Do you think you can find a box to put Casper into Mrs Sanders? Maybe with an old blanket to line it and then we can get Bert in, before I take Casper back to the surgery. I don't want him to have to sit loose on the back seat of my car and I think you need to keep an eye on Bert.'

'There's one that my new garden shears came in that should be about the right size. I won't be a minute, but don't put Casper down until I've sorted it will you?'

'Of course not.' Ben caught Ellie's eye as he spoke and she had to supress a smile. There was no doubting that Bert came second place to the dog that was now licking Ben's face. It was going to be up to her and Ben to give Bert the TLC he needed.

Within a couple of minutes, Hetty Sanders, still wearing her slippers, had sorted out the box and the blanket and was trying to stop Casper from jumping straight out of it. Ben was steadying Bert, who despite several reassurances that Casper was almost certainly none the worse for wear, was still unsteady on his feet.

'Ooh, Casper, don't!' Hetty called out to try and stop the little dog from escaping from the box and running into the house. But it was no use; the dog shot towards the house and came back seconds later with a rawhide chew in his mouth, wagging his tail and jumping up and down as though he was putting on a display.

'I think it's safe to say that he's definitely okay.' Ben laughed as they all followed the dog back into the house, Bert still looking as if he needed to lean heavily on his arm. 'I can still take him to the surgery if you want me to, but I suspect the car missed him altogether. It's probably Bert we need to look after.'

'I'm going to take him down to get him one of the ice-creams they sell in the café by the harbour.'

'I'm not sure that's a good idea, I think Bert probably needs a rest.' Ellie was still worried about how pale he looked, but Hetty was shaking her head.

'Not Bert, Casper! They sell dog-friendly ice-creams down there now.' Hetty had taken off her slippers and pulled on a pair of elasticated trainers. 'You'll be all right here, won't you?'

'I just need to catch my breath, that's all.' Bert slumped down heavily in the seat.

'I'll see you later then and thank you both so much.' Hetty blew a kiss to Ben and Ellie, before planting a very quick one on her husband's cheek and scooping up the little dog who she kissed at least twenty times on the way out.

'Shall I put the kettle on?' Ellie turned to Bert as Hetty closed the door behind her, wondering if he really wanted two strangers in his house, but he was nodding his head.

'Oh yes, a tea with two sugars would work wonders and I think I could use a biscuit too, that flipping dog has taken five years off my life. There should be some biscuits in the tin by the kettle, but, if not, I'll let you into a secret, there's some chocolate digestives hidden on the top shelf of the larder that Hetty can't reach.' He laughed, looking much better than he had a few minutes before. 'After all, a man's got to have some secrets, hasn't he? Even after fifty-two years of marriage.'

'That's a real achievement.' Ben smiled as he stood next to the chair Bert had sunk into, in the sunny kitchen, which looked as though it hadn't changed much since he and Hetty had first got married. It was so retro that it was almost fashionable again and Ellie immediately felt at home.

'Can I get you a drink, Ben?' She didn't miss how patient and gentle Ben had been with both Bert and Hetty, and she couldn't help wondering how Rupert would have reacted in the same situation. He'd almost certainly have been out of the door even quicker than Hetty, if he'd even stopped in the first place.

'I'd love a tea, no sugar for me though, thanks.' Ben picked up the biscuit tin and put it in front of Bert.

'Sit down, lad. It's like having Hetty standing over me otherwise, making sure I don't eat too many of these.' He took the lid off and stacked four biscuits in front of him before passing the tin to Ben. 'Although I know she's only doing it to look after my health. The old girl might not give you the impression she wants to keep me around, but I know she does really.'

Ellie turned her back on Ben and Bert to pour the tea. Even if she and Rupert found enough common ground to stay together, would they last fifty-two years? The possibility that they might made her suddenly shiver. A whole lifetime, that's what agreeing to marry someone was supposed to mean, but the truth was she'd never thought much beyond their five-year plan. Thinking about a stretch of time more than ten years longer than that suddenly made it feel as though she'd forgotten how to swallow. Bert wasn't the only one who desperately needed a cup of tea.

'Here you go.' She set the cups out on the table and took a seat next to the older man.

'So how long have you two been courting?' He looked from Ben to Ellie, as he dunked the first chocolate biscuit in his tea.

'Oh no! We're not a couple. We're just… friends.' Ellie sipped her tea, even though it was far too hot. She didn't even know why Bert's words had made her feel uncomfortable, but they had. Even describing Ben as a friend was stretching the truth to its limits. They'd met once and spoken on the phone twice so far, but at least Ben didn't correct her. That would have been really embarrassing.

'Shame. You'd make a handsome couple.' Bert tapped his nose. 'Just like me and Hetty in our day.'

'Have you always lived in Kelsea Bay?' Ben's seamless change of subject meant that Ellie could finally breathe out.

'Yes, man and boy. We bought this house a couple of years after we got married. We lived with Hetty's parents for the first two years while we saved hard. We brought all three of our kids up here, but now that they're gone, it's Casper who rules the roost.'

'I've always lived here too, but where would you recommend to someone who is new to the area' – Ben smiled briefly in Ellie's direction – 'if you wanted to take them somewhere to show them all that Kelsea Bay has to offer?'

'If you're talking about a young lady' – Bert gave him a knowing look – 'I took Hetty to the picture house the first time I took her out, back in the days when Kelsea Bay had one. But that's no good to you now.'

'I was thinking of something that's a bit more unique to Kelsea Bay, that will help her decide whether it's got enough to offer.'

'Ah, well, my grandson runs boat trips out of the harbour to go seal watching.' Bert looked from Ben to Ellie. 'Although it's not as relaxing as it sounds; it's in one of those big rubber dinghy things and they go pretty fast. When the boat flies up after it hits a wave, your stomach goes up with it.'

'It sounds brilliant.' Heat flooded Ellie's cheeks as the words came out before she could stop them. There was no way Ben could be talking about taking her out, even if he did keep looking over at her, but she hadn't been able to stop herself picturing it all the same.

'It does sound brilliant.' Ben was definitely looking at her again. If he did want her to stay in Kelsea Bay, it could only be because he didn't want to see the farm sold up to a developer or some weekenders. He'd probably come up with the idea after talking to Alan about her and Karen again, sacrificing going on a few dates with her to make sure she stuck around long enough to decide against selling the farm. For a moment she bristled, but looking at him again she just couldn't imagine Ben being that manipulative.

'I'll get you his card.' Bert got to his feet. 'I think it's pinned to the noticeboard over there. I suppose I should warn you that Hetty felt seasick for a week after she went on it and she didn't nag me for days about doing any chores. I keep asking her when we can book up to go again! Although, all that said, I do miss her telling me what to do when she'd not around for a bit. I should have listened when she asked me to put a new latch on the gate and then Casper wouldn't have been able to run straight out of the front door into the road. It's just that the battery won't charge on my electric screwdriver any more and I just can't hold my old manual one tightly enough, since the arthritis has made it so hard to grip properly.'

'I think sorting out your gate before we leave is a fair exchange, seeing as you've solved my dilemma about where to take my friend.' Ben took the business card that Bert handed him.

'It's the least I can do, because I can't thank you enough for making sure Casper was okay. You've both been so brilliant and with you offering to fix the gate too, young man, you might just keep me out of the dog house, if you'll pardon the pun!'

It only took Ben a few minutes to sort out the gate but, when they waved Bert goodbye, anyone would have thought they'd given up a week's holiday just to help him out. Ben had told Ellie that he'd been on the way to Seabreeze Farm, when he'd stopped outside Bert and Hetty's place, and he'd offered her a lift back. It would have looked rude to turn him down, even if the idea of being in such close proximity to Ben, as they sat in his car, made her pulse start to quicken. He seemed so lovely, although she still wasn't sure if she could trust that he was genuine, but that wasn't the only reason she was trying hard not to like him too much.

'Bert's a real character.' Ben turned to her as they got into his car.

'I suspect Hetty is even more of one.' Ellie smiled. 'Although I got the impression he actually likes being bossed around!'

'My grandparents were like that, they bickered all the time and sometimes I wondered if they actually liked each other, but when my nan died, my granddad was lost without her. We think he died of a broken heart, even though the doctors told us there was no such thing.'

'I'm sorry.'

'Thanks, but it was a few years back now and my granddad was so sad after we lost Nan that it was almost a relief when that pain ended for him. Bert reminded me of him so much, though, and I guess it's what we all want, isn't it? The sort of relationship where even the arguments can't change the bottom line, when you love someone, you love them. Even if they drive you mad half the time!'

'I think that's real life, isn't it?' Ellie bit her lip; it was becoming increasingly obvious that it was the bottom line that was missing with Rupert. If he loved her, then it came with a lot of provisos – including ticking off every aspect of the plan he'd set out for achieving their goals. Loving someone should never depend on all of that.

'It is, but romantic movies have a lot to answer for. Us men just can't live up to the promise most of the time.' Ben raised his eyebrows.

'So I take it you're a diehard singleton and steer clear of all of that?'

'That's straight to the point!' He laughed and she could barely believe she'd asked him such a direct question. It was absolutely none of her business. 'I've had a couple of serious relationships, but they didn't work out for various reasons and I suppose I'm not willing to settle for less than what my grandparents had. My parents have got that sort of rock-solid relationship too and it's a lot to try and emulate.'

'I've got the opposite problem. Parents whose relationship was a nightmare from start to finish and a dad who wasn't that inter-ested in the fact he had a daughter.' The words just seemed to be tumbling out of Ellie's mouth, without her being able to stop them. It had taken her months to open up to Rupert as much as this.

'That sounds really tough.' Ben touched her hand for just an instant, before putting it firmly back on the steering wheel, and she found herself wishing that he hadn't taken it away again.

'Mum was brilliant, but it's probably why I've made some stupid decisions along the way.'

'So it hasn't made you steer clear of relationships then?'

'I'm engaged.' She blurted out the words and she was almost certain she heard Ben sigh. 'But I'm starting to wonder if that's one of those stupid decisions I've been talking about.'

'That doesn't sound like the basis for a happy life.' Ben's tone was gentle as he pulled up outside the farmhouse.

'I don't think it is, but my fiancé, Rupert, showed me what it's like not to spend your whole life worrying if you can pay the rent, or if you need to choose between heating and eating. Mum and I haven't always been so lucky, and now we've taken on a farm that is probably going to use up every penny we've managed to save. Maybe the sensible thing to do would just be to sell it.'

'I could see on your face, the first time I met you, that you really meant it when you said you didn't want to sell the farm. It means a lot to you, doesn't it?'

'Mum and the farm mean everything to me.'

'Which leaves Rupert where?'

'Exactly.' Ellie let go of a long breath. 'I've got to work out what to do, but even if we lose every penny trying, we've got to give this place everything we've got. We owe it to Aunt Hilary.'

'If I can help in any way, I want you to know that I will.' There was such kindness in Ben's eyes and she was suddenly certain that none of it was a pretence. 'The least I can do is make sure that all the animals stay well and you can consider free veterinary services my contribution to a good cause.'

'You can't do that without being paid!'

'Oh yes I can. Your aunt was an amazing lady and I'd hate to see you having to say goodbye to the farm. It's just a little thing, but it all helps.'

'It's not little at all and it's going to make so much difference, thank you.' The kiss she hadn't been able to control had only been on Ben's cheek, but her body had reacted to it all the same. She needed to be honest with Rupert. Whatever she might have come to realise over the last week or so, she owed him that much at least. Her new life in the country had only just begun and it had already changed everything. Whatever happened next, there'd be no going back.

6

'Can you just run me through everything on the list again, so we can sort out the absolute essentials first?' Ellie said to her mum.

The number on the calculator *couldn't* be right, and she shook her head as if that might change the figure on the digital display. It looked like the national debt of Greece. The stack of estimates on the kitchen table, detailing the cost of putting things right at the farm, didn't make for pretty reading, either.

'The surveyor said we need new windows, and, because it's a listed cottage, they've got to be handmade wooden casements.' Karen sighed, beating a cake mix as though her life depended on it. 'Then the roof needs replacing – which can only be with Kent peg tiles. The electrics are, apparently, a museum piece, and potentially lethal to boot. And I'm sure you've noticed that the plumbing makes rattling noises, like Marley's chains, as soon as you turn a tap on? I'm afraid, if we want to make it to the end of our first year alive, they're *all* pretty much essential.'

'Just a few little tweaks, then?' Ellie tried to smile, but she could see her pay off from the bank, and the money she'd saved to hit Rupert's target on their five-year plan, disappearing faster than she could say '*Money Pit*'. 'And what about the outside? Do you think there's anything that desperately needs doing out there?'

'Well, the good news is, the stables and most of the outbuildings, including the old barn, seem to be holding up okay.' Karen spooned the mixture into cake papers as she spoke. 'But the bad news is, almost all of the fencing needs replacing – and the absolute worst part of that is that one of us will have to go and see Alan Crabtree, to check which bits of the fencing belong to him and which of it belongs to us. I can only imagine what sort of reaction it will provoke if we get that wrong!'

'That *is* bad news.' Ellie laughed at the expression on her mum's face, despite everything. 'So, what's the plan of attack?'

'What do you think I'm making these fairy cakes for?' Karen raised an eyebrow. 'They're intended as a peace offering, but, if all else fails, I can always throw them at him.'

'It's probably worth having a backup plan where Alan Crabtree's concerned.' Ellie scanned down the list of things that needed to be paid for again. 'I could always ask Ben to have a word with him, he's his godfather after all.'

'You wouldn't have an ulterior motive at all, would you, my love? And there's got to be a reason why Ben is willing to give up so much of his free time looking after the animals.' Her mum winked, and a blush swept across Ellie's face.

Gerald was on the mend and Dolly's pregnancy seemed to be progressing without a hitch, but Ben was a regular visitor. He popped in every day, sometimes twice. Despite such an unpromising start on that first day, he was proving to be one of the nicest things about moving to Seabreeze Farm. Rupert had cancelled his planned trip to the farm, because the chance to visit another small chain of hotels on the Pembrokeshire coast, which his company was interesting in buying, had come up and he'd rescheduled for two weeks' later. She didn't want to finish things over the phone, so officially she was still engaged. But that hadn't stopped her hoping that Ben might ask her out on that trip to see the seals that Bert had suggested. All of which meant her mother's words were spot on.

'Just because I've decided to finish things with Rupert, it doesn't mean I want to jump straight into something else. Promise me you won't drop any heavy hints when Ben's around? Even if he is as nice as he looks.' Ellie's face grew hotter still as she said the words out loud, and suddenly the pile of estimates in front of her seemed really interesting. She was in danger of acting like a school girl when it came to Ben Hastings.

'So it's definite, then, you and Rupert being finished for good?' Her mum didn't sound at all upset at the prospect, but then Ellie knew she'd never really warmed to him. Ben, on the other hand, was a different matter. Every time he arrived at the farm, Karen would announce that the kettle was on, and she never failed to have a large slice of his favourite gypsy tart waiting for him.

'It's obvious now that we don't want the same things and I don't think we ever really did. I wanted a different life and he seemed to offer that, but I'm still trying to work out why he wanted to make that with me.' She shook her head. 'As soon as I told him about the farm, he was thinking of ways to get rid of it, but here I am – a farm girl all the way. I think what he liked about me was that I was so willing to go along with what he thought was best, but I'm not any more. Once I realised the farm meant more to me than Rupert did, it made everything else clear.' Ellie shrugged. She had absolutely no doubt she was doing the right thing. She'd been surprised by how easy the choice had been when it had finally come down to it. 'I suppose it won't be 100 per cent official until I've told him face to face and given him back the ring.' Ellie glanced at the fourth finger of her left hand, where the white gold and diamond band had left a line of slightly paler skin. By the end of their first summer at the farm, that would disappear too, and the last physical reminder of her relationship with Rupert would disappear with it.

* * *

Gerald's head appeared above the stable door, as if he had heard the footsteps crossing the yard outside. The old donkey appeared to be almost smiling at Ellie and Ben when they approached, a piece of hay sticking out between his big, yellow teeth.

'You've done a great job with him, you know.' Ben, who'd come to give him another check over, ran a hand down the donkey's leg. 'I think he's ready to go back outside. Have you fenced off a starvation paddock?'

'We have.' Ellie nodded. 'Although, I still can't get used to that expression. It sounds so cruel.'

'Far crueller to let him get laminitis again.' Ben looked up at her, his warm brown eyes crinkling in the corners. All of the animosity from their first meeting had long since melted away. 'You should be proud of yourself. I honestly didn't think we could save him, what with his age and everything. But you've worked miracles. Bathing his legs every few hours and resisting those puppy dog eyes of his, begging you for just a bit more food, takes commitment and tough love.'

'It's true, he can give you a look that's pretty hard to resist!' Ellie fought the urge to add that it wasn't only the donkey who had that effect on her. She'd told her mum not to drop any heavy hints, but Karen might not be the only person in danger of giving the game away. Concentrating on Gerald was easier and she watched Ben in silence as he continued to examine the donkey.

'I've been meaning to ask you something, only I wasn't quite sure how to say it.' Ben didn't look at her again as he spoke. Instead, he made a great show of checking over the donkey's other legs. 'I noticed you aren't wearing your engagement ring any more, and...'

'It's because I'm not engaged any more.' Ellie patted the donkey's neck, debating whether to admit to Ben that she hadn't actually told Rupert yet, but that didn't really matter. She wasn't going to change her mind. 'He didn't like the idea of life on a farm.'

'You made a decision then?'

'It was easy in the end.' Ellie smiled. 'I'd started to realise I didn't like the idea of life with him much, on a farm or anywhere else, for that matter. But it was only inheriting this place that made it all crystal clear.'

'I can't lie, it makes me really happy to hear that.' Ben straightened up and returned her smile, the dimple deepening in his right cheek. 'In fact it makes it all the easier to ask you another question. There's a barn dance in the church hall on Saturday, and I'm expected to go. I wondered if you might like to come with me, to meet some of the other locals? It's usually a good night, and they do a fantastic hog roast.'

'You had me at *barn dance*.' Ellie laughed, her earlier vow to steer clear of anything new instantly forgotten. 'You might think I'm a city girl, but believe me, I can do-si-do with the best of them.'

'It's a date, then?' He raised a questioning eyebrow.

'I do believe it is, Mr Hastings. I just hope your square dancing doesn't let you down!'

* * *

Balancing a cake box on one arm, whilst trying to climb over a rickety wooden stile, wasn't the easiest of things to do. Thank goodness she was completely over her surgery now. Karen was sure that Alan Crabtree had seen her crossing the boundary into his land, but he hadn't rushed to relieve her of her load, or even called out to see if she wanted any help. She wasn't about to ask *him* for help, either, or give him another excuse to start ranting about something she'd done wrong. At least this way, she'd have a chance to explain the reason for her visit.

He was tinkering under the bonnet of a tractor, which looked as though it had ploughed its last furrow decades before. 'Whatever it is you're selling, I'm not interested.' Alan didn't look up, leaving Karen in no doubt that he'd ignored her struggle over the stile on purpose.

'I'm not selling anything. I brought you these as a gift.' She put the box of fairy cakes on the tractor's step.

'Experience has taught me there's no such thing as a free lunch.' At last, he looked up from the rusty engine and caught Karen's eye. 'So, what *is* it you want?'

'I don't want anything, I needed to ask you something, though.' She could still barely believe he was the same Alan who'd been so much fun when they were teenagers. She'd never have imagined him growing up to be a curmudgeonly old misery guts, but the truth was right in front of her.

'*Want, need*, it's all the same thing, just dressed up a different way.' Alan didn't move to look in the box, and Karen was more desperate than ever to get back to the farm and away from their grumpy neighbour.

'We're getting the fencing replaced, and we wanted to know which of the boundaries belong to you and which to us, so that we don't take down any fencing that's yours.' She glanced around at the ramshackle state of Crabtree Farm, which, if anything, looked to be in a worse state of repair than their own place.

'It's perfectly simple. The fence on the left of your land is assigned to you. It's all in the deeds.' He sounded as though she'd asked him the same question a hundred times before. 'But since the boundary on the right follows the clifftop, you'll pretty much have to replace the whole thing.' If he had any sympathy for what that might cost them, he was doing a pretty good job of hiding it.

'Okay, well, that sounds simple enough. We'll be getting someone in to replace it. There'll be some other building work going on at the farmhouse, too. I hope it won't disturb you.' Karen waited for a moment, in the vain hope that Alan might say something to indicate he was pleased by the news, happy to see the farm being taken care of, at last. But all he did was grunt and continue poking around under the tractor's hood.

So much for the friendliness of neighbours in small communities. Alan Crabtree had as much social grace as one of the potatoes he farmed, and he was about as much fun to talk to.

* * *

'How did your peace mission with Alan go?' Ellie asked as she came into the kitchen, which had been one of the first rooms to receive a makeover.

They'd chosen a soft, baby blue shade for the walls and given the cupboards a new lease of life by painting them buttercream. Whilst a new kitchen would have been lovely, it wasn't high up on their ever-growing list of priorities. It looked like home, though, all the same. The shelves of the dresser were crammed with Karen's recipe books, and the ornaments, which had covered every surface at the old house, had found new homes, dotted around the kitchen and downstairs rooms. They'd kept the things that were precious to Aunt Hilary, too, and pride of place on the mantelpiece had gone to a black and white photograph of her and the original Gerald, on the day they'd got engaged.

'The conversation with Alan went pretty much how you might expect.' Karen smiled as she lined some baking trays with greaseproof paper, seemingly unfazed by her encounter with the neighbour from hell.

They'd both accepted that life at the farm might be a bit isolating. It was never going to be like it had been with their neighbours back at The Copse – Karen going next door for games of cards, or Scrabble, and fish and chip suppers on a Friday evening, whenever Ellie had been out with Rupert. From time to time, she'd worried that her mother didn't have a social life with people more her own age, but she'd always seemed happy baking, looking in on the neighbours, and generally running around after Ellie. Karen's life had revolved around being a mum for so long that it didn't take a genius to work out she'd side-lined her own needs over the years. Luckily, the farm was a fresh start for them both, and it had been a long time since Ellie had needed looking after in that way. Perhaps Alan wasn't the best candidate with whom to start building up a new social life, but Kelsea Bay was a small community, and there would be plenty of opportunities to make friends. Maybe she could persuade Karen to join her and Ben at the barn dance, for a start.

'I take it that, by going as expected, you mean Alan completely ignored you?' Ellie flicked idly through the local paper. It had been delivered whilst she was out at the paddock with Ben, but looking for a job in Kelsea Bay was still proving more difficult than she'd expected. The only local vacancies she'd heard back about had been in a couple of the shops in town, and even those were just a few hours a week, temporarily over the summer, to boost the workforce during the late spring and summer months, when the tourists were drawn to pretty coastal towns like theirs. But she couldn't afford to take on something that would stop her having the chance to earn a full time salary. Although, as the weeks slipped past, she was getting more and more desperate to find something, and soon.

'He didn't *completely* ignore me. He grunted something, insulted me a bit, and *then* ignored me!' Karen laughed, but as Gerald the III gave one of his ear-splitting *hee-haws*, the baking tray she was holding slipped out of her hands. 'My God, he's got a healthy pair of lungs on him. I don't think I'll ever get used to the sound he makes. I jump out of my skin every time!'

As Gerald's braying died down, it was replaced by what sounded like someone running across the gravel outside.

Ellie moved over to the window, but there was no one in sight. 'Did you hear that?' She turned to Karen, who shook her head. 'I'm sure there was someone outside. I'd better take a look, in case it's someone from the fencing company wanting to start measuring up. The foreman did say he'd try and get someone up here this afternoon.'

Pulling back the heavy front door of the farmhouse, Ellie immediately noticed an old pottery bottle sitting in the middle of the large stone slabs that flanked the doorstep. There were five foxglove stems poked into its neck and a piece of paper, folded in half, tucked underneath its base. After lifting them both up, she went back through to the kitchen.

'Where on earth did they come from? They're beautiful, such vibrant colours! And that bottle looks like an antique.' Karen took the bottle from her and set it down on the windowsill, where it looked as though it had always belonged. It fitted the farmhouse perfectly. The foxgloves, in shades of pink, cream and lilac, had rows of flowers, each one like a little bell. 'They're lovely, and, I'm guessing, from Ben?'

Ellie opened the folded paper, wondering if her mum was right. A warm feeling in her stomach at the thought, she read the letter out loud:

Dear Mrs Chapman,

Thank you for the fairy cakes. They brought back memories and were almost as good as my mother used to make.

Regards,

Alan Crabtree

P.S. Do let me know if you need a hand with the fencing when the time comes.

He had surprisingly nice writing for someone whose hands looked like a bunch of bananas, and her mother's cheeks had coloured slightly at hearing the contents of the letter.

'It's a *sort* of compliment, I suppose.' Karen was clearly attempting to shrug it off. 'My cakes are *almost* as good as his mother used to make!'

'I wonder why he didn't knock?' Ellie met her mother's eyes for the briefest of moments, but they both seemed to know the answer. For whatever reason, Alan Crabtree found it very difficult to be friendly – in person, at least – but it seemed he was trying to offer an olive branch in the guise of five foxglove stems.

'It's very kind of him.' Karen didn't sound entirely convinced. 'But I won't be rushing back to his farm the moment the flowers die off, hoping for a repeat performance. I'm not sure I can cope with more than one encounter with Alan in a week.'

'I think that's as much as anyone can be expected to do!' Ellie laughed again at the look on her mother's face. It would take more than the delivery of some handpicked flowers to convince either of them that Alan had changed his spots.

'What about you? How did it go with Ben? I forgot to ask you what the verdict was on Gerald.'

'He's fighting fit.' Ellie glanced at the flyer her mother had pinned to the noticeboard. 'In fact, if he carries on like this, he might even be well enough for a brief return from retirement to make an appearance at the summer fundraiser.'

The leaflet was advertising Kelsea Bay's twice yearly event, where all sorts of stall holders set up shop for a single day to raise funds for the church hall and the mayor's chosen charity for the year. The upcoming fundraiser was for an animal shelter in a neighbouring town. Taking part in the event would be another opportunity to make sure they became part of the community, and Ellie was certain that people would pay to let their children pet Gerald and some of the others, like Dolly the goat.

'That's wonderful news, but, more importantly, how was *Ben*?' Karen gave her a knowing look, making it clear that it was her turn to tease.

'Fine.' Ellie hesitated, although she might as well tell her the truth. She had a feeling that Kelsea Bay was the sort of place where news travelled fast. 'Actually, he asked me if I'd like to go to the barn dance with him on Saturday. Apparently, there's an amazing hog roast. I wondered if you fancied it, too?'

'Absolutely not!' Karen smiled again. 'Not only did I have major surgery a little while ago, but I've got two left feet and I've been known to bring down a whole anniversary reel. Most of all, there's absolutely no way I'm going to cramp your style. Not now you're seeing such a nice chap.'

'I'm not *seeing* him, Mum.' Ellie pulled a face, but Karen just shrugged, and she knew she was on to a losing battle, trying to convince her mother otherwise. 'Can I ask you something, though? You haven't been able to hide your enthusiasm about Ben, but why didn't you ever tell me how you felt about Rupert before I decided to end things? It was you who kept saying I needed to give him enough of a chance.'

'You had to realise for yourself what the right thing to do was. If I'd told you to steer clear of him, you wouldn't have understood why.' Karen squeezed her hand. 'But remember, your old mum knows best, and I think Ben could make you really happy.'

'Mum, I keep telling you, I don't want to rush into anything. It's one date, to a barn dance in the village. We're hardly announcing our engagement in *The Times*.'

'Maybe not yet, but Hilary knew what she was doing when she left us this place.' She squeezed Ellie's hand again. 'Just you wait and see.'

7

By the time the barn dance on Saturday rolled around, Ellie had arranged an interview with an employment agency in Elverham, the nearest big town to Kelsea Bay, for the following week. Some temporary office work would tide her over until she found the thing she really wanted to do – whatever that was. She wouldn't feel guilty about leaving an agency if the right job came up, in the same way she would have done at one of the local shops during their busiest time of the year. The agency had been impressed with her CV and tried to persuade her to go for an interview for a role as Events Coordinator with a large firm of lawyers. The money was good, and it was only half an hour's commute from the farm, but the thought of plunging straight back into the corporate world made her go cold. Apparently, the firm had won a contract to do all the legal work for a new sewage treatment works, a revelation that hadn't done anything to help change Ellie's mind. Despite her growing panic about money, she'd stood her ground and told them that she was definitely only looking for something temporary. She just had to hope they could come up with something before she was forced in a direction she *really* didn't want to go.

'You look amazing.' Karen looked up from the book she was reading and gave Ellie a thumbs up. 'A proper country girl.'

'I don't think the average Kentish farmhand really wears cowboy boots and a pink Stetson, but I'll be able to hoedown with the best of them.' Leaning forward, she kissed her mother on the cheek, breathing in the familiar scent of English Fern. 'I won't be late.'

'Be as late as you like, darling, but know that I'll be waiting up, anyway.' Karen gave her a little wave. 'I'll want to hear *all* the gossip!'

The lights of the church hall were blazing, visible from a good distance away. It wasn't until she got closer that Ellie could make out the unmistakable sound of a barn dance band. It was a relief to discover that she wasn't the only one to go all out and don country and western gear.

Ben stood outside the double doors, waiting for her. He'd come wearing a checked shirt, and Levi jeans tucked into some very authentic looking cowboy boots, with silver spurs to finish off the look. He looked really good, like he wouldn't have been out of place driving cattle on a ranch somewhere. Nerves fluttered in her stomach as his eyes locked with hers and he smiled. She hadn't been able to stop herself from kissing him when they'd been sitting in his car, so what chance did she have when he was standing in front of her, looking like he did?

'Howdy there, pretty lady. Y'all here for the dance?' He grinned, immediately dropping his attempt at a Southern American twang. 'Sorry, I can't keep that up. The only accent I've ever been able to do is the one I've got.' He took her hand as he spoke, and, still determined to keep it casual, she tried not to think about how nice it felt.

'I'll let you off. I like your normal voice, anyway.' She didn't catch his response, as half the town seemed to be in the church hall waiting just to greet Ben. He was the perfect gentleman and introduced Ellie to everyone who came up to say hello. She was usually good with names, but even she was struggling to recall more than three or four – there were just too many new faces to lock them all into her memory bank.

'That's my sister, Daisy.' Ben pointed towards a pretty girl wearing dungarees and a straw hat, with two thick blonde plaits poking out from underneath it. She had painted on freckles and an air of irrepressible enthusiasm, as she almost bounced over to greet them.

'Hi, Daisy, this is my friend, Ellie.' Ben moved aside to let them shake hands, but Daisy immediately enveloped her in a hug.

'Ellie! It's so fabulous to meet you at last. I've heard *so* much about you.' She stepped back and looked her up and down. 'And for once, Benji boy didn't exaggerate.'

Ellie guessed that Daisy was in her late-twenties, but it was hard to tell between the braids and painted on freckles.

'Daisy, I warned you not to be a blabbermouth! You're not too old for hair-pulling, you know, and those plaits would be perfect – just like the old days!' Ben teased his sister in the way that only a brother could.

'Sorry, sorry, my lips are sealed.' Daisy giggled loudly. 'I'll do things the proper way and not let on how much you keep talking about her.' She turned towards Ellie, giving a little bob of her head. 'Welcome to Kelsea Bay. How are you liking it so far?'

'It's great. We haven't got to know the town as much as we'd like, as we've been so busy sorting things out at the farm.' Ellie paused. She'd been about to say that everyone had been really friendly so far but remembered Alan Crabtree. 'We love living so near the sea, and I'm sure it's only a matter of time before we feel part of the community. Ben inviting me here has certainly helped.'

'Ah, yes, he can be very helpful when the mood takes him.' Daisy winked, earning herself another nudge in the ribs from her brother. 'Come on, then, you two, let's see what you're made of. You've got to work up an appetite for the buffet and the hog roast. There's enough food to last until Christmas, by the looks of it.'

* * *

Karen was just settling down to watch Casualty, when she heard knocking at the front door. By then, it had grown dark, and Gerald obviously hadn't spotted the visitor, as there'd been no braying to herald the arrival of a stranger in the yard.

Nerves suddenly prickled her skin; she was home alone, and the farm was a lot more isolated than their old house at The Copse, where the neighbours had only ever been a knock on the wall away. Perhaps they should get a dog, but only once everything was settled and all the fencing had been repaired. The last thing she needed was to have a dog escape into Alan's farm next door and cause havoc. They seemed to have established the beginning of what might be termed a neighbourly relationship, with the exchange of cakes and flowers, but she had no doubt it was just as fragile as the delicate foxgloves he'd left on their doorstep. A marauding hound would soon put pay to any hope she had of building a proper friendship with him. Still, their prickly new neighbour had one advantage – he was distracting her from worrying about whoever it was that was knocking on the door.

Peering through the peephole, Karen almost toppled backwards. Of all the people she'd expected it to be, he was almost the last she'd have thought of. All the same, the relief was tangible. She was getting far too much of an imagination living out in the sticks. Alan Crabtree might not have been the friendliest person in the world, but at least it wasn't a complete stranger waiting outside her door in the dark.

She opened the door wide. 'Mr Crabtree, come in.'

He moved past her, a large parcel in his arms. 'Alan, please. We've known each other for years after all.' He smiled, and his eyes were much greener than she remembered. He looked completely different when his mouth was turned upwards, too, like he had done in the old days of their carefree youth – he should smile more often. 'Shall I put this on the table?'

'Yes, yes, of course.' She pushed the recipe books she'd left spread out on the kitchen table to one side. She'd meant to put them away before she'd settled down to watch television, but these days, it was so rare to have complete control of the remote and watch the programmes she wanted to watch on a Saturday night. Ellie liked those dating shows, full of canned laughter and over-the-top banter between the contestants, but Karen couldn't stand them. Romance should be old fashioned, like delivering flowers to the doorstep. Even as the notion entered her head, embarrassment at having thought it warmed her cheeks. 'Well, if you're to be Alan, then I insist you call me Karen. Mrs Chapman makes me sound like my former mother-in-law, and let's just say that she wasn't the most likeable of people. And, like you say, when we knew each other all those years ago, we definitely didn't call each other by our surnames then.'

'Karen it is, then, although I seem to remember you being Kaz back then.' Alan smiled again, and the transformation to his face was undeniable. Perhaps she was imagining it, but he looked different altogether – closely shaven. Even his nails were spotlessly clean – a rarity for a potato farmer, she'd bet.

'I'd almost forgotten that! It brings back memories just to hear it.' She returned his smile, almost reluctant to ask him the reason for his visit, in case it broke the spell and he turned back into Mr Grumpy. Still, it was a bit awkward just standing there, so in the end she cracked. 'It's lovely to see you, but I was just wondering what brought you here... at this time on a Saturday evening.'

'Sadly, it's been a long time since Saturday evenings had any significance for me.' She hadn't expected his honesty, and he laughed at the look that must have crossed her face. 'Don't look so worried, I came because of the parcel.' He gestured towards the package he'd just placed on her table, and it was her turn to laugh. She'd forgotten about him struggling in with that, in all the shock of it being him at the door.

'Oh, gosh, I hadn't realised that was for us.' Karen leant forward to look at the label, wracking her brains as to what it might be.

'Bill, the postie, asked if I'd take it in for you. Apparently, you weren't in the house when he knocked, and he thought it might be something you needed urgently.' Alan gave a casual shrug. 'It was no bother for me to bring it over, and it's a heck of a drive to the sorting office in Elverham just to pick it up.'

'That's so kind of you.' Karen pulled a chair out from the kitchen table and indicated that Alan should sit down. 'Can I persuade you to stay for a cup of tea? I was just about to make one.' It wasn't strictly true, but, in Karen's world, there was always time for a cuppa.

'Well, I...' He looked as though he was desperately trying to think up a plausible excuse, and it was almost painful to watch. She hated seeing him so uncomfortable.

'Of course, if you've got somewhere else to be, I completely understand. But, if it does anything to persuade you, I've got some freshly baked Eccles cakes on the cooling rack.'

'Like I said, my Saturday nights have been free for a long time, and I never could say no to an Eccles cake.' He took the seat Karen had offered. 'They were always your aunt's speciality, weren't they?'

'She taught me to make them before I could even reach the kitchen counter. They were her fiancé's favourite, so she told me, and she made them every weekend without fail, as if she still expected him to pop around and ask for one. She always wanted a batch ready, just in case.' Karen busied herself filling the kettle, but when she looked across at Alan, he was watching her intently.

'She was a fine woman, your aunt Hilary. I can see a lot of her in you.'

It was definitely meant as a compliment, and she dropped her gaze, not sure how to respond at first. 'It's funny that we never met up again, once we'd grown out of hanging out with the other local teenagers, seeing as I spent so much time here over the years and you were just next door.'

'The older I got the less I wanted to mix with other people.' Alan sighed. 'My mum was a bit too trusting, and then something happened that made me all the more wary. So I've kept myself to myself more and more over the years.' He paused for a moment, as though he was about to say something else, but he seemed to think better of it.

'I'm sure you had your reasons.' Karen filled the teapot. She didn't want to push him. The progress they'd made over the last couple of days at becoming good neighbours was, frankly, incredible. 'How do you take your tea?'

'With milk, no sugar and two Eccles cakes.' He smiled, lighting up his face again.

'Coming right up.' She glanced at the clock. It was nine fifteen.

By the time she looked at it again, it was ten thirty and they hadn't just reminisced about the past, they'd caught up on the present too. If someone had told her the day before that she'd pass over an hour in easy conversation with Alan Crabtree, she'd have called them crazy. As it was, it had turned out to be one of the most enjoyable evenings she'd spent in a long time. She only hoped that Ellie was having as much fun.

* * *

Ellie half collapsed onto one of the hay bales that had been set in a rectangle around the inside of the church hall, her face flushed from twirling around the floor with so many partners during the mixer. Her head still spun when she sat down.

'Having a good time?' Ben handed her a cool glass of cloudy lemonade, which he'd got from the makeshift bar at one end of the hall.

'I really am.' She took a sip of her drink, and it tingled on her tongue. 'This is delicious and just what I needed.'

'We aim to please, Madam.' He gave her a mock bow. 'It's the least I can do, considering how many times I've stepped on your feet this evening.'

'You're in luck.' She laughed at the genuine look of concern on his face. 'I think these cowboy boots were designed with buffalo ranching in mind, and I don't think even a charging herd of cattle trampling over my feet would register in these things!'

'Just as well, because I was hoping it wouldn't put you off coming out with me another time?'

She was about to answer, when Daisy bounded over again. She must have been a Labrador in a past life. Ellie had no idea where Ben's sister got her energy from, but, despite her leading every dance, it didn't show any sign of waning.

'Grub's up, Benji.' She yanked her brother's arm. 'We've got to show Ellie how we do hospitality in Kelsea Bay, and Nathan is in charge of the hog roast, so he's promised to save us the best bits of crackling.'

'We've had the royal command.' Ben gave an apologetic shrug. 'And if you think Daisy is full-on, just wait until you meet Nathan. You'll do well to get a word in edgeways between the two of them.'

The hog roast and buffet had been set up in an open-sided marquee just outside the church hall. If the smell wafting in through the open skylights, whilst they'd been dancing, was anything to go by, then they were in for a treat. Daisy hadn't been exaggerating about how they did hospitality in Kelsea Bay – the buffet table was heaving with food. There were at least six different types of salad, and potatoes cooked in four different ways. Loaves of French bread were stacked on top of one another, like a bakery-related avalanche just waiting to happen. There was a separate table laden with desserts, too – cheese-cakes, chocolate brownies, and cupcakes thick with icing – all of which looked capable of rivalling something Karen would produce.

'Ah, Benji boy, there you are!' A tall sandy-haired man waved a large pair of serving tongs in their faces, when they finally made it to the front of the queue. 'No wonder you've been keeping this lovely lady all to yourself. If I wasn't an engaged man, you'd have to watch out. I'm Nathan, by the way.' He wiped his hand on his apron and held it out to Ellie.

'It's lovely to meet you. I'm Ellie Chapman. My mother and I recently moved into Seabreeze Farm.'

'We all know who *you* are.' Nathan gave her a leisurely smile, immediately putting her at ease. The flirting was clearly just part of his charm, and Daisy certainly didn't seem to mind. 'You're all Benji can talk about these days.'

'Really?' It was the second time she'd been told that in one evening, and Ellie turned to Ben, who attempted a casual shrug. He'd already said he wanted to see her again, so perhaps there was some truth in what Nathan and Daisy had been saying – although she was pretty certain they were laying it on thick, just to embarrass him.

'That's not strictly true.' Ben picked up two plates and passed one to her. 'I've also been talking about this highly anticipated hog roast. Nathan's an architect by trade, but it's his first year in charge of the roast, and he fancies himself as a bit of a Michelin-starred chef when it comes to barbecuing.'

'You're such a philistine, Ben.' Nathan used his tongs to pull some pork from the spit and loaded up their plates. 'Hog roasts and barbecues are, at best, distantly related cousins. Luckily for you, I'm a master at both.'

As it turned out, Nathan was as good as his word. The pork was delicious and the rest of the buffet didn't disappoint. At least, not until Ellie sampled two of the deserts. Neither of them tasted as good as they looked, and the cupcakes made her feel as if she was trying to swallow wood shavings, they were so dry. Perhaps it was just because she'd been spoilt by her mum's brilliant baking but, when she looked around, there were plates of abandoned desserts everywhere.

'Not quite up to your mum's standard, are they?' Ben set down his barely touched cheesecake on the table closest to their hay bale.

'I didn't like to say anything, in case they were made by one of your friends.' Ellie breathed a sigh of relief that Ben had mentioned it first and put down her plate next to his. She'd been wondering how she was going to hide them, and had even considered the pink cowboy hat at one stage.

'Not a friend, no, but they all come from Daisy's Deli. Everything in the buffet does.' Even though he laughed, she wanted the ground to open up and swallow her, hay bale and all. 'Mum and Daisy run it together, but since the lady who used to supply all their homemade desserts moved to Devon last month, they just haven't been able to find a reliable supplier. Don't tell anyone, but most of this stuff comes from a frozen food firm. The cupcakes were from a new supplier they were hoping would work out, but I think we can safely say that won't be the case.'

'I'm sorry. I wouldn't have said anything, if you hadn't mentioned it, and I'm sure it's not really that bad.' Ellie looked at her abandoned dessert again, wondering if she could force down a mouthful.

'You only said what everyone else is thinking, Mum and Daisy included. They're both great at cooking the savoury stuff, but desserts just don't seem to be their forte, and so they've always bought those in.' Ben gave her a rueful smile. 'If only we knew someone who was a dab hand at knocking up a sponge cake. Someone like your mum.'

'Do you think they'd give Mum a trial, if she was prepared to give it a go, I mean?' Ellie touched his arm, as the possibilities began to race through her head. Being a regular supplier to a well-established deli like Daisy's could be just the way to expand Karen's business.

'I think they'd jump at the chance. I could bring Daisy up to try out some of your mum's cakes next week, if you think she'll be interested?' He put his hand over hers and her skin tingled in response. 'And maybe afterwards I could take you out for that second date.'

'That would be lovely.' Ellie curled her fingers around Ben's, as couples promenaded past them following the band leader's commands. It had never been this easy with Rupert, despite the voice in her head reminding her that not only was she supposed to be steering clear of new relationships, she was technically still engaged. Despite all of that, throwing away the chance of something that felt this right would just be stupid. She had no idea what Ben was looking for, but for once in her life she was determined to just have fun finding out. Not everything in life needed a step-by-step plan after all.

8

The temping work Ellie had taken on so far had helped towards paying some of the bills on the farm, which seemed to come in with alarming regularity, but it had also served to remind her that she really didn't want to have to end up having to work full time in an office. She spent the whole time she was cooped up in an air-conditioned box, with artificial lighting, longing for the moment when she could get back to the farm.

Worrying about work wasn't the only thing on her mind. Dating Ben would have been perfect, but for one thing. She still hadn't told him that she hadn't officially broken things off with Rupert, who had cancelled his second planned visit to the farm, citing another business trip. She'd realised just how many times over the years he'd done that to her. It was probably the reason Rupert had picked her in the first place – the fact she was so willing to go along with his plans and fit in with them whenever he decided he had time to see her. Had she really been so desperate to prove to herself that a man could love her, that she'd settled for whatever scraps he could spare? But that's all she'd had from her father over the years, too, so maybe it was no surprise it had taken her this long to realise it wasn't okay.

Ben was everything Rupert wasn't, choosing to spend every spare moment he had with her and planning things because he thought she'd like them, not the other way around. They'd even been on the boat trip to see the seals, that Bert had suggested to them. As soon as she could make the breakup with Rupert official, she'd finally be able to stop looking over her shoulder and wondering when all of this might go wrong. If Rupert cancelled his next scheduled visit, she'd just have to go back to London and meet up with him there because it couldn't wait any longer. She needed to draw a line under that part of her life and the person she'd been back there. She still wanted to do it face to face, though, anything less went against the way Karen had brought her up – to take responsibility for her own mistakes, not run away from them.

Either way she needed to clear her head and exercise had always been Ellie's go-to strategy for doing that. There might not be any gyms in Kelsea Bay, but there was no better place to go for a run than in the lanes and hilly countryside that stretched out from Seabreeze Farm.

Forty minutes in and the run had worked its magic, draining her of the energy to do anything much other than put one foot in front of the other. Slowing down to a gentler pace as she started the final descent back into the bay, she passed a piece of scrubland almost hidden behind a row of ramshackle sheds. There was a rickety wooden gate at the entrance to the land, with building rubble dumped over most of the grass. She'd never been this way before and it was a bit of an eyesore compared to everywhere else around Kelsea Bay. There was a 'sold' sign on the corner of the land and it had no doubt been snapped up for redevelopment.

Ellie was about to pick up the pace again when she saw a

piebald horse standing in one corner of the scrubland. Its head was hanging low and it was standing awkwardly, unable to get a steady footing amongst the rubble. There was no way she could just leave it. Ellie could almost hear Aunt Hilary's voice in her ear again and she had to check the horse was okay.

Not wanting to risk opening the gate in case it fell apart altogether, she managed to scramble over it, putting her weight on the fence post that looked reasonably sturdy and nearly falling on the other side as she landed on the rubble. This was no place to keep an animal and the horse didn't even react when she walked towards it.

'You okay, boy?' As she got closer, she could see the horse was male and that he was in an even worse condition than she'd feared. The poor thing had ribs visibly sticking out even through his unclipped coat, and the head collar he was wearing had obviously been cutting into his flesh for some time. Tears stung the backs of Ellie's eyes when the horse eventually moved its head and gave her a mournful look, too listless to actually move, even if she had presented a threat.

'What the hell do you think you're doing?' A shout from behind made Ellie turn quickly, and she nearly lost her footing again on the rough ground. 'This is private property and I could have you arrested for trespassing. If you're one of those bloody surveyors again, measuring up for what the new owners are going to put here, you can get lost. They don't officially own it until next week and I might still pull out if they keep sending idiots like you round here.' The man was probably only middle-aged, but he looked as if he'd had a rough life. His face was bright red with indignation and, when he'd opened his mouth to shout at Ellie, it was clear it had been a very long time since he'd seen a dentist.

'I'm not from any surveying firm, but if we're talking about arrests, I'm the one who should be having you arrested for keeping an animal in these conditions.' Ellie suspected her own face had gone quite red too and she should probably have been more worried that the irate man in front of her might turn nasty, but she hadn't been this angry for a long time.

'Oh you're one of *those*! I suppose you care more about animals than people, don't you?'

'Definitely more than *some* people.'

'Where were you when they told me I couldn't live in one of my sheds any more? I wasn't bothering anyone, but it brings down the tone of the neighbourhood they said. That's all people around here care about – the value of their bloody houses and roaring up these lanes in their overpriced cars, polluting the atmosphere with chemicals.' The man shook his head and his fist at the same time. 'Me and Joey were quite happy here until all this.'

'If Joey's the horse's name, he looks anything but happy to me.' Ellie's fingernails dug into her palms. She'd have no chance if the man came for her, but with fight or flight kicking in she was willing to stand her ground for Joey's sake. The head collar had rubbed away patches of hair all over the horse's head and the skin underneath was raw and bleeding; his hooves were overgrown and his flanks hollow. He was in a very sorry state, and frankly Ellie couldn't have cared less if the man's shed was bulldozed with him inside. It would have been no less than he deserved for treating the horse the way he had.

'He'll be out of his misery soon, so there's no point in reporting me. The knacker's yard have offered me thirty quid for him.' The man narrowed his eyes, daring Ellie to object. 'You're to blame, you nosy little cow, you and all the others like you. Poking your nose in where it isn't needed and messing up my life, forcing me to stop living like I was, and now I've had no choice but to sell the land. I've got nowhere to keep Joey now, even if I wanted to.'

'Sell him to me instead.'

'I wouldn't sell him to you for three times the price they've offered me.'

'What about ten times the price?' As Ellie asked the question the man's face changed. Greed overtook his indignation. With the costs mounting up the way they were at the farm and so little money coming in from her temping, she couldn't really afford the thirty pounds, let alone the three hundred, but one more look at Joey's sorrowful face and she knew she'd do whatever it took.

'You'd pay three hundred quid for that mangy bag of bones? All he's good for is dog food but, if you've got more money than sense, then far be it from me to stop you.'

'If you come down to Kelsea Bay with me now, I'll get the money out of the cashpoint and we can come back and I'll take Joey straight away. Otherwise the deal's off.' Ellie held her breath, hoping her bravado would pay off and thanking the habit she had of keeping a bank card tucked into the zip pocket of the leggings she wore for running. It had started when she'd first begun running in London, after work some days, and had got such a bad cramp that she'd needed to get a cab back to her office to pick up her stuff. After that, she always took it with her – to pay for a taxi home if she got injured out running – but she'd never once imagined it would result in her coming home with a horse in tow. God knew what her mother was going to say. But she didn't have time to consult with Karen, because she didn't trust Joey's owner to keep to the deal if she didn't get him the money straight away. He might just have been vindictive enough to have disappeared by the time she got back and ended up sticking with his original plan for Joey.

'Whatever.' The man grumbled, but he grudgingly turned towards the gate and Ellie followed him. 'But if you think I'm jogging down there after you, you've got another think coming.'

* * *

'How much did you pay for him?' Ben finished looking inside
Joey's mouth and turned to Ellie. She'd called him as soon as she
got back to the farm and he'd arrived within ten minutes.

'Three hundred pounds.'

'I'd say they saw you coming, but I think he'd have been dead
within a week if you hadn't stepped in, even without a trip to the
slaughterhouse.'

'Is he going to be all right?' Karen looked close to tears as she
stood next to Ellie, watching Ben checking the horse over. It
hadn't really been a surprise to Ellie that her mother had immediately agreed that she'd done the right thing, never mind the
cost, and that they'd do whatever they could to give Joey a loving
home at Seabreeze Farm for the rest of his life, however long that
might be.

'I think so. We'll need to treat his wounds and get a farrier up
to sort his feet out as soon as possible, and feed him up of course.'
Ben shook his head, still looking as if he was struggling to take in
how Joey had been treated. 'He can only be about six or seven. So
if he's got the will to survive, he should be able to make it
through. I've already spoken to one of my friends who works for
the RSPCA and he wants us to take some photographs, so that
they can pursue a case against Joey's old owner, to make sure he's
banned from keeping animals again.'

'That's great, but I'm going to pay the going rate for his treatment though, because it sounds like he needs a lot of it. I don't
care what you say.'

'We'll talk about that later, let's just concentrate on getting
Joey well first. Thank goodness you found him; he's finally had
some luck at last.' Ben's eyes met hers as he spoke and there was
so much warmth in the look he gave her she couldn't help

thinking that Joey wasn't the only lucky one. But the horse's real good fortune would be in having Ben take care of him; he was gentle but incredibly determined and if anyone could get the horse on the road to recovery it was him.

'He's quite a handsome chap, isn't he? Underneath all that missing fur.' Karen's voice caught on the words and Ellie could tell how much Joey had got to her too. 'I hadn't realised until just now that he's got one blue eye and one brown eye.'

'They call it a wall eye, but I think it gives him extra character, like David Bowie.' Ben lifted up one of Joey's hooves.

'Joey Bowie, that's got quite ring to it.' Ellie laughed as the horse finally lifted his head in response; he clearly approved of his new name too. 'That settles it then, I think he's found a new home and a new name all in one afternoon.'

'I think he'd make a great mascot for the veterinary surgery too, so how about free treatment in return for some promotional pictures of him on the road to recovery?' Ben raised a questioning eyebrow. 'It would help with fundraising for the animal shelter too. I'm sure your aunt Hilary would approve of all that.'

'We can't let you do that.' Ellie and Karen spoke in almost perfect unison, but Ben was already nodding his head.

'Yes I can; it'll help raise the profile of the surgery no end and get us more equine work in the surrounding area. Plus any traction on social media that gets donations in for the shelter can't be turned down. You'd be doing me a favour.' Even if Ben had been asking for something from Ellie, instead of offering free treatment for Joey, it would have been almost impossible to turn him down. She really wanted to kiss him, right now, with Joey looking on wearing that mournful Eeyore-like gaze, to show Ben just how much he was starting to mean to her. And, if her mother hadn't been standing less than two feet away, then she would have done.

'It's good to know that there are still some good guys around.

You and Alan are slowly restoring my faith in men.' Karen's cheeks definitely coloured as she seemed to realise she'd given more away than she'd probably planned to.

'It's entirely down to your brilliant daughter that he's got a second chance.' Ben reached out and squeezed her hand. All the holding back she'd been doing, not wanting to jump into a relationship with both feet and speed things up too quickly, suddenly felt in danger of breaking loose. If she didn't distract herself, she was definitely going to end up kissing him like she'd never kissed anyone before, whether they had an audience or not.

'Joey's the real star hanging on through everything, but we're officially a team now, he's going to need all of us.' As Ellie spoke, the familiar warm glow she had whenever she looked at Ben got even stronger. She liked the idea of her and Karen's team of two welcoming in a new member and that was something else Rupert would never have been.

'He definitely does need us all. I'll start by calling the farrier and getting him over here as soon as I can.' Ben touched her arm again briefly and she had the overwhelming feeling that she could trust him with anything and it would be okay. She just needed to find the right moment to tell him that she still hadn't spoken to Rupert, although she had to admit there was a big part of her that didn't want anything about her old life to taint the way things were going at Seabreeze Farm. Her biggest fear was that Ben might not like the person she'd been back then, which made the decision to say very little about her life with Rupert an easy one to make.

9

It was so hot in the kitchen, Karen had opened all the windows. Every spare surface was covered in trays of cooling cakes and pastries, and her cheeks were flushed as red as the strawberry jam in the tray of tarts she'd just removed from the oven.

'Tea?' Ellie wanted to do something to help, but Karen was rushing around like a whirling dervish, and she shook her head at the offer of a drink. Her mum saying no to a cuppa meant things were really serious, and Ellie wondered if she'd been wrong to put her under so much pressure. 'It'll be okay, Mum. Even if they don't want your cakes for the deli, I'm sure you'll soon have some new clients lined up. Wedding season is about to get underway, after all.'

'The bills keep coming in, though, Ellie and heaven knows where we'd be if Ben wasn't being so incredibly generous with his time.' Karen took another tray of golden fairy cakes out of the oven as she spoke, and the delicious smell of vanilla filled the air.

'The employment agency seem certain they'll find me some more work next week, and, if I have to, I'll get something permanent. I don't want you worrying about money, Mum. You've sacrificed enough my whole life. Let me worry about this.' Ellie crossed her fingers behind her back, hoping that it would be as simple as that.

They were okay for now, but maintaining things on the farm would continue to cost a lot of money, and they'd need to find a long term solution eventually. Still, that was a worry for another day. Today, their job was to impress Daisy.

Ben's mum had stayed behind to manage the deli, so the entire decision rested with his sister. Ellie had met their mum, Joy, at the barn dance. She was quiet and softly spoken, and it was clear that Daisy was the driving force in the business, the one who made all the decisions.

It was almost a relief when the distinctive crunch of tyres on gravel heralded Ben and Daisy's arrival. They'd done all they could do to prepare for the grand tasting session and perhaps Karen would be able to relax once she'd met Daisy and realised how friendly she was.

'It's a lovely place you've got here.' Ben's sister breezed into the room and made herself at home immediately by sitting down at the kitchen table before she was even invited to do so. 'And the smell of all this baking is just divine. We were getting it from halfway down the drive.'

'I'll put the kettle on, and you can decide what you want to try first.' Karen moved towards the other end of the kitchen and Ellie could see that her hands were shaking. It was odd to think of her mum feeling nervous. She'd held their little family together for so long that she'd always seemed invincible to Ellie.

'I can recommend the gypsy tart.' Ben took a seat opposite Daisy, next to Ellie. He was sitting so close that their legs were touching. The small intimacy immediately alleviated some of the nerves she had on her mother's behalf.

'Help yourself, then, Ben. Someone needs to dig in.' Karen

didn't join them at the table, clearly too anxious to sit down. She'd never had a contract as big as the one that Daisy's Deli could potentially offer, and Ellie knew as well as she did that there was a lot riding on Daisy's verdict.

'Mum's cupcakes are the best I've ever tasted, and that's not bias talking.' Ellie took one of the cakes, peeling back the cake paper and revealing an inch and a half of perfect golden sponge, with another inch of expertly swirled icing resting on top. Just as well that she wasn't planning on selling her body to make ends meet at the farm. Although, at this rate there'd be plenty of it to go around.

'They do look incredible.' Daisy helped herself to a cake from the same plate as Ellie. 'What flavours do you make?'

'I've made almost everything over the years, from banana to lemon, carrot to chocolate, coffee to strawberry and everything in between. I even made walnut and lime once, not a combination I'd ever thought of, but it was the bride's favourite. And what a bride says goes on her big day.'

'Oh, wow!' Daisy spoke with her mouth full. 'This sponge is so light. Please tell me I didn't mishear you... do you really make wedding cakes, too?'

Karen nodded, and Daisy crossed the room in a flash, flinging her arms around the older woman.

'I take it you like the cakes as much as I said you would?' Ben laughed, and Karen looked a bit dazed from being on the receiving end of one of Daisy's enthusiastic reactions.

'You didn't tell me she made wedding cakes! You know how stressed I've been about the plans for the wedding. Nothing seems to be going right. All I've got so far is a theme and the dress. And being able to tick the cake off my list would be at least one thing going in the right direction.' Daisy finally let go of

Karen. 'And now it looks very much like I've found my wedding cake maker, as well as a new supplier for the deli.'

Ellie, who couldn't imagine Daisy every truly getting stressed, was glad of the opportunity to make herself useful at last. Disappearing into the lounge, as the others tucked into more of her mum's samples, she dug out a small photo album, which she quickly took through to the kitchen and set down in front of Ben's sister.

'There are pictures in there of some of mum's celebration cakes. They're mostly weddings, but there are some birthday and anniversary cakes, too. It'll give you an idea of what she can do.'

For once, Daisy was silent as she flicked through the album, and Ellie was prouder of Karen than ever, watching Daisy's face as she took in each new photograph.

'These are amazing. Are the flowers real?' Daisy pointed to a three-tier cake, which had a waterfall of daisies cascading all down one side.

'No, I made them from icing sugar.' Karen smiled. 'The groom proposed on a picnic, by threading the engagement ring onto a daisy chain and presenting it to his bride-to-be. They wanted it to be captured in the wedding, somehow, so I came up with this design.'

'Could you do something like this for me? Maybe with a little cottage on top to represent the design Nathan has done for our house, with a garden full of wild daisies?'

When Karen nodded, Daisy clapped her hands together in delight.

'I think,' said Ben, taking another slice of gypsy tart, 'that this is cause for celebration. And the only way to mark that appropriately is to have another piece of cake.'

* * *

Within an hour, they'd made pretty impressive in-roads into Karen's samples, and Daisy had settled on a final design for her wedding cake.

'I don't know about you, but I could do with walking some of these calories off.' Ben sat back in his chair and massaged his stomach. 'A brisk walk to John O'Groats and back again should just about do it.'

'I'm not sure if I can commit to that.' Ellie laughed. 'But I need to go down to the starvation paddock and check on Gerald and then maybe we could look in on Joey too?'

They'd moved Gerald down to the far end of the farm. Alan had come over with one of his tractors and cut the grass as short as an army crewcut, to ensure that the old donkey couldn't overeat and risk getting laminitis again. His willingness to help had shocked Ellie, but Karen hadn't seemed nearly as surprised. She was sure something else had happened after the mysterious appearance of the foxgloves on the doorstep and every so often her mother would disappear over to Crabtree Farm on the pretext of asking for some advice, but they'd both been too busy to talk about what was going on between her mother and Alan. Ellie just hoped that their neighbour wasn't taking advantage of her mother in any way, because she was too soft by half. The decision to move Gerald farther away from the house had been, at least in part, to help Karen avoid the temptation of feeding him titbits. His mournful braying wasn't easy to resist, and, since her mother had always equated feeding people with love, Ellie had decided it was best for them both to move Gerald out of earshot.

'Would you mind if I tagged along, too?' Daisy grinned, obviously deciding to ignore the warning look her brother had shot her. 'I haven't seen any of the donkeys since Hilary shut the sanctuary down, and I used to love coming here.'

'Of course not.' Ellie got to her feet and pulled on the light summer jacket she'd draped over the back of her chair. 'We've started working to replace the fencing, and we've done a lot of tidying up out on the farm, but we've still got a way to go. Alan has been really helpful lately, though, hasn't he, Mum?' As Ellie spoke, Karen nodded, but she didn't seem keen to elaborate and was saved from having to do so by an interjection from Ben's sister.

'Alan has been *helpful*? Without a gun to his head? I mean he always does stuff for Ben, being his godfather and all, but ask anyone else around here and they'd tell you he's got more spikes than a porcupine. Yet he's willingly helping you out?' Daisy looked incredulous. 'Mind you, having tasted your cakes, I think you might just have the sort of magical powers it would take to bring about a miracle like that.'

The trees that marked the end of the farm, just out of reach of Gerald's starvation paddock, were in full foliage, and the sea was as calm as a mill pond at the base of the cliffs. The view was so clear, it looked as if France was close enough to swim to, although even the thought of getting in the water made Ellie's toes curl up. It might look inviting, but the Channel could bite back at any time of year, and it was never anywhere near as warm as she wanted it to be.

'He looks well.' Ben held out a hand to stroke the donkey's ear, and Gerald regarded him with a knowing look, as if he knew Ben held responsibility for his strict diet. 'Are you still restricting him to a pad of hay a day?'

'Yes, exactly as the doctor ordered.' Ellie glanced at Ben, and they exchanged a smile.

'It's beautiful here. I never realised quite how lovely. I suppose you don't notice those things as much when you're a child.' Daisy stood on the other side of her brother, leaning against the top rail of Gerald's paddock and looking out towards the sea. 'If you had a gazebo over there, at the end of the woodland, with the view of the sea and France beyond it as a backdrop, it would make a stunning venue for a wedding. You could use the hay barn for indoor ceremonies and it wouldn't really matter how rustic it was – that sort of thing is really popular now. I've looked at loads of places, but nothing as nice as this. The barn would work for receptions, too, with a bit of sprucing up, or you could pitch a huge marquee close to the clifftop.' Daisy had that dreamy look that lots of brides seemed to get, as if she really could visualise it all.

'Do you actually think people would want to get married *here*?' Ellie was suddenly seeing the farm through fresh eyes too.

It *was* beautiful, and the way the land looked out towards nothing but miles of water made it so private. Perhaps, with a lot of hard work and some financial investment, it *could* be turned into a wedding venue. She couldn't believe she'd never thought of it before. The barn was probably in better condition than the farmhouse, and it had beautiful oak beams, which would look stunning hung with floral displays. It wouldn't take that much to bring it up to scratch, not in the grand scheme of things, compared with the money they'd already spent on the farm.

'You'd be run off your feet with bookings. Your mum could do the wedding cakes and desserts, and the deli could supply the rest of the catering.' Daisy's enthusiasm was infectious, and she spoke as though it was already a reality – just as simply as saying so.

Part of Ellie wanted to rein her in, and the other half wanted to run with her, throwing caution and all the boring practicalities that went with it to the wind. 'That's always been my dream job, being a wedding planner. I love the idea of being part of the most important day of someone's life.' Ellie began visualising it, too, her cautious side on to a losing battle. Just maybe it was doable, even if she had no idea how she could actually make it happen.

'Leave you two alone together, and you'd be ruling the world within half a day.' If Ben was trying to sound a gentle warning note, it fell on deaf ears.

'Come on, let's see what you need to do to register it as a venue. I take it you've got Wi-Fi?' Daisy had already linked her arm through Ellie's and was heading back toward the house. 'I'll tell you something: if you can get the approval in time for my wedding, I'll be the first in the queue. We might even get our pictures in *Kent Life*.' Daisy picked up the pace, leaving Ben trailing in their wake. 'Keep up, we've got loads to organise!'

* * *

It had been the sort of day that changed everything. Not since discovering they'd inherited the farm from Aunt Hilary had so much happened in one day. First, there was the offer of a contract at the deli and the commissioning of Daisy's wedding cake. Now, Ellie and Daisy were back at the house, looking into how to register the farm as a wedding venue. It was exciting but exhausting. Just listening to the pace of their conversation wore Karen out. Ben had disappeared to take evening surgery at his veterinary practice, and she'd taken the opportunity to escape, too.

It had been staying light until almost 9 p.m., but by the time she set off towards the cliffs for five minutes of quiet contemplation away from the excited chatter of the two girls, the pink sky was slowly fading to a deep mauve.

It was easy to see why Hilary had loved the farm so much. Where the land ended, a vast sea stretched out, and it almost felt as though you owned it all. Daisy was right, it would make a stunning venue for a wedding, and Karen could just imagine what Ellie would achieve with it. It could be her dream come true.

As she passed him by, the old donkey was scuffing his mouth against the ground, getting what little grass he could between his teeth and making the most of it. They had to be cruel to be kind, and, as hard as that sometimes was, she could admit he was looking much healthier. She'd even seen him kick up his back legs in response to a horsefly landing on his rump – something he would never have been able to do a month before.

Just outside Gerald's bald little paddock, to the left of the gate post, a large flat rock made the perfect place to sit and ponder whilst the sky gradually darkened to plum. Karen's mind drifted, thinking how pleased her aunt would have been to see the farm used for weddings. Hilary was a person who believed in one true love and soul mates – so much so that she'd never even considered finding someone else after she'd lost her fiancé.

A lump formed in Karen's throat as she thought about her own wedding. She'd truly believed it was love, back then, at least. But she knew for certain now that it wasn't. Fifty-five years old, and she'd never really been cherished by someone in the way that Hilary and Gerald had loved one another. It was stupid to cry over things like that at her age, but rational as she tried to be, it still hurt. Thank heavens Ellie had seen the light and finished with Rupert. He'd never have made her the centre of his world, either. The only person Rupert loved was himself. She wanted the best for her daughter, someone whose eyes lit up every time Ellie walked into the room, and Karen could see that when Ben looked at Ellie, in a way Rupert never had.

'Did you know that when you left us the farm? That somehow you'd break the hold Rupert had over her?' Karen whispered the words into the still night air, and in the quickly descending darkness, she could just make out Gerald's ear twitching in response.

Suddenly, his head shot upwards, just as a large cracking sound came from the woods at the other side of his paddock, as if someone had snapped a branch in two.

She pushed up from the rock and took the torch out of her pocket, shining it towards the woods, her heart hammering in her chest. The beam from the torch was weak, and it was getting really dark, but for a moment, she thought she saw two figures standing on the edge of the woodland, one of whom looked familiar.

She rubbed her eyes – she had to be seeing things – and when she opened them again, there was no one there. Maybe it was the dark playing tricks on her, making the trees look a bit like people, but she could have sworn she'd caught a glimpse of Rupert.

It had to be because he'd been on her mind. After all, why on earth would anyone be lurking in the woods in the dark, let alone Rupert? He wouldn't want to get his shoes dirty. He cancelled two planned visits to the farm too, so there was nothing to suggest he'd be broken hearted by Ellie calling this off, although Karen wouldn't trust him as far as she could throw him.

Adrenaline rushed through her veins, all the same, and it no longer seemed such a good idea to be sitting alone on the edge of a cliff, as the sky turned darker still.

Turning, she pointed her torch towards the path. It flickered for a second, or two, then went out. By now, it was hard to see where she was stepping, and, in her haste to get back to the welcoming lights of the farmhouse, she caught her foot on what must have been a tree root and hurtled forwards in the dark. After her surgery the one thing the doctors had warned her to avoid at all costs was a fall, but she was about to find out what the consequences of that would be.

Just as she expected to hit the ground, something, or someone, caught hold of her. They steadied her for a moment before letting her go.

'Are you okay?' The deep voice was familiar, and she let out the breath she hadn't realised she'd been holding.

'Alan! I was scared half to death for a moment, there.'

'I was going to call out when I saw you, but then you tripped and there wasn't time. Sorry.' He sounded out of breath himself, like he'd shot towards her with lightning speed when he'd seen her about to fall.

'Don't be sorry. I'm just so relieved it was you.' She took his arm to steady herself again, still shaken by tripping and the fright of what she thought she'd seen back at the woods. 'It seems like you're destined to be my hero, always turning up when I need you. You must have some kind of sixth sense.'

'Not really.' He gave a low laugh, and she thought briefly of how much she enjoyed hearing the sound. 'I'm here because I phoned and spoke to Ellie, who told me you'd gone for a walk. I wanted to know how it had gone with Daisy this afternoon. When I rang back twenty minutes later, Ellie said you were still out, so I got a bit worried and thought I'd head over and see if you were okay.'

'You might pretend to be all bluster and disinterest, Alan Crabtree, but I know your secret now.' She squeezed his arm as she spoke. It was nice to have someone to lean on for a change.

'Not many people do, so I'd rather you kept that to yourself.' There was a teasing tone to his voice. 'You should be a bit more careful, though. If you'd fallen out here in the dark and hit your head, it doesn't bear thinking about. You were hurtling back towards the house like Usain Bolt, and running around in the pitch black is never a good idea.'

'I thought I saw someone, or maybe just something, down at the edge of the woods.' She shivered at the thought. 'But it must have just been a trick of the fading light, or the shadows of the trees.'

'Are you sure? I can check it out, if you like.' Alan swung round in the direction of the woods, but it had suddenly got much darker and Karen couldn't even make out his features clearly, despite the fact he was standing right next to her.

'Maybe tomorrow? You could come over, and I'll do you a bit of lunch.' She already felt better for having told Alan. It was almost certainly nothing, but it was nice to share her worries with someone all the same. 'But for now I think we should head to the house and see if those girls have left us anything to eat. I'm sure you could use a cuppa as much as I could.'

'It sounds like a good plan to me.'

With his arm linked back through hers, they made their way towards the farmhouse, and all thoughts of someone lurking at the edge of the woodland were temporarily forgotten.

10

'I thought I might find you down here, doing a Snow White and singing to the animals!' Ben leant over the five-bar gate as Ellie filled up the donkeys' water trough and flicked a stream of water in his direction, making him jump back out of the way. She had been singing away to the animals as she often did, but she hadn't been expecting Ben to make it to the farm so quickly after she'd called him, much less catch her in the act of putting on an impromptu one-woman show.

'You should never insult a woman when she's got a hosepipe in her hand, not unless you want to end up soaking wet!'

'I'm not insulting you; I think it's great that you sing to the animals, but then I think everything about you is great.' Ellie couldn't help smiling at Ben's words and it had been on the tip of her tongue to say she loved everything about him too, but it was far too early for the L word, even in that context. It would probably send him running back to the surgery and she needed his expertise.

'Thanks so much for coming up to see Dolly again. I can't

believe she hasn't given birth yet, she looks fit to pop, and you'd be a much better judge than me about whether she's okay or not.'

'I'm sure she's okay, but you know I never need an excuse to come up to the farm, because you're here.' Ben moved closer to Ellie as he spoke.

'I wish you'd let me pay you something for all your time.'

'I'm just helping out a good friend that's all.'

'I thought we were beginning to be a bit more than that.' She'd been about to kiss him, when a squawking seagull suddenly decided to see if Gerald and the other donkeys had left any of their food. The whoosh of air, as it swooped down, made it feel as if it was only inches above Ellie's head and she dropped her bucket in shock, the bird phobia she'd been convinced she'd cracked kicking back in.

'Are you okay?' Ben put a hand under her chin and she wondered if he could feel her shaking.

'I got attacked by a bird as a child and they just make me really nervous when they get too close. I'm trying to get over it, but it's just a stupid, irrational fear.'

'No it isn't. Something bad happened to you and that changed the way you see things that wouldn't worry other people. It doesn't make it stupid. Trying to move on from that makes you brave.' He could have been talking about so much more than just birds and, for a split second, she almost told him everything – why she'd clung on to Rupert when deep down she'd known he wasn't right for her and why she'd stood by and watched as he ruthlessly bought up businesses that took advantage of their owners' desperation. Even working for the bank had gone against her principles at times, but she didn't want Ben to know that version of her, because it had died the moment she'd inherited Seabreeze Farm.

'Why are you always so lovely?' Without waiting for him to

answer, she closed the gap between them, her eyes never leaving his face. Tilting her face upwards, she kissed him, the resulting sensation tingling right down to her toes. In the next moment her hands were in his hair and her body was arching towards his. No one had ever made her feel like this. Ben was everything she'd really wanted, even when she'd been looking for something that she'd thought she needed.

When she finally pulled away, she promised herself that the first thing she was going to do after Ben left was call Rupert and tell him it was over, even if it was terribly bad form to end things over the phone. He'd barely responded to the messages she had sent him to check that he was still going ahead with his visit to the farm this time, so there was every chance he'd already moved on once he'd realised she was serious about keeping the farm. She couldn't be sure though because she'd stuck to texting Rupert, not wanting to call him before now, in case she'd ended up blurting everything out over the phone. But with so little contact for so many weeks, surely no one would think things between them could go back to the way they were? Knowing Rupert, he'd want to be the one to say he'd ended it though and he'd definitely want his ring back. If she had to give him the chance to end things first, then she was more than willingly to do that. Right now, she'd do almost anything to pretend that her life with Rupert had never really happened at all.

* * *

'Is she okay?' Ellie leant on Dolly's stable door as Ben checked the goat over.

'She's in labour.'

'Oh, wow, really? What do I need to do? I'm guessing it's not

like the films where women give birth, but if we do need towels
and hot water, I'm ready to swing into action!'

'It's definitely not like the films. Dolly's doing a great job and
there's no need for anyone to intervene unless it looks like she's
getting into trouble.'

'Do you think it will stress her out, us standing and watching
her?'

'I think she's got too much else to think about and this way we
can step in, if she does need us for something.' Ben took hold of
her hand. 'Any excuse to hang out with you is a good one as far as
I'm concerned.'

'I think I could get used to it too!' She grinned, leaning into
him, more grateful than ever that he was there. Her mum had
gone to the cash and carry in Elverham, with Alan, to stock up on
supplies for her fledging catering business. So it would all have
been down to her if Ben hadn't turned up.

They stood, mostly in companionable silence, as Ellie
watched Dolly in amazement, delivering three kids, without
needing anyone's help. Anyone who didn't believe in love at first
sight had clearly never seen anything like the three little black-
and-white bundles who were soon on their feet and feeding.

'Wow, Dolly's amazing, she's done all of that without a scrap
of fuss.'

'Nature is fantastic, isn't it?' Ben put his arms around her.

'It certainly is.' Moving in to kiss him again, Ellie jumped as a
car horn suddenly sounded, making Dolly and her kids danger-
ously spooked.

Seconds later gravel sprayed up as a distinctive red BMW
skidded to a halt outside the farmhouse.

'Who the hell is that?' Ben turned back from the car to look at
Ellie, and she shook her head, barely able to believe who it was.

'It's Rupert.'

'Your ex-fiancé?'

'Yes, but—'

'Look what it takes for me to get my fiancée to answer my calls!' Rupert shouted as he got out of the car, laughing loudly in an obvious attempt to draw even more attention to himself than his arrival already had.

'He doesn't know, does he?' Ben muttered the words almost under his breath, but there was no missing the tightness of his tone and he'd never looked at Ellie like that before.

'Not yet, but—' For the second time in less than a minute, Ellie didn't get the chance to finish her sentence.

'There are no buts that will explain this away. You can call me if anything happens with Dolly or her kids, but I think it's already way past when I should have left.' Ben didn't even look at her this time, but he raised a hand in greeting to Rupert as the two men strode purposefully past one another. Even in a moment like this, Ben didn't have it in him to be rude or arrogant. But the antithesis to that was now striding towards her and Ellie had a horrible feeling she'd messed everything up.

* * *

Even as Ellie was making Rupert the coffee he'd asked if she was ever going to offer him – after Ben had left the farm without a backward glance – she was trying to think of an excuse to sneak off and send Ben a text to explain why she'd done what she'd done. One small mercy was that Rupert hadn't even tried to kiss her. After she'd shown him Dolly's kids, he'd pulled a face about her being in such close proximity to 'all that mess', as he'd put it, even though she'd been on the other side of the stable door the whole time.

Part of her had wanted to tell Rupert that it was all over,

without even inviting him in, but he'd told her at least three times already how long it had taken him to drive down to the farm and what a horrendous journey it had been. The least she could do was make him a drink.

'I thought you weren't coming down until Saturday.' Putting the coffee in front of him, she sat opposite and tried to run through the conversation she'd practiced so many times in her head.

'I thought it would be a nice surprise.' Rupert reached out across the table, but she kept her hands firmly glued to the sides of her own coffee cup.

'I wish you'd called me first.' She'd nearly added that it would have saved him a journey, but she didn't want this descending into an argument, before she'd even had a chance to say everything she needed to say.

'I've only had a handful of messages from you and I didn't *want* to call, I wanted to come and see you myself to try and work out what's going on.' Rupert gave her an appraising look and she suddenly wished she could be certain what time her mum and Alan would be back. It made her uncomfortable just being on her own in a room with someone she'd been so intimate with, now that the thought gave her goosebumps for all the wrong reasons.

'What's going on is that Mum and I have been working all hours trying to get this place straight and it was you who cancelled coming down here twice because you had better things to do.'

'You know business has to come first; it doesn't mean I don't still want us to carry on the way we were.'

'Even if you really wanted that and, based on how things have been between us since I told you about the farm, I really don't think you do... Even then, it would never work with me at the farm and you in London, or away on business all of the time.'

'I still think we should sell the farm.' He held a hand up as she started to protest. 'I know what you're going to say, but it would push our plan along so much. But even if we decide not to sell this place, I think there are ways we could make it work for us.'

'Rupert, you must see that there isn't an us. There can't ever be, not now.'

'Oh what, because of that man you were draped all over when I pulled up?' Rupert laughed, drowning out her attempt to answer. 'We're going to have dalliances from time to time, God knows I've had plenty. As long as they don't interfere with our plans, I think they might actually benefit us. They've certainly helped me seal deals more than once.'

'Are you saying you've cheated on me?' It was a strange sensation for Ellie, asking what should have been such a painful question and feeling nothing but relief. Any remaining guilt she'd felt about falling for Ben, before she'd been upfront with Rupert, drifted away.

'It was business and it served a purpose, but the same can't be said for you and that *farm boy* of yours.'

'Ben doesn't work on the farm, he's a vet, but it doesn't matter what he does for a living, I lo—' She stopped herself just in time, blushing furiously as Rupert laughed again.

'You *love* him! Oh come on El, you hardly know him. What we've got is the perfect partnership and we've got a plan, both working hard to get enough capital behind us to make some serious money. Then, if you want to stay down on the farm, that might even work to our favour. Like I said when we got together, I've always thought you'd make a good mother when the time came. It was another reason I chose you, because I knew that, deep down, being a stay-at-home mother would be enough for someone like you. Not like most of the women I meet. You can make a home here with the children and a base for us all to be together when that works for me, and the little dalliances we have along the way don't need to interfere with any of that.'

'Please tell me you're joking?' Ellie screwed up her face, already knowing he was deadly serious. She'd heard of a marriage of convenience, but she'd had no idea that was what she was signing up to when she accepted his proposal. Surely he couldn't really have been planning all of this back then? He'd set their whole relationship up as though it was a business deal, with clauses and addendums, and yet he'd laughed out loud at the mention of love. Except she knew with absolute certainty now that she'd never really loved him either, she'd just loved the idea of stability and she'd convinced herself that the rest would grow in time. All along the way ignoring the warning signs and the things she hated about the choices both of them had made to get to where he said they needed to be. She hated the idea that she might be just as bad as him, but it was hard to shake it.

'I never joke about a proposal, business or otherwise.' Rupert was still wearing that cocky grin of his, as if he expected her to suddenly agree with his every word, the way she had so many times before, but just looking at him made her skin crawl.

'It's all business to you, Rupert, that's the trouble.' Getting the engagement ring out of the old toby jug on the kitchen shelf where she'd put if for safe keeping, she slid it across the table. 'Let me put this in words you'll understand. The merger is off. I'd like to say that I hope you'll find someone else who makes you happy, but I honestly think only an offshore bank account will ever do that.'

'You're making a huge mistake.' The cocky smile had finally slid off Rupert's face and his jaw was set in a firm line. 'Do you honestly think that some village idiot who spends all day with his arm up a cow's arse can offer you more than I can?'

'This isn't about Ben.'

'I think you'll discover that I can make this all about Ben if I want to.' Rupert got to his feet, pushing his chair in so hard against the table that his coffee mug juddered, spilling a pool of liquid across the solid oak surface towards where the ring was still sitting on the table, abandoned.

'What do you mean you'll make this all about Ben?'

'Don't you worry your head about any of that, you just concentrate all your efforts on trying to hold on to this farm, because I've got a really strong hunch that you're going to be in for a very bumpy ride.'

11

Ellie had barely been able to sleep the night after finally breaking things off with Rupert. She'd sent a couple of texts to Ben, but there'd been no reply, and she hadn't even been able to bear to tell her mum all the details of her final conversation with Rupert. She'd been such an idiot and as much as she tried to forgive herself, even replaying Ben's words in her head about fear making her react differently to other people couldn't make her feel better. Not when Ben was no longer speaking to her. She'd longed for a situation where she and her mother never had to worry about money again, or worse still, losing their home a second time over, but she couldn't believe what she'd been willing to sacrifice to make that happen. A life lived by Rupert's principles would have been far worse.

Getting up even earlier than usual she'd made sure all the animals were fed. Not even the chickens squawking and flapping as she let them out into their run bothered her. None of that mattered when she had so much on her mind. The sight of Dolly feeding her three kids, their little tails wagging with excitement as they tried to nudge each other out of the way, made tears well up in her eyes. What Rupert hadn't known when he'd dismissed her as being someone who'd be happy 'just' being a mother, was that he was actually paying her a huge compliment, but only if she could be half the mother Karen had been. Seeing Dolly with her own babies had brought those thoughts rushing back to the surface, and the tears had come with them.

Heading down to Joey's paddock, the sky was ablaze as the sun made its ascent above the horizon. It looked as if it was going to be another beautiful day. Aunt Hilary had clearly known the best way to try and distract herself from a broken heart, when she'd taken on Seabreeze Farm and filled it with her menagerie of animals in need. Just the sight of Joey's face lifted her spirits. He was already looking much better than he had and the haunted expression in his mismatched eyes had all but disappeared. They had to build his food up slowly, but with Ben's help he definitely seemed to be on the road to recovery. She just hoped she hadn't let Joey and the other animals down too, if Ben decided he could no longer help out.

'I thought I might find you down here, when I drove by and the lights in the stable yard were already on.' Ben's voice, behind her, almost made Ellie fall over as she spun around to look at him. 'Sorry, I didn't mean to make you jump.'

'Were you on a call out?' It was an innocuous question after their last conversation, but it felt like safe ground to ask about work. At least Ben wasn't still looking at her the way he had when Rupert had turned up and he'd realised she hadn't broken off the engagement.

'No, I couldn't sleep and I wanted to speak to you, but not over text. I was half-hoping that if I drove up here as soon as the sun started to rise that you might be up early too. But, if I'm honest, most of all I was hoping that I wouldn't see Rupert's car still sitting in the driveway.' Ben smiled and it was all she could do not to throw herself at him. The relief that he still liked her enough to care about that was almost overwhelming.

'He's gone for good. I'm so sorry that I didn't tell you that I hadn't spoken to him. He and I had drifted so far apart and we'd barely even spoken since I told him I was moving to the farm, it was almost like we had already broken up. But I wanted to speak to him in person, because for once I didn't want to take the coward's way out.'

'You could never be a coward.' Ben pushed a stray strand of blonde hair away from her face and she could feel her heart beating. 'It's me who should say sorry. I should have given you a chance to explain, it's just when I thought you might still go back to him and I saw that flash car he was driving, I thought, how can I compete with that?'

'You don't have to compete with anyone, you're a million times the man Rupert will ever be! He's the one who couldn't begin to compare to you. I promise.'

'That just makes me want to say sorry again for thinking you could ever be that sort of person; someone who's impressed by all of that. I know that's not you.' Ben put his arms around her as he spoke, and she swallowed down the guilt that was bubbling up inside, concentrating instead on the flecks of amber in his brown eyes. 'It's just that there's something I should have told you too, but I hate talking about it. Most of all I hate how it's changed my trust in people and made me doubt someone as wonderful as you.'

'If you don't want to talk about it, you don't have to. We've obviously both had relationships in the past that we wish we hadn't. Maybe all we need to do is to agree that it's all behind us.' That's all Ellie wanted after all, to forget that she'd ever agreed to marry Rupert, but Ben was shaking his head.

'I *want* to tell you. It's important to me that we've got it all out in the open and been completely honest.' He took a deep breath, his eyes never once leaving her face. 'I was engaged to a girl called Pippa. We met at veterinary school and we had our whole lives planned out. I moved to the West Country, where she was originally from, to be with her and we were going to set up our own practice. But we were trying to save, living in rented accommodation, paying off a mountain of uni debt and working all the hours we could. Somewhere along the line I think we forgot to just live our lives. One night in our local pub, Pippa met a guy who owned one of the biggest estates in the county, and the moment she realised I'd never be able to come close to all of that, I lost her. He was thirty years older than us and he'd made his money as a venture capitalist, buying up businesses and farms, and not giving a toss what that did to the communities around them. I always thought Pippa had the same sort of values as me, but it turned out she didn't.'

'That must have been so hard.' Ellie tried not to think about how similar Rupert's plan had been to what Ben was describing. That wasn't her life any more.

'It was, but they're married now and I genuinely hope they're happy, because I realised a long time ago that someone who wanted all the things Pippa did was never going to be right for me. I'm much happier back living in Kelsea Bay, but just seeing Rupert yesterday took me right back to that moment when Pippa left and her new boyfriend came to collect her from our tiny flat in his brand new Maserati. But you're not Pippa, you're the most amazing woman I've ever met, and I'm just so sorry for being such an idiot.'

'The only idiot is Pippa.' Ellie pushed down the confession she knew she should make – that she'd been every bit as shallow as Ben's ex-fiancée, but that she'd realised how little any of that meant since she'd met him and taken on the farm. But there was a huge risk that he wouldn't be able to get past the first half of what she so wanted to say, and the thought that he might turn around and walk away again was just too big of a risk to take.

'You can forgive me, then?' Ben smiled again, as Ellie nodded. 'It feels great now there's no more secrets between us.'

'Let's just keep moving forward.' Ellie tried not to think about Rupert's final threat as she pressed her body up against Ben's. He'd just been trying to scare her by saying her could make things all about Ben; their worlds had nothing to do with one another's and with any luck they'd never see each other again.

'I'm all for moving forward.' Ben kissed her slowly, pulling away slightly to look at her again. 'But only when you're ready. There's no rush.'

'I'm ready right now, if you are.' Taking his hand, she led him back towards the farmhouse and they crept up to her room, at the opposite end of the house from her mother's, like a couple of teenagers sneaking in after staying out late. Ellie had never been more certain of anything and, the moment she lay next to Ben, nothing else mattered.

* * *

It had been too long between FaceTime calls for Ellie and Olivia. With everything going on at the farm, and Olivia studying for a Master's degree, it had been even harder for them to find a time of day that worked for them both with the difference in time zones. But they'd finally found time for a proper catch up. Ellie had so much to tell her best friend and she was determined not to leave so long between calls again, whatever else was going on in their lives.

'So, how's the life of a farmer suiting you?' Olivia grinned out of the screen at Ellie, from the other side of the world.

Aside from enabling them to research the likelihood of it gaining approval as a wedding venue, getting online had brought her best friend home – well as near as damn it – via their frequent FaceTime calls.

'It's great, and, actually, I've had an idea, which, if it comes off, might mean I can make a living from it.'

'Don't tell me, you're going to start a yoga retreat, or a sanctuary for retired bankers.' Olivia laughed. 'After all, they've got to have somewhere to splurge their bonuses, and you do have a lot of connections in that world.'

'Not quite. We're thinking of turning it into a wedding venue.' Ellie couldn't miss the look of delight that crossed her friend's face as she spoke.

'That's brilliant. Seabreeze would be a fantastic place to get married.' Olivia paused and smirked, raising one eyebrow in the process. 'So, tell me, was this inspired by a certain handsome vet I've heard so much about?'

'In an indirect way, yes.' Heat flooded Ellie's cheeks, and she knew exactly what Olivia was thinking. 'But not because I've got any designs on getting engaged again, just yet.'

'*Just yet*?' Olivia laughed again, and Ellie wished she was there in person, so she could give her a nudge in the ribs.

'All right, all right, you're worse than Mum!'

'Well, who wouldn't imagine themselves staring into those dark eyes of his and exchanging vows on a clifftop, wearing a Vera Wang wedding dress and a very self-satisfied smile?' Olivia, who had seen pictures of Ben on Ellie's Facebook page, feigned a swoon.

'Do you know what, Liv? Sometimes, I think you haven't changed at all since we were eight!' Ellie laughed, though, and she was sure that when her friend came home at Christmas, she'd like Ben just as much in real life. After all, he couldn't have been more different from

Rupert. 'It's actually his sister, Daisy, who gave me the idea. She wants to get married here, but the only trouble is, we don't have much time.'

'If anyone can pull it off, El, you will.'

'I really hope so, but, in the meantime, it's back to all that corporate bull for me, as you so succinctly put it. I've got to do some temporary work to keep this place running.'

'You'll escape it for good before long, I'm sure of it.' The tone of Olivia's voice suddenly changed, as she said, 'and when you do, you can help me formulate my own escape plan. Deal?'

'Deal.' Ellie sighed. As fantastic as FaceTime was, it couldn't quite do the job when what was really needed was a hug from your closest friend.

* * *

Every time Ellie took on another temping job, being stuck in an office somewhere felt like torture after the freedom of the farm. Especially as it was starting to look like the temping work wasn't going to be so temporary after all. The warm weather had been more or less continuous, aside from the odd thunderstorm, since they'd taken over the farm, and she wished for the first time in her life that she had a desk facing a wall, rather than looking out onto everything she was missing.

Cooper and Co were a large firm of accountants, situated right next to a public park in Elverham. The employment agency had got her a month's contract helping one of the partners out with a new marketing campaign, but trying to make taxation services sound exciting was almost a challenge too far, even for Ellie. When her mind wandered from the advertising campaign, which it frequently did, she found herself watching mums with their little ones, playing in the park. They wheeled their pushchairs in the sunshine and fed the ducks in the large pond that dominated the centre of the park, making her wish she could be back at the farm with her own little family.

It was a funny word *'family'*. For so long, it had just been Ellie and her mum – along with Aunt Hilary and her grandparents, of course – but it felt as though that little unit was starting to extend. Gerald, Joey, Dolly, her three kids, and the other menagerie of animals were like part of the family, too, almost as if Aunt Hilary was still with them. Then there was Alan Crabtree, who Ellie had genuinely grown fond of since their first meeting back in the spring. He'd helped them so much with getting the farm straight, and she'd never seen Karen laugh as often as when Alan was around. Not to mention Ben and his family. Their relationship was still in its early days, but despite trying to hold back on saying the L word out loud, she loved being with him and the bonus was that she loved his family.

She and Rupert had barely spent any time with his family when they'd been together. From what she could gather he'd been packed off to boarding school at six and his relationship with his parents was distant, both physically and emotionally. It probably explained a lot, but she barely gave Rupert a thought these days and thankfully his threats had come to nothing so far. Ben had been true to his word and the way she'd handled the situation with Rupert was forgiven and forgotten. Ben was so different in every way from her ex-fiancé. He came from a close and loving family, and watching him interact with his godfather, the way they ribbed each other and had the sort of in-jokes only a family shared, was like seeing Alan in a different light. Daisy and Nathan were both full of energy and great fun to be around. His parents were quieter, but just as welcoming of Ellie into their lives. Suddenly it wasn't hard to picture the little family that she and Karen had always been, becoming part of something much bigger.

Karen's baking for the deli was selling, somewhat ironically, like hot cakes, and that had really helped establish them in Kelsea Bay, too. Ellie had applied for a grant of approval from the council to establish Seabreeze Farm as a licensed venue for civil weddings. So they'd been working really hard to make sure it was ready for the inspection and could meet all the fire and safety provisions they'd set out. Alan had started on the construction of a gazebo, too, for outside ceremonies. Ellie was keeping everything crossed that it would be approved in time for Daisy's wedding, especially as she was doing absolutely nothing else to secure a venue as a back-up plan.

Ben's sister was one of those upbeat people, who just put their faith in everything turning out okay, and she had assured everyone that it almost always did. That didn't stop Ellie waking up in the night, sometimes, wondering what on earth they would do if the council turned down the application. She could just imagine Daisy's face if they suggested a quiet registry office wedding in Elverham, instead. So they'd provisionally booked a registrar to conduct the ceremony, and Daisy was poised to send out invitations as soon as they got the official go ahead. It felt increasingly to Ellie as though she was trapped in one of those reality shows where there were only ten days to pull off a wedding that fulfils all the bride's long held dreams.

Running a wedding venue at the farm was the equivalent to winning the lottery for Ellie – there was nothing she'd rather do. But they'd need a healthy slush fund in the early days, to keep the business afloat. The money from her savings and the pay-off from the bank had dwindled fast, especially with the work they'd had to do to make the barn a stand-out wedding venue, even with Alan putting in all the hours that God sent and refusing to take anything for it. In the meantime, Ellie had no choice but to take the temporary contracts the employment agency offered. She was about to finish her month-long stint with Cooper and Co, hoping against hope the agency would come up with something a little less dull this time. Even proofreading tax returns sounded more appealing.

When her mobile rang, on her last afternoon at the accountants, she would have bet her last pound on it being the agency, with details of her latest assignment, but it was Ben.

'Have you accepted a job for next week, yet?' He didn't start with his normal *hello*, or *how are you*, and he sounded uncharacteristically stressed.

'No, I'm just waiting for the agency to ring. In fact, I thought the call was going to be them.'

'Thank God.' He let out a long breath. 'Our receptionist has put her back out, and I know it's a bit more basic than the sort of work you normally do, but I wondered if you'd step in. I need someone reliable and first thing on Monday morning. We'd pay you the going rate for a temp, of course. And I'm desperate.'

'Saying that you're desperate is not the way to convince a girl she's the one for you.' Ellie laughed, but if he'd been there, she'd have hugged him. The pay might not be as good as the work the agency could get her in events or marketing, but working in Kelsea Bay, with Ben, was well worth the pay cut. 'Still, seeing as you asked so nicely, how could I say no?'

'Really?' He sounded as though he couldn't quite believe his luck. 'I could kiss you!'

'Maybe later, Mr Hastings. Although, now that you're my boss, I'm not sure that's appropriate any more.'

'I'll add it to the job description in that case. Although technically I'm only a junior partner, so it's Nigel and David who'd be your bosses.'

'I don't want it in my contract that I have to kiss them too!'

'Definitely not. You're one in a million, Ellie, you know that, don't you?' His voice was warm, and she could picture his dark brown eyes crinkling in the corners as he spoke, and for once in her life she found herself wishing it was already Monday morning.

'So I've been told. I'll see you later, boss.' Putting down the phone, she stood up and did a little dance around the office. Goodbye, Cooper and Co – things were looking up.

12

The stile that crossed into Crabtree Farm came into view, and Karen smiled to herself, thinking about the first time she'd climbed over it, carrying a huge cake box, whilst Alan did his best to ignore her. Now he was already waiting to help her over it, and not just because he didn't want his beloved Eccles cakes to get squashed. He'd been more helpful than she could ever have imagined since that night he'd brought over the package he'd taken off the postman for her. Reminiscing about the old days, when they'd had nothing to do but hang out with friends and when summers had seemed endless, had made Karen feel like that carefree teenager all over again. When she looked at Alan, she could see the boy she'd known back then too and, once the barriers had come down, they'd got very close, very quickly.

There was a protective side to Alan too; he wanted to take care of her in a way she hadn't been since she left home. Ellie's father had never been like that and it felt so good to have someone to lean on, someone she could share her hopes and fears with, in a way she couldn't with Ellie, without risking adding more worry to the load her daughter was already carrying. The day after she thought she'd seen Rupert down by the woods, Alan went to check it out, afterwards reassuring her that there was absolutely no sign anyone had been down there. It was still as overgrown with brambles and trees as it had always been. The only trace of anyone having been there was a patch of green material caught on one of the spikier branches. They'd agreed it could have been there for years, and it was ridiculous to think that Rupert might have been lurking about, anyway. He'd never exactly been shy when it came to getting what he wanted. If he'd had an urge to see Ellie, he'd have just turned up at their door.

All the same, Karen had been relieved when she'd heard that Ellie had finally made the end of the engagement official. She'd always know that Rupert wasn't right for her only daughter, but she'd hated the fact that Ellie's upbringing meant she craved financial stability so desperately that, for a long time, she couldn't see that money was all Rupert would ever really have to offer her, because nothing else mattered to him anywhere near as much. There were similarities between Rupert and Ellie's father, which had worried Karen even more. Ellie's dad had been more concerned with getting his next gambling fix, and wearing the right watch and driving the right car when he was on a winning streak, than keeping a roof over his daughter's head. It meant that Ellie also desperately needed to believe she was the centre of *someone's* world and Karen had done her absolute best to show her daughter how true that was for her. The trouble was that Rupert was capable of putting on that kind of show too and making Ellie feel like the centre of his world, for snapshots of time just long enough to keep her hanging on way beyond when she should have done.

That was all behind them now, though, and as soon as they got the wedding venue license everything would be perfect. The gazebo Alan was building was taking shape nicely, too. Hexagonal, with ornately carved struts, it had a low fence with vertical posts, and a red tiled roof. He'd made some rails inside, from which swathes of organza could be hung, and Ellie was planning to start painting the woodwork in antique cream on her next weekend off.

Karen had wanted to find a way to thank Alan for his help, and after he'd refused to accept any money, in her usual manner, she'd shown her appreciation through food. Making sure the farm ticked over while Ellie was at work and keeping up with the demands from the deli kept her busy enough, but she could always find time to make Alan his favourite things. She'd taken to cooking for him every lunchtime – whether he was working on something at Seabreeze, or on his own land – and sharing a meal with him every day meant that they'd grown closer still. Yet, she still didn't know the whole story, why he put up the façade he presented to almost everyone and how he'd changed so much from the boy with the ready laugh to the man she'd met the first time they came to the farm after finding out about the inheritance. The gruff and unwelcoming persona made no sense when, at heart, he was one of the kindest men Karen had ever known.

'I've got your favourites today.' She accepted his hand, as he helped her over the stile, and didn't object when he kept hold of it. 'Thickly cut ham on fresh brown bread, and a nice Eccles cake for afterwards.'

'And a flask of tea, if I know you, Karen.' He grinned, and she nodded. He'd joked more than once that they should change the words of the nursery rhyme so it said, *'Karen put the kettle on'*, instead of Polly.

Alan had set up a little makeshift picnic area, using some bales of straw, from which he'd fashioned two seats and a table, of sorts. The weather had been so good of late, they seemed to have come to an unspoken understanding that it was too nice to waste by having lunch indoors.

'So, what have you been up to today?' Karen asked, as Alan eagerly tucked into his sandwich, waiting while he finished his mouthful.

'I've been planting trees, down at the far end of the farm, where it borders the caravan park.' He said the words '*caravan park*' much like someone might say '*rubbish dump*', as if the two things were on a par as far as he was concerned. 'A few of the trees that screen it from the farm came down last winter. I like to be able to see as little of that place as possible, so I've replaced the missing trees with some mature fir trees I had delivered, that are already eight feet tall. They cost me a fortune, but they were worth every penny.'

'Is that why you aren't keen on strangers – having a holiday park so close by?' It had never looked like a rowdy sort of place when Karen had driven past it, but maybe it was different when you lived right next door.

'It's not so much the people who are there now, but the memories of how the place got set up that mean I can't bear to look at it.' He put his sandwich down, as if talking about the caravan park had robbed him of his appetite. 'I suppose you want to know the whole story?'

'Only if you want to tell me.' Karen had never been the sort to push people into confiding in her, but she hoped Alan would. She hoped that their friendship was good enough for that.

'I find myself wanting to tell you everything.' He took her hand across the straw bale table, his green eyes meeting hers. 'I don't know how much you remember about my mother, but she was a wonderful woman – too wonderful for her own good, in many ways. She saw the good in everyone, trusted what people said to her as the truth, and in the end she paid the price. Growing up, it meant that I saw a few things happen to her that shouldn't have done. She'd get ripped off when mechanics came to work on the tractors – that sort of thing – or get a lower price for the potatoes than she could have done. My dad had a weak heart and by the time I got to my late teens and stopped hanging out with the crowd from Kelsea Bay, Dad had taken a back seat in things. Neither of them had had much schooling, either, and they didn't read as well as they might. So it fell to me to look out for their interests.'

'That must have been hard for a young lad?' Karen squeezed his hand, encouraging him to go on.

'It was, and it meant I was distrustful of people, which must have looked to others like I was standoffish. It took me a long time even to realise that I could completely trust your Aunt Hilary, but she had a heart of gold – just like her niece.'

Their eyes met again, and she couldn't deny that what she felt for Alan had shifted beyond friendship a while back. 'I know she was fond of you, too, and of your parents.'

'For a long time, I managed to keep the people who wanted to take advantage of my parents at bay. Having genuine friends like Hilary helped with that. But, of course, people have their own lives to live, and when I got to my early twenties, I wanted to start living mine.' Alan cast his eyes downward. 'It was selfish of me, knowing how much my parents needed me, and it was something we all suffered for in the end.'

'What happened?' As Karen spoke, Alan's grip on her hand tightened.

'I had the chance to work in Africa, on a volunteer project, digging irrigation ditches organised by a charity that the Farmers Union supported. I wanted to see a bit of life, experience the world outside Kelsea Bay.'

Karen kept hold of his hand. 'That doesn't sound selfish to me.' The regret in Alan's voice was obvious, though.

'Oh, but it was. I left Mum and Dad to it. Whilst I was away, some chap visited the farm and told them he worked for an organisation that could offer them a way of releasing part of their capital to update the farm equipment. They thought it was some sort of government grant.' Alan gave a deep sigh. 'Of course, it wasn't. Just a shady chancer, who got them to sell off almost a third of the land in return for a nominal payment – less than you'd get for a barren piece of scrubland, never mind for prime arable land.'

'Wasn't there anything you could do?' Her scalp prickled at the thought of someone as vulnerable as Alan's mother being taken advantage of.

'We tried. I came home from Africa straight away and did everything I could think of to try and put it right. We lost a small fortune fighting it through the courts, but because they'd been paid for the land, no matter how small an amount, and because Mum was too proud to admit she could barely read, the court found in his favour.' Alan cleared his throat, emotion almost getting the better of him. 'The thing that galled me most of all was that he didn't even want to farm. The firm he worked for sold off the land to a developer within months of the court case concluding, and, eventually, planning permission was given for the caravan park. I'm sure everything he put my parents through was what made them ill.'

'Not everyone's like the man who defrauded your parents,' Karen said softly. Alan had missed out on so much by closing off from the world over the years.

'I know that now. After what happened, I just forgot how to differentiate the good people from the bad. Until you came back into my life.' Wrapping his half-eaten sandwich up again, he put it back into the picnic basket. 'Do you fancy a walk? We could go somewhere different to finish lunch?'

She nodded and he picked up the basket. They crossed the field, to the spot where the woodland started. Both farms had a small patch of dense woodland in one corner, which marked the point where the cliff edge fell away most steeply. The patch of woodland was only about two hundred feet deep at Seabreeze, and Karen assumed the same was true of Crabtree Farm.

They didn't speak as Alan led them down a cleared pathway through the trees. At first, the canopy of leaves made it dark, but the dappled sunlight started to get stronger, the farther down the path they went. Suddenly, with only that subtle warning, they emerged into a large clearing in the woods, where the ground was alive with colour. Hundreds of wildflowers fought for attention, all standing tall as if each were trying to outdo the other to get to the sunlight first.

'It's beautiful, Alan.' She turned towards him, as he set down the basket, bringing their faces only inches apart.

Very slowly, very tenderly, in the middle of a sea of wildflowers, he kissed her. The sun wasn't the only thing shining a light on everything in its path. In that kiss, she knew, for the first time in her life, that someone loved her in the way Hilary had loved her fiancé.

'I wanted to show it to you. I've never shown anyone before.' He held her face in his hands. 'I cleared the land, knowing it was hidden away from prying eyes and could never be found by accident. I scattered thousands of wildflower seeds, so I could have a place to remember Mum and Dad, and they flourished beyond my wildest dreams. It's always been a place of beauty I could escape to, when the rest of the world only seemed to offer its ugly side.'

'Thank you for sharing it with me.' She took his hand again, not feeling the need to say anything else. It must have taken a lot for him to show her the clearing, and to tell the story of what had happened to the farm, and to him, but she was really glad he had. Now everything made so much more sense.

* * *

'Do you fancy coming up to Julian London's place with me?' Ben perched on the edge of the reception desk, whilst Ellie filed the last of the case notes away. It was Friday afternoon and the end of her first week as a temporary veterinary receptionist.

'Is that the sheep farm on the way out to Elverham?' She smiled when he nodded. 'Well, I had thought you might suggest a nice meal, or a trip to the cinema, but I suppose this *is* country life.'

'Julian's invited us to dinner.'

'Us?'

'Yes, *us*. Is there a problem with using such a scary word?' He was teasing her, but she shook her head anyway. 'Well, that's good, because as far as I'm concerned, there's very much an *us*, and I thought it would be good for you to meet Julian whilst you're working here. He's one of our most regular clients, and we were best friends at school. I'm often up at the farm, and no doubt, he'll have me looking at some of the ewes whilst I'm there tonight.'

'Umm, an evening of sheep husbandry. It's certainly different to how I used to spend my Friday nights when I worked in London.'

Ben stood up, slipping his arms around her waist. 'And how was that?'

'Oh, I don't know... in some wine bar, with loads of boring corporate types.' Ellie relaxed into his arms; that whole world was a million miles away now and he didn't need to know how much of who she was she'd had to compromise just to survive in that environment.

'Any regrets?'

'Not one.'

'That's exactly what I wanted to hear.' His smile reached all the way up to those beautiful brown eyes of his, and she fixed her gaze on his face, as he leant into her body.

Forgetting all her principles about staying professional in the workplace, she pressed her mouth to his. This was officially the best job she'd ever had.

Coppergate sheep farm was about five miles outside of Kelsea Bay, and the farmhouse itself was down a long bumpy track that cut a swathe between two small hills. By the time they reached the farm, kangarooing down the track in Ben's four wheel drive truck, Ellie felt as though she'd spent ten minutes inside a cocktail shaker.

'Evening, Ben!' A tall wiry-haired man with ruddy cheeks was out in the yard when they arrived, two collie dogs close on his heels. He clapped Ben on the back by way of a welcome. 'And you must be the famous Ellie we've heard so much about! I'm Julian.' Much to Ellie's surprise, he clapped her on the back, too, leaving her feeling more shaken than ever.

'It's lovely to meet you.' One of the collie dogs snaked its body between Julian's legs and nudged Ellie's hand with its head, clearly looking for some affection.

'We can do the niceties later, even though my wife, Caroline, will tell me off for being rude, but right now we've got an emergency on our hands.' Julian ran a hand through his hair. 'It's

Maisie. She's kicking up blue murder because I've got to take one of the ewe lambs off her for slaughter.' Without another word, Julian stalked off towards the nearest of the barns with the two collies in hot pursuit, leaving Ellie and Ben to follow on behind.

'Who's Maisie? One of the ewes?' Ellie didn't like the idea of being the one to separate the lamb from its mother for the final time, and as Ben laughed, she slowed her pace.

'No, Maisie's my goddaughter. She's six years old, going on thirty, and heaven help us all if she's screaming blue murder.'

Julian had already disappeared inside the double doors of the barn by the time Ellie and Ben had crossed the yard, and a very determined voice could be heard arguing her point, as they followed him in.

'Daddy, you can't take Holly, you promised you wouldn't take any of the lambs I fed. You pinkie promised!' The little girl's voice was high-pitched, and she was clearly on the edge of tears.

'Yes, but I didn't know at the time she'd have a damaged stifle joint. She won't be able to have lambs of her own, Maisie, and you know we can't keep animals as pets on the farm. Even the dogs have to earn a living.'

'But I fed her for ages before she could start eating by herself. She knows me.' Maisie turned tear-filled eyes towards them. 'You agree, don't you, Uncle Ben. It would be cruel to send her away from the farm to *you know where*.' She whispered the last few words, as though the sheep themselves might overhear and get upset.

'Well, I agree with your dad that you can't have sheep as pets on a working farm, just because you feel sorry for them.' Ben crouched down beside his goddaughter, who'd started openly sobbing. 'And it's time to stop feeding her, too. She's more than twelve weeks old, and the lambs who weren't rejected by their mums were weaned a long time ago.'

'But that's the whole point! Even her mummy didn't want her. We found her under a holly bush, which is why I called her Holly, and all of the other girl lambs I fed are getting to stay on the farm.'

'So they can have lambs of their own.' Julian threw his hands up in the air and whispered an aside to Ben and Ellie. 'I've only ever let her handfeed the ewe lambs rejected by their mums, and kept the rams separate, so she didn't have the upset of them going off to market. But I didn't realise this lamb was going to end up a hop-a-long.' Maisie's hearing was far too good, though.

'What about if I'd been born with a limp, Daddy? Would you have sent me away from the farm, too?' She might only have been six, but she was already an expert at manipulation, with her bottom lip sticking out and a look of desolation in her eyes.

'Of course not.' Julian sounded worn out, as if his argument was running out of steam, but it would be really hard for him to back down. If he did, he could end up with a whole flock of unproductive sheep by the time Maisie was old enough to leave home.

'Hetty, Hilda, Hilary and Hermione all get to stay.' Maisie threw her arms around one of the sheep in the pen next to her, covering its ears with her hands. 'But you're sending Holly for the chop!'

'We named them all with the letter aitch after finding Holly,' Julian offered by way of explanation, and Ellie nodded.

She hadn't missed the mention of the name Hilary, wondering if it was another sign. If she'd had any doubts about where her thoughts had just raced to, that was enough to convince her. Ellie turned towards Julian, aware of Maisie's eyes on her as she asked, 'How much would you get for Holly at market?'

'About eighty pounds, give or take, depending on the weight.'

'How about if I matched that, to take Holly off your hands?' Ellie turned to smile at Maisie, who was regarding her with an air of suspicion.

The little girl tightened her grip on the lamb. 'You're not going to eat her, are you?'

'No, I could take her back to my farm; I've got a whole collection of animals there that needed a home for one reason or another. I've got a horse called Joey who was destined for the same place as Holly before I found him.' Ellie moved a step closer to the pen and rubbed the lamb's soft black head. Holly had long since lost the prettiness of new born lambs, but she had the same mournful look in her eyes as Joey, when she'd first got him, and Ellie could imagine the two of them getting along just fine.

'So, *you've* got pets on your farm?' Maisie shot her dad an *I-told-you-so* sort of look.

'Yes, but mine's not a working farm like this. It's a sort of retirement home for donkeys and other animals, and we're hoping we might start having weddings there soon, too.' Ellie smiled when Maisie nodded sagely in response.

'Sounds like a much nicer farm than this one.' Finally releasing her grip on the lamb, she hopped over the fence of the pen and slid her hand into Ellie's. 'Can Uncle Ben's friend buy Holly, Daddy? Please!'

'If Ellie really wants to waste her money on a good-for-nothing ewe, then I'll not stand in her way.' Julian gave another shrug of the shoulders, sneaking Ellie a quick thumbs-up sign when he knew Maisie wasn't looking. Everyone was happy, and Julian had been able to save face. Giving in to his very determined daughter was clearly a precedent he wanted to avoid.

'That's settled, then, and you can come and visit Holly any time you like.' Ellie was nearly knocked backwards, when Maisie released her grip on her hand and threw herself into her arms, instead.

'Really? I'll come all the time, then. Uncle Ben can bring me. Mummy says you're his girlfriend.' Maisie giggled as she said the word, and Ben nodded.

'That's right Maisie, and I promise to take you to see Holly as soon as she's settled in. She'll love it at Ellie's farm.'

'Thank God that's all sorted. We'll get dinner before midnight, after all.' Julian lifted Maisie out of Ellie's arms and hoisted her onto his shoulders. 'Let's go and see how Mummy's getting on with dinner, while Ben checks over the rest of the ewe lambs.'

After Julian and Maisie left the barn, Ellie had another look at Holly. She was definitely lame, but otherwise she looked fine – like any other sheep, in fact – and she had a powerful bleat on her that might even give Gerald's braying a run for its money. 'Did you invite me up here because you know I'm soft-hearted and wouldn't be able to refuse a little girl, or an injured lamb?' She turned to Ben, who knotted his hand into hers, much like Maisie had.

'No, I had no idea that any of the lambs Maisie had bottle fed were due for slaughter. I suspect that Julian was the one manipulating us. Well, more me, really. I think he wanted me to tell Maisie from a vet's point of view that it was kinder to put Holly down. After all, he had no way of knowing how lovely you are.'

'Lovely or gullible?' She stared up at him.

'Definitely lovely. No question about it.' Then he kissed her again, leaving her in no doubt at all that he meant every word.

13

Holly settled into life on the farm extremely quickly, alongside Betsy, the only sheep left from Aunt Hilary's time on the farm. But Holly soon acquired a new second name that also began with an aitch. Holly Houdini was an expert escapologist, capable of squeezing between the narrowest of gaps in the post and rail fence. Even with a lame back leg, within a week of arriving on the farm, she'd twice managed to navigate the stile and get onto Alan's land. Thank goodness they were all now friends.

Olivia had demanded frequent email updates on Holly's adventures, too. She'd told Ellie they cheered up her day no end, and even the kids in her class looked forward to hearing the latest instalment. Luckily for Olivia, she never had to wait long.

Holly, Betsy and Joey were housed in the paddock next to the one with Gerald and the other donkeys, and they would often lean across into one another's fields, like neighbours chatting over the garden fence. Sometimes Ellie would put Dolly the goat out there too, when she needed a rest from her three incessantly hungry kids for a little while.

One Saturday morning, Karen and Ellie were doing the

morning rounds at the farm, checking on the animals, and had headed down to the bottom paddocks. Gerald saw them coming and began braying, Dolly bleating in unison with him, Joey watching them both with interest, but there was no sign of Holly.

'Looks like she's disappeared again.' Karen grinned at Ellie. They'd both grown fond of the newcomer, who seemed to have inherited some of Maisie's wilful ways, and she hadn't strayed too far in her little adventures. 'I'll give Alan a ring and see if she's turned up over there.'

Ellie couldn't make out much of the one-sided conversation her mother was having with their neighbour, but one thing was clear: Holly hadn't escaped to Crabtree Farm this time around.

'You don't think she could have fallen down the cliff edge, do you?' Ellie was suddenly gripped by panic. What would Ben say if the sheep was badly injured, and more to the point, how would Maisie react? The little girl was due to visit later in the afternoon, and she could just imagine Maisie's face if her beloved Holly was nowhere to be found – or, worse still, was lying at the bottom of the cliff.

After dashing to the other side of the field, Ellie peered over the cliff edge and down onto the beach below. There was no sign of Holly, thank goodness.

'If she's not there. What about the woods?' A look of panic suddenly crossing her face, too, Karen pulled her mobile out again and had another hurried conversation that Ellie couldn't quite pick up on. 'Alan's going to check the woods on his side and we can have a look on our side,' she said once she'd ended the call. 'She can't have gone far, can she? After all, it's not like people wouldn't notice a sheep walking down the middle of Kelsea Bay High Street. Especially not on a Saturday morning, in the middle of market day.'

They ran down to the woods, Ellie convinced that Holly

would be lying in a heap somewhere. Only having to tell Maisie could actually be worse than finding the sheep in that sort of state.

The search in the woods proved fruitless, too. The only animal life they saw was a rabbit, which shot down the nearest hole as soon as it caught sight of them, and a couple of squirrels scampering along the branches, high above their heads.

Ellie felt like Bear Grylls as she searched for sheep droppings, or some other sign to give them a clue as to which way she'd gone. It was all glamour in the country. She wanted to call Ben, but it was hardly a veterinary emergency, and a big part of her didn't want him to know that she'd lost the sheep.

Her mum caught hold of Ellie's elbow, after they'd spent at least half an hour searching for Holly, to no avail. Karen's mobile had rung at one point, and Ellie's heart had soared, hoping it would be Alan saying that the runaway sheep had arrived, after all. It was him, but only asking if they'd had any luck, as there was no sign of Holly in the woods on his side of the fence, either. 'Do you think we should go back to the house and call the police?' her mum asked.

'I don't think they'll send out an officer for one lost sheep.' Ellie's throat was tight from calling out for Holly, not to mention the emotion that burned every time she thought of having to face Maisie when she arrived later. 'Maybe we could give Daisy and Ben a call and ask them to spread the word, in case Holly has wandered down the road and is currently working her way through someone's prize marrows on their allotment.'

They headed back to the house, Ellie hoping that Holly would be waiting for them up at the yard, on the lookout for a bucket of sheep nuts, or whatever treat she could get. Dolly the goat would eat absolutely anything, including the local newspaper, when the delivery boy left it on the step, but Holly wasn't far behind her in the gastronomic stakes. The yard was totally empty, though, and even five minutes of rattling a bucket filled with Holly's favourite food didn't bring her running from her hiding place. Ellie knew she wasn't on the farm. If she had been, she wouldn't have been able to resist the lure of sheep nuts.

She gave in and rang Ben as soon as she got inside the house. 'It's me. Have you finished morning surgery?'

'I've just seen the last patient.' He hadn't needed her receptionist assistance that morning, since he only saw a few emergency patients on Saturdays, anyway. 'What's wrong?'

'I didn't say there was anything wrong.' Ellie gripped the phone, trying to convince herself that she meant what she was saying. She hated the idea of anything bad having happened to Holly.

'No, but I can hear it in your voice.' They might have only been together a few months, but he already knew her better than Rupert had – perhaps because Ben actually listened.

'Holly's missing.' She bit her lip. Stupid to get so attached to a sheep, especially one that spent all her waking hours trying to escape, but she couldn't help it.

'Again! Don't worry, she'll just be over at Alan's.' His tone was soothing, but he had no idea how long they'd already been searching.

'He's been looking everywhere on his farm, too. There's no sign of her anywhere.'

'Do you want me to come up?' She could hear him already jangling his keys in the background.

'If you can, but can you spread the word around town first please, and ask Daisy if she can put the word out, too? Maybe someone else will have seen her.' Ellie bit her lip again. 'What do you think Maisie's going to say?'

'Let's not worry about that until we have to, okay?' Ben was still using soothing tones. 'I'll go and see Daisy, then I'll be straight up.'

* * *

Every time there was a noise on the gravel in the yard, Ellie jumped up and looked out of the window, hoping it would be someone bringing Holly back. It had been the postman the first time, bringing a pile of letters she didn't even glance at as she threw them onto the kitchen windowsill. The bills could wait until later.

The second time it was Ben, arriving in his truck to help with the next phase of the search. 'Are you okay?' He gave her a hug, and she wanted to lean on him and not have to worry about tracking down Holly, suddenly worn out.

She'd been working long hours at the surgery, and doing whatever she could on the farm in between, even helping out Karen with some of the deli orders. Her repertoire was far more limited than her mother's, but she could whip up a mean Victoria sponge cake and flaky pastry that was light and crisp. Trying to spread herself between three jobs was hard, though, and she was starting to wonder if they'd ever hear from the council about the venue license. She didn't want to think about how much of Daisy's big day was hanging on the outcome. The disappearance of Holly was enough to worry about for now.

'I've had better days. I keep thinking about how upset Maisie's going to be.'

'We've got a while yet and, if the worst comes to the worst, we can always distract her with Gerald, Dolly, and the others.' He gave her a half-smile, but they both knew there was no fooling Maisie.

'Let's go and have another look. She can't have gone that far.'

As a light but persistent drizzle began to run down the windows outside, Ben passed Ellie her jacket before turning towards her mum. 'Are you coming as well, Karen?'

'I'll wait here in case anyone tries to call the home phone.' She frowned, obviously feeling as helpless as her daughter. 'I don't suppose you happen to know what Maisie's favourite biscuits are, do you?'

'Gingerbread, and they're bound to help distract her.' Ben slung a comforting arm around Ellie's shoulders. 'Not that we'll need it. We'll be back soon, with Holly in tow. She might even have broken into her own paddock. I wouldn't put it past her.'

'Me neither.' As Ben removed his arm from her shoulders, Ellie shrugged into her jacket and followed him out of the house.

Two hours later, they were wet through, and there was still no sign of the runaway sheep.

By the time Ben set off to pick Maisie up at three o'clock, the sun had come out. Holly was still on the run, and, for once, Ellie wasn't looking forward to the sound of Ben's car on the gravel.

Like an impending trip to the dentist, or a deadline you just knew you weren't going to make, Maisie's arrival came all too soon – and the tooting of Ben's horn meant there was no chance of pretending she hadn't heard them arrive. Deciding that the best thing to do was just to get it over and done with, Ellie headed outside, leaving Karen to put the finishing touches to the gingerbread men she'd baked for Maisie. Although, she doubted even her mother could bake her way out of this one.

'Holly!' Maisie flung her arms around the sheep, who was standing nonchalantly in the middle of the yard, looking as though she'd been there all day, and completely oblivious to all

the fuss she'd caused. Relief flooded Ellie's body and she was so
overjoyed to see the errant wanderer that she couldn't even be
angry about how much hassle Holly had caused. Suddenly she
understood Aunt Hilary's unconditional love for her animals
better than ever.

'Where did you find her?' Ben silently mouthed the words to
Ellie, who just shook her head.

'Does she get to wander around and do what she likes all the
time?' Maisie turned towards them, her face shining as she was
reunited with her favourite lamb.

'No. She's usually in the paddock with Joey, but, as this was a
special occasion, we thought she'd want to be here to greet you.'
Ellie crossed her fingers behind her back. This was the okay type
of lie to tell, one that protected a child and kept the magic alive –
like Santa Claus or the tooth fairy.

'She looks really happy, and she's even got a friend!' Maisie
pointed to what looked like a ball of fur lying on the ground just
behind Holly. As she spoke, the furball moved and a little brown
head emerged to reveal a small dog, some kind of terrier, and as it
struggled to its feet, Ellie could see how fat it was.

The dog waddled forward, and Holly gently nudged it with
her head, pushing it towards where Ellie stood.

'Hello, little one. Where did you spring from?' She knelt down
and stroked the dog's ears.

'She's probably lost.' Maisie gave a little sigh. 'I bet Holly told
her how kind you are to animals, and that's why she's here.
Animals can talk to each other, you know. Mummy has been
reading me a book called *Babe* and all the animals talk in that.' It
wasn't the kind of logic you could argue with, and Ellie couldn't
help smiling at the thought. Wherever Holly had been on her
adventure, she seemed to have made friends with the little stray
dog along the way, and perhaps Maisie's explanation wasn't so

wide of the mark. Either way, the dog looked like it could do with Ben's attention.

'Shall we put Holly in the stable for a bit, and you can give her some sheep nuts later, once her lunch has gone down?' Ellie could only imagine what the sheep had been stuffing her face with since she'd escaped, and she wasn't about to take any chances. A stable with two bolts and a padlock seemed the best place for her.

'Sounds like a good plan to me.' Ben scooped the little dog into his arms. 'And Maisie can demolish some of Karen's gingerbread, whilst I take a look at this chap. Then we can all have a tour of the farm. I'm keen to see if Gerald looks well enough to make the fundraiser.'

* * *

'Well, one thing was immediately obvious when I took a proper look.' Ben came into the kitchen ten minutes later, the little brown dog still tucked under his arm. 'He's a she and she's very pregnant. About to give birth any day, I'd say.'

'I've made her a temporary basket.' Ellie pulled a cardboard box out from under the table that she'd lined with blankets, and the little dog set about making herself a bed, as soon as Ben put her inside.

'It looks like she might already be nesting.'

'Don't we need to find her owner, then? She'll want to be at home, with the people she knows looking after her.' Karen looked concerned, but Ellie knew it was nothing to do with her being worried about getting saddled with yet another unwanted animal.

'By the looks of it, I don't think anyone's been taking proper care of her for a very long time.' Ben took the drink that Karen had poured for him.

'See, I told you Holly had brought her here. She knew you'd look after her.' Maisie had been busy colouring in a large sheet of paper that Ellie had given her, but she didn't miss a trick.

A knock at the door made the little dog's ears prick up, and she started to shiver, clearly a nervous wreck.

'That'll be Alan. I told him about Holly...' Karen just caught herself in time as she added, '...waiting out in the yard for Maisie to arrive, and he said he'd pop over for a cup of tea to celebrate. He doesn't even know about the dog, yet. It's been quite a day!'

Moments later, Karen ushered Alan into the kitchen. He shook hands with Ben and gave Ellie a warm smile, listening intently as Karen explained about the little dog. Peering into her basket, he rubbed his chin with one hand, as if he was trying to remember something.

'I might be mistaken, but I'm sure I've seen the dog before. I kept hearing yapping in the night last week, and when I looked out of my bedroom window at the caravan park, there was a little terrier like this chained up to one of the caravans. I complained, but the manager said he'd sort it and not to worry. The people who'd been staying there were moving on the next day, anyway.' Alan sighed deeply. 'I wonder if they left her behind.'

'If they did, you can bet your life they did it on purpose.' Ben had a murderous look on his face, and for a moment Ellie was taken back to the first day she'd met him, when he'd been so cross about the state that Gerald was in. The only time she'd ever really seen him get angry was when people mistreated animals, and when he'd realised she hadn't ended her engagement with Rupert. She tried not to think about the fact that Ben still didn't know the whole story and that Maisie wasn't the only one she'd lied to by omission; like the truth about Santa Claus, there were definitely some things that were better left unsaid. Right now they had more urgent things to think about anyway.

'We'll keep her tonight.' Ellie glanced towards her mother, who nodded swiftly in response. 'But then we ought to try and find out who she belongs to, just in case someone is desperately looking for her.' Glancing at the dog, Ellie suspected that Ben was right, though. Sadly, the little terrier didn't look well loved. 'Unless of course you think she'd be better off at the surgery.'

'No, she'll be shut up in a cage there, and this way, we can keep an eye on her if she shows more signs of going into labour.' Ben smiled at her. 'I suppose we better give her a name, for tonight, at least.'

'What do you think, Maisie? What's a good name for a lost dog?' Ellie looked across the table at the little girl's drawing, where she'd added a sheep that was a remarkably good likeness to Holly and a little brown ball of fur, which was unmistakably the dog curled up a few feet away from her.

'I think Ginger would be a good name. She's almost the same colour as the gingerbread men that Karen made for me, and she turned up on the same day.'

'Ginger it is, then.'

The little brown dog lifted up her head, as if she'd been paying attention. It was as good a name as any, and Ellie already had a feeling that the dog might end up staying far longer than the one night they'd agreed to. Whatever knack it was that Aunt Hilary had for finding and taking in the waifs and strays of the animal kingdom, Ellie seemed to have inherited it. The latest instalment in the adventures of life at Seabreeze Farm had only just begun.

* * *

Ben took Maisie home at seven o'clock, by which time she'd been around the farm three times, completed the almost impossible task of plaiting Gerald's mane, and thought up names for seven boys and seven girls to cover all eventualities with Ginger's puppies. She'd also fed Holly some sheep nuts and brushed her coat with an old dog brush, until the lamb resembled a giant powder puff.

Karen invited Alan to stay for dinner, and Ben was coming back to join them, after dropping Maisie off. They were all on puppy watch, waiting to see if Ginger's digging at the side of her cardboard box really was a sign that puppies were on the way.

They had an enjoyable meal together and were just playing cards, when Ginger started to pant much more strongly. Ben told them it was best not to interfere with her, unless it looked as if she was getting into trouble, so they watched from a safe distance as five puppies emerged. First came a ginger one, two jet black ones, and a couple of almost tabby-looking puppies, which were a mixture of several colours. The identity of the puppies' father was destined to remain a mystery, but clearly he hadn't been the same breed as Ginger.

When Ben was sure that there were no more puppies to come, he checked them over – two boys and three girls, as it turned out – and they were all feeding well within an hour of being born. Ginger might not have been well looked after during her pregnancy, but she was doing a pretty amazing job of being a mum.

'This calls for a proper celebration.' As Karen stood to put the kettle on, Alan put a hand on her arm and reached down inside the rucksack at his feet. 'None of your tea malarkey. I brought a bottle of champagne over, when you told me about Holly turning up. Only it didn't seem appropriate to open it whilst Maisie was here, especially with her not knowing about the sheep escaping in the first place. It's been in the cupboard for years. I can't even remember what it was bought for originally, but champagne is supposed to get better with age, isn't it?'

'Alan, you never cease to amaze me!' Ellie planted a quick kiss on his cheek, and he beamed in response. She had a suspicion he might become a permanent fixture one of these days – he was like an adoring puppy himself when Karen was around. Much to her surprise, Ellie found herself liking the idea more and more. Alan was one of the good guys, and that was what her mum deserved. 'I'll get the champagne glasses. Sit down, Mum, Alan's right. This definitely isn't a time for tea.'

As she crossed the kitchen to the cabinet where they kept the glasses, the pile of letters she'd propped on the windowsill, hours before, caught Ellie's eye. She picked them up and dropped them onto the table, placing the champagne glasses beside them, and a brown envelope slithered out from the middle of the pile.

'Look at the franking, it's from the council. It'll be the results of the inspection.' Karen picked up the envelope, turning it over carefully in her hands before handing it to her daughter. 'You should be the one to open it. It's you who's put all the hard work into this.'

'I don't think I can.' Ellie ran a finger along the flap sealing the envelope. It would be so easy to rip it open and read the council's verdict on whether Seabreeze Farm would make an appropriate venue for civil wedding ceremonies. Yet, there was so much riding on it, so many of Ellie's dreams, that she was sure the words would swim in front of her eyes, even if she was brave enough to read it. 'Can you do it, please?'

A bit like pass the parcel, she handed it to Ben, who peeled back the envelope slowly, like one of the presenters on an awards show. She had to sit on her hands to stop herself snatching the envelope out of his grasp and tearing it open. The anticipation was killing her.

'They've granted the license!' Ben had a huge grin on his face, but she still made him repeat it three times before it finally sank in.

'I still can't believe it!' Ellie was struggling to catch her breath, as Ben pulled her into his arms and kissed her. This was the news she'd been longing for and hearing the words out loud more than lived up to her every expectation. It was like the final piece of the puzzle she'd been looking for, for so long, had finally dropped into her lap. She had everything she wanted – her mum, Ben, a farm full of animals, and even lovely Alan – and now she could have her dream business too.

Squashing down her natural tendency to worry about what could go wrong, or just how hard it might turn out to be, she kissed Ben again. Sometimes you just had to celebrate the moment and worry about the rest later.

'Well, I don't know about you, but I think that's even more cause than ever to open this champagne.' Alan carefully released the champagne cork, muting it with a tea towel, so as not to frighten Ginger or her puppies. As they raised their glasses, he made a toast. 'To the Chapmans of Seabreeze Farm and their new venture.'

Karen raised her glass a second time, making Ellie's suspicions official as she added, 'And to Ginger, the newest member of the family.'

14

By the time the summer fundraiser, for the church hall and Elverham animal sanctuary, came around, Gerald was in rude health. His coat was shiny – at least, as much as an old donkey's coat ever could be – and Maisie had plaited his mane again for the occasion. Ellie was also taking Joey down to the green that ran parallel with the sea wall, where the fundraiser was being held. It was too risky to take Holly Houdini down with them, too, though. If the lamb slipped her lead rope, she could disappear in minutes, which would either cause panic in the crowd, or, knowing Holly, she'd steal everyone's picnic lunches and knock down the hotdog stand, if it got in her way.

Ben was bringing some guinea pigs, who were looking for a new home, and his own dog, Humphrey – a black and white Great Dane, who stood nearly as tall as the donkey. They would be asking for a donation for people to pet the animals of their choice, all in a good cause, and Ben would be doing a talk on animal care.

Karen and Alan had offered to help out, but since her mum

had already baked several cakes for the tea tent, Ellie was keen for her to have a day off and just enjoy the fundraiser.

By 3 p.m., the old ice cream tubs, which they'd used to collect the donations, were brimming with coins. When someone dropped a ten pound note into the tub without saying anything, Ellie looked up into the face of the last person she'd expected to see.

'Rupert!' She put a hand on Gerald's neck to steady herself. 'What an earth are you doing here?'

'I came to see how country life was treating you.' He looked her up and down in the way that had always made her feel so self-conscious, as if he was actively searching out her flaws. 'It obviously suits you. You look really well – slimmer.'

The bottom line for Rupert clearly hadn't changed, and Ellie felt the tension in her shoulders relax. He was part of her old life, and, seeing him, she was more certain than ever that she'd done the right thing by moving to Kelsea Bay.

'I thought about calling you to let you know I was coming down, but I thought you might try to put me off. You've changed so much, El.' There was an odd note of surprise in his voice, as if he still couldn't quite believe it.

'I can't see why you'd want to come down.' She couldn't bring herself to say she was pleased to see him, when she was anything but, and was vaguely aware of Ben standing a few feet away, talking to a couple about the importance of considering, very carefully, what would be the right pet for their child.

'Because I've been thinking about how much the farm means to you and I think I get it now.'

'Okay, but that doesn't change anything. We broke up months ago.' As Ellie spoke, she could tell that the pace of Ben's speech was quickening, too. He was clearly keen to get away from the couple and to find out what was going on. She'd have wanted to be in on the conversation, too, had their roles been reversed.

'Of course it does; I've really missed you El.' Rupert moved to take her hand, but she snatched it away. 'And I hoped you might have missed me too. I thought that maybe once you knew I understood why you'd want to live at the farm, that you might change your mind about us.'

'And are you telling me that you'd be willing to move to Kelsea Bay full time, if I had? That you'd want to help me run the farm? Because it needs all hands on deck.' Ellie laughed, as Rupert pulled a face. Absolutely nothing had changed. She knew how he was motivated. She was just an acquisition that had got away, something that made him want her all the more. He was the same with properties he had his eye on. She'd seen it time and again. There was probably still an ulterior motive with the farm too, thinking he could work on her slowly and eventually persuade her to sell it, just like he'd planned all along. It was a pointless conversation, anyway, she felt nothing for him except regret that they'd ever been together. She didn't want him to taint the life she had now and she definitely didn't want him talking to Ben.

'It must be hard work up at the farm, making ends meet? It looks like it needs a lot of upkeep, especially all those outbuildings and the fencing where the land drops away at the cliff edge. It could be very dangerous if it isn't taken proper care of.'

'When did you look at all of that?' He'd only ever visited the farm once, on the day she'd ended their engagement. By the time he and Ellie were together, Hilary had banned anyone from visiting her there. 'Have you been up there, then?'

'I drove by on the way down here and, when no one answered, I had a little look around. I didn't think you'd mind.' He gave a causal shrug and Ellie disliked him even more.

'Well I do mind, it's private property, and you obviously didn't get a *proper* look, because we're doing just fine. In fact, we had some really exciting news last month. We've been approved by the council as a wedding venue, and we've got our first wedding soon.' She didn't know why she was telling him any of this, she just wanted to wipe the self-satisfied smile off his face.

'Lovely.' Rupert's mouth formed the word, but there wasn't a trace of sincerity. It was probably his idea of hell, getting married on a farm, surrounded by animals who had seen better days.

They'd never got as far as agreeing on a venue for their own wedding, but it would have been sleek, modern and soulless, if Rupert had got his way – she knew that now. It was funny, looking at someone she thought she'd loved and realising she never really had. She'd just craved the certainty of being loved, but he'd never done that either.

'I'll call you about meeting up.' He paused, searching her face, as if waiting for some sort of sign that she still had feelings for him. 'We can sort out the ring, then, if you really want to give it back.'

'There's absolutely no point, Rupert.' Ellie held out the ten pound note he'd dropped in her ice cream tub – there was no such thing as a donation without strings, as far as he was concerned – but he shook his head, ignoring the gesture and the words that had come with it.

'See you soon, Ellie.' Turning on his heel, he disappeared into the crowd, leaving her with a distinct feeling of unease.

Seconds later, Ben slid an arm around her waist, having finally escaped from the clutches of the couple, who'd been trying to decide between a guinea pig and a rabbit for their children.

'What on earth was Rupert doing here?' He pulled her in

closer, concern in his voice rather than any anger that her ex had shown up out of the blue.

'He just hates that I'm the one who finished it I think. He said he was hoping I might have changed my mind.' Ellie sighed. She didn't want her old life coming to Kelsea Bay. 'Nothing's ever as straightforward as it seems with Rupert. He didn't come all this way just to see how I was. I might actually feel sorry for him if I genuinely thought he missed me, not that I'd want to go back in a million years.'

'I'm very glad to hear that, because if I lost you, I'd keep trying to convince you to give me a second chance as well. So I can't blame him for trying.' Ben's lips brushed against hers, and she knew without a shadow of a doubt that he would.

'You're not getting rid of me, I'm afraid!' They still hadn't said the L word yet, but she'd been close a hundred times and, if they hadn't been surrounded by families queuing up for their turn at the makeshift petting zoo, she might even have told him there and then.

* * *

'You could have bought half a dozen coconuts for the amount of money you've spent trying to win one.' Karen laughed, when yet another one of the small red balls that Alan had aimed at the hairy brown target went wide of the mark.

'That's not the point!' He was laughing, too. 'I wanted to win one for you, and it's all for charity, in any case. If I'd just wanted to buy a coconut, we could have nipped to the supermarket and been home before lunch.' He hurled the last of the three balls forward, without really looking, and this time it made contact with the coconut. The hairy fruit wobbled for a bit, and for a horrible moment, Karen thought it was going to stay put, before it finally toppled down to the grass below the stall.

'Bullseye!' Alan swung her round in a circle – something no one had tried for years, much less achieved. He didn't even make a groaning sound as he lifted her off the ground. Years of building up his muscles farming had obviously paid off.

'If this is what you're like when you win a coconut, remind me never to be around if your lottery numbers come up. I don't think my spine could take it!' Karen gave a little curtsey, as he handed her the coconut. 'Why, thank you, kind sir. I'll treasure it for ever.'

'Actually, I was hoping for some coconut macaroons, so we'll have to smash it open at some point.' Alan grinned. 'But in the meantime, can I interest you in a visit to the tea tent?'

'Always. You know me.' Putting the coconut into her bag, she linked her arm through his.

A brass band played outside the tea tent, where several people walked past with slices of her cakes on their plates. It still gave her a warm glow inside to think of people enjoying something she'd baked, especially when she saw someone smile in satisfaction as they tasted the first forkful.

'Do you want something to eat?' Alan pulled out a seat for her at one of the small garden tables that had been set up outside the tent.

'No, thanks. I'm saving myself for the coconut. Just tea would be lovely.'

'I'll go and queue up, if you promise to save me a seat.' He squeezed her shoulder, and she turned to look at him. She wanted to say something significant, something about always saving him a seat next to her, but shyness still ruled her sometimes, as if she might be pushing this quiet man faster than he really wanted to go. Any movement in their relationship had always been on his terms, and, as much as she wanted to tell him how she felt, it was less scary that way.

Several groups of people drifted past, as Karen sat waiting for Alan. She was starting to recognise a lot of the locals from Kelsea Bay, some of whom she'd been introduced to when she'd been delivering her cakes to the deli. There were also a few of the old crowd she'd reconnected with still living in Kelsea Bay, from the days when she and Alan would hang out with other local teenagers, when Karen spent time at her aunt's farm during the holidays. She could see Ellie across the green too, chatting animatedly to the children who were petting Gerald. The old donkey looked perfectly content to be the centre of attention, even if he did occasionally have a rummage in someone's pocket with his nose, or a conveniently open handbag that happened to pass him by.

Karen smiled. Ellie had been even more successful at integrating herself into the community. Working at the veterinary surgery with Ben had helped, and she'd embraced local events like the barn dance, too. She was a natural networker, and now that she was out of Rupert's shadow, she was blossoming, on the cusp of starting her own business.

Almost as soon as his name had entered her head, Karen saw him. This time, there was no mistaking Rupert. Standing bold as brass, on the other side of the tea tent, he chatted to Daisy, who couldn't keep anything to herself if her life depended on it. By now, Rupert would know everything that Ellie had done since she'd arrived in Kelsea Bay, but the important question was, what was Rupert doing there?

As it had her daughter, less than half an hour before, seeing Rupert again left Karen with an uneasy feeling.

* * *

'Sorry it took so long.' Alan set the tea tray down on the table. On it were two mismatched cups and saucers and a plate of short-bread, which clearly wasn't homemade. 'The queue stretched right around the inside of the tent, and by the time I got there, all the good stuff – and by that I mean everything you made – was long gone.'

'Never mind. I was saving myself, anyway, and there's always the coconut macaroons to look forward to.' She put her hand over his, pushing thoughts of Rupert out of her mind. She wasn't going to let an unwanted visitor spoil a perfectly lovely afternoon.

'You're always making things for me, so I'd like to give you something in return.' Alan's voice had dropped in volume, as though he was worried someone might overhear.

'Don't be daft, you've done far more for me than I ever could for you. All the things you've helped us with, and building that beautiful gazebo. It's stunning now it's finished.'

'I built it for *you*.' He stumbled over his words a bit. 'I mean, with you in mind. I wanted it to be the perfect place for you to choose, if you ever wanted to get married again.'

Karen gave a nervous laugh. 'Who'd ever want to marry me?'

'I would.' He cleared his throat, his nervousness evident. 'No, scratch that, I mean I *do*. I do want to marry you. The truth is, I've loved you since we were kids. I always wanted to pluck up the courage to ask you out and then Dad's health deteriorated and I stopped hanging out with the old crowd in Kelsea Bay, so I never saw you when you visited. I thought I'd lost my chance of being with the one girl I ever loved.'

'I'm the only girl you've ever loved?' Karen could have wept for the years they'd lost, because she'd imagined Alan asking her out a thousand times back when they were young. Their lives might have turned out so differently, but then she'd never have had Ellie and she wouldn't change that for the world. Maybe now was meant to be their moment all along.

'I'm not saying there haven't been a few short-lived relationships, but I've never felt like I did back then, not until now. Except now the feelings are even stronger and I'm more certain than ever.' Alan ran a finger inside the collar of his shirt. 'I've rehearsed all of this, but I'm still making a hash of it! I wish I could be one of those people who made a big show of things by asking the brass band to play "Isn't She Lovely" while I drop down on one knee, but I'm just not like that. I've hidden something under the shortbread instead.'

Karen picked up three biscuits before she saw it. A gold ring, in the middle of the plate, set with rubies in the shape of a flower and a cluster of diamonds in the centre. 'I...' She could scarcely speak, but when she looked at Alan, she realised there was only one answer. 'Yes!'

15

'Are you sure you're not rushing into this?' Ellie didn't look up at her mother as she spoke. It was taking all her concentration to keep the paint inside the heart shaped outlines on the metal jug she was decorating.

There were ten centrepieces to prepare for the tables at Daisy's wedding. In the high of getting the go ahead for the venue, it had seemed like a good idea to hand paint them. However, as she struggled to decorate only the third jug, Ellie was definitely starting to wish she'd bought them online.

'Maybe it seems quick because we've only been back in touch for a few months, but I've been on my own for twenty-five years, Ellie, so I'm not prone to rushing into things. I've known him since we were both kids too and deep down he hasn't changed a bit. It's been like reconnecting with an old friend, only better. One of the things I love most about Alan is that there's no pretence with him. He says what he means and he wouldn't have asked me if he didn't believe it would be for keeps. And I really want that, I don't want to be on my own forever.' Karen busied herself as she spoke and, when Ellie eventually glanced up, she was folding green fondant icing over little square cakes, her face shining with happiness. The preparations for Daisy's hen night might be turning out to be almost as time consuming as coordinating the wedding itself, but nothing could wipe the smile off her mother's face.

'You wouldn't be on your own. You've always had me and you always will.' Ellie put the paintbrush down for a moment. Her hand had started to shake with the effort of keeping it steady. It wasn't that she wasn't happy for her mother and Alan, she just had to be certain that Karen wasn't making the same mistake that she'd made with Rupert and leaping into an engagement out of anything other than love.

'And you were all I ever needed. But when you got engaged to Rupert, and even after you broke up, I realised that one day, very soon, you'd be moving on with your life, and you wouldn't want me holding you back. I've been lucky to have you at home with me for far longer than most mums do, and we've always been close, but I'd hate for you to come to resent that. When we inherited the farm, it meant we had time together again and I treasure every moment. You will always be the love of my life, my sweet girl, but I think there's even more for both of us.' Karen wrapped her arms around Ellie, holding her tight for a moment before letting her go again. 'I know you don't like me making assumptions about Ben, but even if you two don't end up together – although I have to say I hope you do – one day you *will* want to settle down into a life with your own family. Meeting Alan has been like a second chance at love for me. I'll never regret marrying your dad, because we had you, but I know what it's like now, to have someone put you first, and I've never had that before.'

Ellie smiled, the worry that her mum was rushing into the engagement with Alan lifting off her shoulders. She'd already talked it through with Olivia. But despite her best friend's reas-surances that Karen's new fiancé sounded perfect, the desire to protect her mum from any sort of hurt had left a lingering sense of unease. Now it was finally passing. 'It's about time someone did that for you, and there's no denying he's a lovely man.' She picked up the paintbrush again. 'It looks like I'm going to have to get a bit better at painting these love hearts. With your wedding on the cards, we've suddenly got a rush on.'

'There's no hurry for us, and we're certainly not about to steal Daisy's thunder.' Karen rolled out another piece of green icing. 'You and Ben might even beat us yet...'

'Mum! How many times do I have to tell you?' The tip of the brush slipped as Ellie protested, making the last of the love hearts look distinctly wobbly. That one would definitely be relegated to a position in the darkest corner of the marquee.

Her mum had a habit of knowing what Ellie really wanted, even before she realised it herself. Not this time, though, because she'd already imagined what building a life with Ben might be like, not long after they'd started dating. As much as she'd told herself it was far too early to think like that, she couldn't help it when Ben seemed so much like her matching half. She'd fallen for him watching him taking such great care of Gerald and the other animals, but the more time she spent with him the harder she fell. He made her laugh harder and smile more often than she could ever remember doing. But it was seeing him with his goddaughter, Maisie, that had made it even harder to stop herself picturing the life her mother had described – building a family of her own, with Ben. She wasn't about to admit that out loud though, not even to Karen.

* * *

Surprisingly, for Daisy, she was having a very relaxed hen night. They were using the seating area in the deli as the venue, and she was having a meal for family and close friends. At the bride-to-be's request, Karen had made some cakes for the party, the little square ones she'd decorated earlier. Half of them were covered in green fondant icing, with a large daisy in the centre, and the other half had little houses on top, to represent Nathan's job as an architect. They were like a prequel to the wedding cake, and each one was a miniature work of art.

One of Daisy's friends leant across the table, nearly knocking over her drink in the process. 'So, are you going to tell us about the wedding dress?'

'Let's just say, the big day is all about *me*. Everything, from the flowers to the cake, is daisy themed!' She giggled and took a sip of champagne. 'And, if it wasn't for these ladies...' Daisy swept her hand in the direction of where Karen and Ellie were seated, at the far end of the table. 'I would never have got my dream wedding. If Jamie finally gets around to asking you to marry him, Pru, I can't recommend them enough!' Daisy, who was exuberant even without the aid of several glasses of champagne, could probably have been heard three streets away.

'I'll bear that in mind.' Poor Pru looked distinctly deflated, and Ellie immediately felt sorry for her. It must have been hard having a friend like Daisy, who was the life and soul of every occasion and who could be about as tactful as Gordon Ramsey in a failing restaurant. Whenever she was with Daisy, she couldn't help thinking about Ben and how different the pair of them were, despite growing up side by side.

Ben never seemed to feel the need to compete with his sister. He was full of life, too, just in a less obvious way, never trying to dominate the conversation, or make sure he was the centre of attention. He always wanted to hear Ellie's opinion on things, as much as his own, and it was like a breath of fresh air after Rupert.

She hadn't heard from Rupert since the village fair and, as relieved as she was that he seemed to have disappeared again, it was oddly unsettling. There had to be some reason why he'd gone to all the trouble of coming to Kelsea Bay and she just wished he'd show his hand, tell her what he was really after.

'Time for a song, I think!' Daisy, who, by then, had drunk the best part of a bottle of champagne, got to her feet. 'Just because I decided not to go dancing for my hen night, it doesn't mean we can't have some fun. Ellie, can you put on track thirteen, please?' She gestured towards her iPhone, that was linked into the deli's sound system. They usually played classical music – apparently, it made the customers buy more, or so Daisy said –but there were obviously a few of the bride-to-be's other favourites on there, for occasions such as this.

'All done for you.' Ellie smiled at her friend, as she selected the requested track. 'Take it away!'

'I'd like to dedicate this song to my wonderful fiancé, Nathan Hardy!'

Daisy began to join in with the track. It was a love song, but one Ellie didn't recognise, and even if she had, the way Ben's sister was murdering the tune, it would have been difficult to make out.

She could see people walking past the window in the glow of the streetlight above, most of them stopping to see where the caterwauling was coming from and smiling at the sight of Daisy in full swing.

Ellie's mouth went dry as a familiar figure paused outside the window. It was Rupert, and he was looking straight at her. She'd seen that ruthless look on his face before and she knew he wouldn't stop until he got what he wanted. If she'd felt oddly unsettled at his silence following the fair, now she felt completely sick.

* * *

'If that's Kelsea Bay's Got Talent, then I think you need to draft in some ringers from a neighbouring town.' Rupert smirked, but she didn't even attempt to laugh at his joke.

Daisy was still inside the deli, launching into a second tune. Even with the party still in full swing, it had taken all of Ellie's powers of persuasion to convince Karen not to follow her outside to confront Rupert.

'What are you doing here *again*? There's nothing left to say.' Every muscle in Ellie's body was tensed so that he wouldn't see her shaking. If he knew how much of an effect his behaviour was having on her, she had a horrible feeling he'd ramp things up even more. She had to pretend that him turning up was just a minor inconvenience, in the hope he'd get bored when his actions didn't seem to be having the desired impact.

'Oh but I think there's plenty left to say.' Rupert took a step towards her, and she took two steps back. 'You made a verbal contract when you agreed to marry me and you've broken that, so I think I deserve some compensation.'

'What do you mean, compensation?' If he was after money, like some scorned woman from the history books, suing for breach of promise, then he was out of luck. She didn't have a penny that wasn't tied up in the farm and, even if she had, he was being completely ridiculous. He'd all but told her that he'd been cheating on her all along. So, even if she'd never met Ben or chosen a life on the farm that Rupert would have hated, that would have dealt the hammer blow to killing off their engagement anyway.

'You've humiliated me and the least you can do is find some way to make it up to me. You owe me that. What price does a broken heart fetch, do you reckon?'

'Please don't come here pretending to be heartbroken. It's been months and we've both moved on.' She turned to leave, but he caught hold of her wrist.

'Well, I know *you* have. Things are still looking very cosy between you and the local vet. I was speaking to his sister at the fundraiser and I heard all about his practice. It could be an interesting investment for my firm if we bought it up to become part of one of our franchises. From what Daisy tells me, he loves the personal relationship he has with his clients the way things are run now and all of that would change.'

'He'd never sell to you in the first place!'

'No but his partners might, with the right offer, and then he'd have no choice but for lover boy to go along with it.' Rupert smirked again. 'Think how your precious boyfriend would feel if he found out it was information I got from you that sealed the deal. You took a job there according to Daisy, so it wouldn't take much to convince him.'

'He'd never believe that!' Part of Ellie wanted to run, but Rupert was still holding on to her wrist, his fingers digging into her flesh, and she was suddenly terrified of what he might be capable of. She'd never seen him quite like this before, but then she'd always gone along with what he wanted when they were together.

'Why wouldn't he? Doesn't he know how many businesses your department at the bank put the squeeze on, shutting down their credit, and making them prime targets for my firm to buy up?'

'They were never my decisions—'

'No, but you were part of it. Does Ben know what sort of person you really are? If not, then maybe I should tell him.'

'Why are you doing this?' Ellie finally managed to wrench herself free of his grip. He didn't really stand to gain anything from following through on his threats, it was pure vindictiveness. The trouble was, Rupert reacted badly to not getting what he wanted. So, even if there was nothing for him to gain from this, there was still a very good chance that revenge would be enough of a motivation.

'Because you broke a promise, Ellie. You want to be careful with that little business of yours too – people don't take kindly to broken promises. Daisy's clearly got high expectations, and it would be a real shame if you couldn't fulfil them.'

'You know I could report you for threatening me, Rupert, don't you?' She was determined not to let the tears stinging her eyes fall. She had to call his bluff, because if he sensed a shred of weakness, he was going to feed off it.

'Just a warning, from a friend, that's all.' The look on Rupert's face was anything but friendly, before he finally turned and walked away. Watching him disappear into the darkness, Ellie's stomach churned and the tears she'd fought so hard to hold back felt like acid on her skin. There was no way she'd seen the last of him and she had absolutely no idea what to do.

The day after the hen night, and with less than forty hours to go until the wedding, Ellie was working her way through the checklist. Ben had helped her finalise the decorations in The Old Barn, where Daisy and Nathan would be signing the register, and all the official paperwork would be completed to make things legal. It would also be the backup venue for the ceremony itself, if the weather finally broke and the glorious Indian summer they'd been enjoying suddenly disappeared – making a wedding in the gazebo, overlooking the cliffs, out of the question.

After getting the go-ahead from the council, she'd bought a hundred gold chairs for the ceremonies, which were burning a hole in her credit card. They were a necessary expense though and the chairs could be moved from The Old Barn to outside the gazebo depending on where the couples chose to say their vows. Alan had put the use of a tractor and trailer at their disposal to make all of that easier. Thankfully, Daisy and Nathan were only having sixty guests, so it wouldn't be such a military operation to move the location for their ceremony, if the need arose. That said, Ellie had been keeping an almost obsessional watch on the weather, and so far, it looked as if Saturday was going to be a good day.

She'd thought about telling Ben what Rupert had said, but everyone was so consumed with the wedding and she needed to find the right moment and the right way to explain everything. She wanted Ben to know how different things had been in her life when she'd got together with Rupert. It almost felt now as if she'd been under his spell because that person didn't feel like her at all. Ellie was sure Ben would understand, but on the slim chance he reacted badly, the last thing she wanted to do was to ruin Daisy's wedding, by creating a terrible atmosphere between her brother and the wedding coordinator. She hadn't even told her mother the full story, just that Rupert seemed determined to make a nuisance of himself. It would all get sorted as soon as the wedding was out of the way, there was no way she was giving Rupert the satisfaction of putting a dampener on Seabreeze Farm's first big event.

The Elverham Marquee Co were coming to erect the reception venue the next day, just twenty-four hours before the wedding, and it would be dressed with flowers early on the day of the wedding itself. As Daisy had told anyone who would listen at the hen night, the flowers would be themed with her name, and there were daisies on everything, from the place cards to the confetti that was going to be scattered on the tables. Ellie had eventually managed to paint all of the old milk jugs with love hearts, and they would also be filled with daisies and put as the centrepieces on each of the ten tables. Daisy didn't want a top table, so they were having ten tables of six instead, including one for the bride and groom and their parents.

The pièce de résistance – the wedding cake, covered in hundreds of icing sugar daisies – would be put out on display at the same time as the flowers, so that everyone could admire it as soon as they entered the marquee. Everything had been thought out to the tiniest detail, including the positioning of an air conditioning unit, to ensure that neither the marquee, nor the cake, got too hot.

Karen had finished the cake a few days earlier, and had almost completed the handmade chocolates – unsurprisingly in the shape of daisies – that were going to be put in miniature cake boxes and used as favours on the tables. There was no chance of anyone forgetting the bride's name at this wedding!

16

The morning of the wedding dawned bright, just as the forecasters had promised. Every sound in the night had woken Ellie up, and she'd had to keep peering out of the window to make sure the marquee was still there and hadn't been blown into the Channel by some freak storm.

She hadn't heard a thing from Rupert on the day before the wedding, so the marquee had gone up without distraction and everything was going according to plan. The caterers had dropped off the food for the buffet, and every spare inch of space, in the two new fridges Ellie had bought for the business, with more help from her credit card, was taken up with their platters. The florist had been in to dress the marquee and The Old Barn, and had also left a large display of daisies, which were due to be moved to the gazebo on the clifftop just before the ceremony. They weren't taking any chances with a last minute change to the weather. It was all going perfectly – too perfectly, as it turned out.

Karen had gone down to the bottom paddock, with Alan driving the tractor and trailer, to set the chairs up for the wedding ceremony, once Ellie had finally stopped checking the weather like a woman possessed and had accepted that a freak thunder-storm was very unlikely to break out, after all. Her mum's scream, a few moments later, carried all the way up to the house, and Ellie ran out and straight down towards the gazebo, in only her socks.

Terrified that something awful might have happened, and half-expecting to see the tractor lying on its side with Alan pinned underneath, or that Rupert had ramped up his threat and had set fire to one of the outbuildings, she was shocked to see everything looking perfectly normal. Except for the fact that all of the bottom paddocks were empty.

'Someone's cut the chains on the gates for both these fields. All the animals are gone, even Gerald!' Karen was breathing really quickly and shrugging off Alan's attempts to comfort her. 'He was Aunt Hilary's favourite. If anything happens to him...'

Ellie felt surprisingly calm, having expected to be met with a scene of devastation. If Rupert was behind this, he hadn't managed to derail the wedding, but for now she wasn't even going to give a hint that it could be to do with him – they had enough to deal with. 'It'll just be some kids, thinking it's a laugh to let them go. No one is going to steal our motley collection of animals. An ancient donkey, a goat with ADHD, and a lame sheep aren't high up on the steal-to-order list. They'd have taken Joey or some of the other donkeys if anything, but all the other animals are still in the paddocks and even an open gate couldn't entice them to leave. They'll just have gone to the nearest source of food and stopped there.' Almost as soon as the words were out of her mouth, Ellie's heart sank towards her shoe-less feet.

The marquee. It was filled with flowers, and, *oh, God*, the wedding cake.

It was as if she was in one of those cartoons, where she was running without actually moving. She must have been, though, because as she got closer to the marquee, she could make out the outlines of shapes inside, then the unmistakeable sound of a bleating goat.

Maybe they wouldn't have touched the cake. The consumption of the flowers would have been a disaster, but a small one in comparison to the demolition of the pièce de résistance.

Sadly, as she finally got to the entrance of the marquee, any last vestige of hope disappeared.

Gerald and Dolly both had their heads buried in the ruins of Daisy's wedding cake, and Holly was wandering around with half a dozen daisies hanging out of one side of her mouth. Every single centrepiece had been upended, and almost all of the flowers were gone.

'*No!*' Ellie shouted the word and held on to the single syllable for what seemed like an hour. However long it was, it was enough time for Karen and Alan to make it to the marquee by the time she finally stopped. Suddenly she was certain this was Rupert's doing and if he was capable of this, he might be capable of following through on the rest of his threats. But if she thought about that, her legs might stop cooperating with her altogether. She couldn't give way to the anger or fear battling inside her to be the first to bubble over, she had enough to worry about. She was just going to have to keep repeating the mantra that had been running through her head since the hen night – she just needed to get through the wedding, then she could sort everything else out.

'I'll get the animals back to the field.' Alan spoke first. It was a practical suggestion, but it didn't begin to cover what needed doing to put things right. Even as she tried to hang on to the thought of getting through the wedding, Ellie could feel the prospect slipping through her fingers. It was already too late and hot tears were streaming down her face as she surveyed the carnage again.

'Oh, Mum, what are we going to do?' As Alan led Gerald out of the tent, Ellie picked up a piece of squashed wedding cake – there were strands of grass and half-chewed daisies all mixed up with it.

'I've got a cake, for a Christening next week. It's the same shape, but it isn't decorated yet, only with plain white icing. I don't know what we can do about the daisies, but it's something.' Karen sounded almost as shocked as Ellie was.

They'd put so much work into everything, and she'd wanted it to be so right – not least because it was Ben's sister who was getting married, and she loved him so much. It was a funny time to finally admit just how completely in love with him she was, standing in the middle of what looked like a small earthquake, but she knew it was true. There was no one else she wanted to be with more at that moment, with his arms around her, telling her it would all be okay, but the thought of letting him or his family down made the tears flow all the faster.

'The wedding is only four hours away and there's no time,' she said. 'Look at the centrepieces, and Maisie's headdress was here, as well, but that's gone, too.' Ellie bit her lip, trying to stop herself from actually starting to sob.

Ben was due to bring the little girl to the farm an hour before the wedding, so she could get ready. She was a bridesmaid, and Daisy had decided that her parents, Julian and Caroline, couldn't be trusted to get her to the ceremony on time. Apparently, Julian had been late to his own wedding, after one of his sheep had managed to get herself wedged in a ditch. The florist had left Maisie's headdress in the marquee, saying that the air conditioning should help the daisies stay looking fresher for longer. Of course, they hadn't reckoned on them coming into contact with Holly.

'I can call the girls from the deli. It's been closed for the day for the wedding, so they've got the morning off to get ready, but I'm sure they'll be prepared to spend a bit less time on their hair and makeup, if I explain it's an emergency. Luckily daisies aren't the trickiest flowers to make out of icing. If I can show the girls how to do it and get a little production line going, whilst I work on recreating Nathan's cottage, we might just about do it in the time.' Karen was already reaching for her mobile, and Ellie had more respect for her mum than ever. She'd always been able to cope, making sure they survived, even in the toughest of times. And here she was again, not panicking, but working to put everything right and make sure Ellie was okay, when it was mostly her hard work that had been destroyed.

'Shall I ring the florist whilst you're doing that?' Ellie had to get a grip and follow Karen's lead, but she didn't hold out much hope that the florist would somehow have over-ordered on wild daisies and be able to come and replace everything that Holly and her chums had devoured.

'Were all the flowers daisies?' Alan was back in the marquee, clipping a lead rope onto Dolly the goat this time.

'Yes. The biggest displays are in the barn, but all the centrepieces will need redoing. There were bunches of daisies in all of the jugs, and we need some to go in the gazebo, and some more to make Maisie a replacement headdress. Why couldn't Daisy have got something easier to get hold of, like roses, or lilies?' Ellie blinked back the tears again. Crying wasn't going to help anyone.

'I know where we can get hold of plenty of wild daisies.' Alan put a hand on her shoulder, and the urge to cry subsided. She realised this must be what it was like, having two parents to look out for you. 'I might need some help with the picking, though. So, maybe you could ring around and see if you can get some volunteers for that?'

An hour later, a small army had been mustered and operation wedding recovery was underway, as the community in Kelsea Bay rallied round.

Daisy's perfect day might just be back on, after all.

* * *

'How are you getting on?' Ben popped his head around the corner of the marquee, just as Ellie was putting the last of the centrepieces back in place.

Alan had pulled off a small miracle in finding so many wild daisies, and, if anything, they were prettier and far fresher than the originals. She'd opened her mouth to ask him where he'd got them from, in the midst of thanking him profusely, but her mum had put a finger to her lips and Ellie had got the message. She'd hear the story eventually, but the look Karen had given her had suggested that now wasn't the time.

'I think we're almost there. I just need to sort out Maisie's headdress – although I should probably prioritise my own bird's nest first.' She made a vain attempt to flatten down her dark curls, which were suffering the effects of the mad dash they'd had to do to try and put everything right. 'Did you and Alan manage to finish things up at the gazebo?'

'We did, and Alan's still up there now, keeping Maisie entertained whilst I came to check on how you were doing. I can't believe the change in him since he met your mum. He's helping Maisie finish off plaiting Gerald's mane again. If she can manage that, maybe you should let her have a look at yours!' Ben laughed, and she couldn't help joining in.

He was so easy to be around, and it was obvious his

comments were no reflection on what he felt about her. It was nothing like the way Rupert used to comment on her appearance. So she might look like something the cat had dragged in, but the marquee looked beautiful, and, judging from the laughter coming from the kitchen, her mum's gang of willing helpers were getting on well, too.

When Ben had arrived at the farm, with Maisie in tow, Ellie had hastily explained about the animals escaping, but he'd just kissed her, telling her it would all be okay and asking what he could do to help. She should have known there'd be no reproach from him, just support. She wanted to tell him what she'd realised earlier, that she was 100 per cent certain now that she loved him, but it wasn't the time. She needed to tell him the rest about her old life first, and she wanted to get in before Rupert did. But it was all hands on deck for now, that was the only way to describe it. They'd pulled together, about fifteen people in total making up her mother's chain gang and Alan's team of flower pickers.

'There's a princess bridesmaid out here, all ready to get into her gown,' Alan called from the yard, and Ben took Ellie's hand, leading her out into the sunshine that was still upholding the forecasters' promise.

'Never mind a princess, she's a miracle worker, if she did that to Gerald's mane!' The old donkey looked distinctly unamused to be sporting short, sticky-up plaits, threaded through with daisies. Maisie, on the other hand, looked proud as punch.

'He's so pretty, don't you think? I wanted to make a daisy chain for Holly, too, but Alan said we haven't got time. He did put all the flowers around Gerald's head collar, though.'

'He looks beautiful, sweetheart, and if we can't manage it ourselves, maybe Alan could help with your headdress, too. He's done such a good job with Gerald's head collar!' Ben took hold of

Maisie's hand, just as Karen and some of her helpers emerged from the kitchen to have a look at Gerald's makeover.

'My goodness!' Karen laughed, her cheeks flushed red – a clear side effect of how hard she'd been working for the last few hours. 'Aunt Hilary would have loved to see this. She would have laughed herself hoarse.'

'Thanks for everything, Mum.' Ellie crossed the yard and folded herself into her mother's arms. 'And I don't just mean for the cakes.'

'No need for thank yous, love. We're a team.' Karen stroked a hand across Ellie's unruly curls. 'We're a bigger team these days, though.'

'And all the better for it.' Ellie cuddled closer to her mum, as the girls who'd been helping her in the kitchen crowded around Alan and the donkey. 'I'm going to help Ben get Maisie ready and grab a quick shower, but can you thank Alan for me? He's been amazing. If I had any doubts about you rushing into things with him, there's not a shred of that left.'

'I will, and that means a lot to me, too, Ellie. You've earned the right to enjoy this wedding, though, and you're all the more likely to do so if you're dressed up for the occasion. I can sort out the last few bits down here.'

'Did you really decorate his head collar like that?' Karen took Alan's hand, as they looked across the stable door at Gerald. For safety's sake, they'd decided to put the old donkey, Joey and Holly Houdini into the stables. Dolly was back with her kids, who thankfully hadn't been in the paddock with her when they'd been set free. Either way, Karen was clear that there wouldn't be a repeat of the morning's events; it was more than any of them could bear to think about.

'Maisie said it spoilt the look of his mane when I put the head collar on.' Alan grinned. 'She's quite a character that one. I just threaded a few daisy stems through the buckle and eyelets, that's all.'

'Don't make light of everything you've done today, or over the last few months, Alan.' She squeezed his hand. 'I know you find it hard to take compliments, but you better get used to it. Ellie wanted me to tell you how grateful she is, too.'

'I'd do anything for the pair of you. When you first arrived, I was so angry, thinking you'd come in to strip Hilary's place bare, and that you'd turn out to be like everyone else, just in it for yourselves.'

'Seeing everyone working together today, you can't still think that surely, that most people are in it for themselves? Look at how many people have given up their time to help us.' Karen turned to face him. 'It restored my faith, anyway.'

'You're right, but I've only seen that, thanks to you. You've made me feel like part of a family again, part of a community. It's been years since I felt like that.'

'Me too. And I've been so busy with the farm that I've barely had time to go down into the Bay, but I bumped into Lizzie the other day, and she and Pete still live here too. I thought the old gang had all moved on, but it's as if I've gone back in time being here. It's like I'm getting the chance to start my life again, the way it should always have been.'

'Maybe we could meet up with them some time?' Alan's words took her by surprise. He was so different these days, but it was obvious he'd do whatever it took to make her happy.

'I never thought I'd hear you say that; you want to be careful where all this being part of community might lead!' She was teasing him and he knew it, laughing at the look that must have crossed her face.

'It's true, I feel like Kelsea Bay is my home again for the first time since I lost Mum and Dad. Mind you, if I ever find out who let those animals out today, and put you and Ellie under so much stress, I won't be responsible for my actions.' He kissed her gently and then pulled away. 'Now, go and get ready, I'm expecting a dance later, and the sight of Alan 'Crabby' Crabtree on the dance floor will cause even more of a stir than Gerald's fancy hairdo. People will have to start seeing that I'm a changed man at some point, though, and it's all down to you.'

17

Ellie was ready with minutes to spare. Ben had once more come to the rescue, saying it was part of his role as usher to make sure the guests knew where to go once they'd parked their cars. Watching him for a moment from her bedroom window, she was more certain than ever that her feelings for him had shifted into a whole new dimension. He looked so handsome in his suit, and his ready smile, as he greeted arrivals to the farm, made her want to rush out and throw herself into his arms, to tell him how she felt, but that probably wouldn't be a good impression for a newly appointed wedding planner to present.

By the time Ellie was ready, groups of guests were already thronging around the gazebo, chatting and laughing before they took their seats. Champagne glasses were lined up on a table in the barn, ready for toasting the happy couple as they signed the register. Gerald was serenading all the arrivals with enthusiastic braying, and the wedding cake mark II had been put back in position in the marquee. It was difficult to believe that only a few hours earlier, everything had been chaos.

When the vintage Rolls Royce pulled up, with Daisy and her

dad in the back, even Gerald had the grace to stop making so much noise and look inquisitively over the stable door.

The bride wore an antique dress, with a pattern of daisies fashioned from lace, whilst her dad sported a large daisy in his buttonhole, and even her tiara had daisies picked out in diamantes. Thank goodness they'd been able to replace the cake and all the centrepieces in time, as not having daisies there, too, would have been so obvious.

Ellie had tried to push the fact that it was almost certainly Rupert who'd set the animals free out of her head, but, as her eyes followed the bride on her slow walk towards the gazebo, she saw the severed chains that had secured the gates to both paddocks, hanging loose. However much she might rather it was the case, there was no way it had been children playing a prank. Whether it was Rupert, or someone else he'd put up to it, they would have needed some heavy duty bolt cutters to get through the links. She'd stepped up security following Holly's numerous escapes, and letting the animals out of the fields was no longer an easy task.

The thought of Rupert suddenly turning up again made her shudder. She had to keep telling herself that not even he would make a scene in the middle of the wedding to confront her or Ben. That was the sort of thing that viral videos were made of, and Rupert had a certain image to protect.

By the time Daisy and her father reached the gazebo, with Maisie just behind, all the guests had taken their seats and were turning to witness the arrival of the bride. Daisy had asked Ellie to book a harpist. It was strangely hypnotic, hearing the sound of the 'Wedding March' played like that. As Ellie caught Ben's eye, tears threatened for the second time – only this time they were happy ones.

The farm really was a stunning place to get married, everyone said so. There was a buzz of excitement about it. Once the service was over, the guests followed the newlyweds back to the barn for the signing of the register, to make it all official, and yet more photographs. Ellie had already been asked if she'd consider hiring out the barn, and a plot where a marquee could be pitched, for a ruby wedding anniversary, as well as for a twenty-first birthday party.

The guests' reactions to the centrepieces and Karen's amazing wedding cake were exactly what she'd hope for, too. As least ten people asked if the flowers on the cake were real, and the stack of business cards that she'd discreetly placed on a small table in one corner of the marquee, at the base of yet another jug of daisies, had all been taken.

There'd hardly been a chance to speak to Ben all evening. As the wedding coordinator, Ellie had to keep an eye on everything, so just being a guest, like everyone else, wasn't an option. She was determined to manage at least one dance with him, though.

'So, how's your first wedding experience been?' He held her close as they moved around the dance floor. It was the first time they'd ever danced together so closely – do-si-do-ing at the barn dance didn't really count – and Ellie wasn't disappointed. She'd seen some fairly awful dancing and some attention-seeking moves, not least from the bride herself, but Ben just held her close, as though he didn't want to let her go.

Alan had been a revelation earlier, too, looking surprisingly light on his feet as he'd led Karen around the floor. She had a funny feeling that it wouldn't be long before she'd be helping her mother organise another wedding. As much as she'd promised Ellie she wouldn't rush into it, anyone with half a brain could see that Alan and Karen were made for each other, so why wait?

'My first wedding has been... exhausting, terrifying and amazing, all at the same time. What does it look like from the guests' side of things, do you think?'

'It's gone without a hitch. Except for those of us who know, no one would have a clue what kind of drama went on in this tent this morning.' He stroked her hair as he spoke, but he still didn't know the half of it.

'I owe you a favour. In fact, I owe half of Kelsea Bay a favour.'

'Funny you should say that, because I've been tasked with decorating Daisy and Nathan's car, and I wondered if you'd give me a hand? I know your duties as wedding coordinator don't stretch that far, but I thought perhaps you'd do it as the girlfriend of the bride's brother instead?'

She liked the way he said that, it almost made her sound like part of the family. 'It would be my pleasure, Mr Hastings, and I know just where I can lay my hands on a can of silly string. I'll meet you in the yard in ten minutes.'

* * *

'I know I've said it already, but you really are a miracle worker!' Ben stood back to admire their handiwork. 'Where did you get all this stuff?'

'I had a hunch it might all still be in the loft.' Ellie put the finishing touches to another daisy design on the back windscreen. 'Aunt Hilary used to go all out for Christmas, when I was younger. She had snow spray in every colour and used to spray pictures onto all the windows in the farmhouse. Plus she liked a silly string fight as much as the next person! I used to have so much fun visiting her here. It was an amazing place to be as a kid.'

'I'm sure Maisie thinks the same, and you're her idol, ever since you saved Holly from turning into lamb chops!'

'She's a lovely girl. It sounds like we've pulled off decorating the car just in time, too.' Ellie grinned.

Suddenly the DJ made an announcement from inside the marquee, his voice booming over the sound system. 'Apparently, the bride and groom are about to leave for their honeymoon. So get ready to give them a big send off!'

'I think that's our call to action.' Ellie led the way back into the tent. It had been a great wedding to start the business with. Daisy had wanted it all traditional, with the bride and groom leaving before the party ended and everyone waving them off. It might just have been another way for Daisy to ensure that she was centre of attention, but Ellie liked the idea, anyway.

'Right, get ready, ladies, I'm going to throw my bouquet!' Daisy was already standing in the middle of the black and white checkerboard dance floor, with her back to the rest of the guests. 'One, two, three!' She hurled the bouquet of wild daisies over her shoulder and they sailed past most of the guests' heads, landing, whether he wanted them to or not, straight into Alan's arms.

Six months before, he would probably have thrown them right back, but, as it was, he seemed to enjoy his own few minutes in the spotlight, joking that he'd be picking out a wedding outfit any day, before presenting the bouquet to Karen.

There was a flurry of congratulations and kisses, as the bride and groom bid farewell to their guests, most of whom followed them outside to give Daisy exactly the sort of send-off she'd been after. She clapped her hands with delight at the sight of Nathan's almost unrecognisable BMW, decorated with daisies made from multi-coloured snow spray and what looked like a thatched roof of silly string.

'It's brilliant, Benji, you clever old thing!' She threw her arms around her brother's neck, and it took him a moment or two to break free.

'It's all down to Ellie. She's a wedding coordinator like no other. She can even lay her hands on silly string, and snow spray in every colour of the rainbow, without a moment's notice.'

'In that case,' announced Daisy, to anyone within in shot. 'I think she's officially a keeper.'

'I hope so.' Laughing, Ben submitted to yet another of his sister's hugs. 'And I promise I'll keep you posted.'

'You do that! And as for you, young lady.' Daisy turned her attention to Ellie. 'You've given me the best bloody wedding ever. I know I'm demanding, but I also knew you could pull it off. That's why I wanted *this* wedding, and for you to organise it so badly. It's also why I couldn't bring myself to book anywhere else. After all, why settle for second best?'

Daisy's words took Ellie right back to that day down at the paddock, when Aunt Hilary had explained why she'd never wanted anyone but her lost fiancé. She hadn't understood it back then, or even when she'd got engaged to Rupert. It was only the last few weeks that it had really begun to make sense, and it was perhaps the most important of all the legacies Hilary had left.

* * *

The party had gone on for a couple of hours after the newlyweds set off, and it had been far too late to start the clean-up operation by the time the last of the guests left. Alan and Ben had both headed home a little after midnight, with a promise to return the next morning and help get everything straight again – in exchange for one of Karen's famous cooked breakfasts.

By the next morning, Ellie had received several texts congratulating her on organising such a fantastic wedding. She'd read the latest, just as Ben arrived, and slid the phone into her pocket as she went to the door, bringing him straight through to the kitchen.

'Tea?' She'd been assigned the duty of making drinks, with Karen at her usual place in front of the cooker, where she whipped up bacon, sausages, three variations of eggs (scrambled, poached and fried), mushrooms, tomatoes and fried bread. Offering the relatively simple options of tea, coffee or orange juice seemed like the good end of the deal to Ellie.

'I could murder a coffee, actually.' Ben's warm brown eyes crinkled in the corners, in the way that had always got to Ellie, as he gave her a rueful smile. 'I stayed at my parents' place last night, and Mum wanted to sit up half the night talking about the wedding and how brilliant it was. You're everyone's favourite wedding planner, by the way.' He smiled again, as she handed him a strong cup of coffee. 'I can hardly keep my eyes open as a result, and then some boy racer in a bright red BMW nearly ran me off the road on the way up here. Maybe it was my fault, though. I was probably still half asleep.'

'Did you see the driver's face?' Ellie had gone cold at the mention of the red BMW. She'd almost been able to forget about Rupert when the wedding had gone so well, but she was fully expecting him to turn up. After all, if he had been the one behind the animals escaping, he was going to be as mad as hell that it hadn't had the desired effect. If he did show up, he'd be determined to make trouble and she still hadn't told Ben about the last time he'd shown up.

'No. It all happened so quickly.' Ben shrugged. 'Still, no damage done.'

'Can I get you another drink, Alan?' Ellie poured tea into his mug when he nodded, her mind still on Rupert and the fact that he was almost certainly still in Kelsea Bay. There might have been no harm done yet, but Rupert didn't look like he had any plans to give up. If only life could be tied up as neatly as things on the farm, but it was Alan who'd taken care of most of that.

A typical farmer, despite the late night the evening before, he'd been up at the crack of dawn and had already moved all the chairs back down from the gazebo and made sure everything down at that end of the farm had been cleared away. They just had the tent to tidy up, ready for the Elverham Marquee Co to dismantle after lunch, and a few things to put straight in the barn. All in all, Alan was worth his weight in gold.

'How are you feeling this morning?' Ben took a seat next to the older man. 'Have you recovered from catching that bouquet, yet?'

'Just about. And I wouldn't put your wedding suit back into mothballs just yet, because I'm trying to persuade Karen to make ours the second one at Seabreeze Farm.'

'That's brilliant. Congratulations!' At the very moment Ben shook Alan's hand, a loud braying came from the yard outside.

'Sounds like Gerald wants to join in with the congratulations, too.' Ellie smiled. 'Either that, or he's reminding us he's been shut in the stables since yesterday morning.'

'I wouldn't put it past him, after getting a taste for wedding cake yesterday, to be giving his breakfast order!' Karen put a large plate of food in front of Alan, and the old donkey brayed again, as if in agreement.

'I'm going to go out and check on him, just in case he's feeling the aftereffects of yesterday.' Ellie wouldn't have put it past Rupert to try and pull the same trick twice.

'I'll come with you.' Ben put his coffee down, but Ellie shook her head.

'No, finish your drink first. Gerald's probably fine, but I'll come and get you if there's a problem.' If Rupert was lurking outside, the last thing Ellie wanted to do was to give him the opportunity to confront Ben, before she had the chance to speak to him herself.

'Okay, but just call me if you need me.'

'I will.' Ellie could feel her pulse quickening as she headed across the gravel and into the yard. There was no sign of Rupert, but walking around the back of the stable block, she saw him, leaning against the wall as if he owned the place.

'You always were drawn to me, weren't you El? You must be, to have known that I was here.' Rupert laughed at the look that had clearly crossed her face. 'Now, now, don't pretend you didn't know I'd be waiting here.'

'Ben saw your car this morning; you nearly ran him off the road.'

'I'll try a bit harder next time.'

'For God's sake Rupert, just stop it! What are you hoping to achieve from all of this?'

'Like I said before, compensation for the way you've humiliated me.'

'I've got nothing to give you. Every penny I had has been sunk into this place.'

'More fool you. The best way to make money out of this place would be to sell it on for development.' Rupert curled his lip. 'In fact I think that's the best plan all around. Sell the place to me. I'll give you a fair market price and when the development work is finished... let's just say I'll be handsomely compensated.'

'I wouldn't sell you Seabreeze Farm if my life depended on it!' Ellie curled her fingers into a ball, fighting the urge to run at him, fists flying, and get as many punches in as she could before he overpowered her.

'Well that's a shame, because I'm not leaving Kelsea Bay without acquiring at least one new business, so I'll just have to follow up the email I sent to the two senior partners at the veterinary clinic instead.'

'Stop threatening me! I know you're lying.'

'I can show you the emails we've exchanged on my phone if you like. I contacted David and Nigel the day after I spoke to you, and told them you'd given me their details and that they might be interested in selling their share of the business. And, guess what? They were. I said I just needed to see how an approach to another business worked out first, but if you aren't going to do the sensible thing and sell me this place, then I'll just have to seal the deal with them instead.'

'Please Rupert, you don't have to do this, just let me get on with my life and you can get on with yours.'

'Is everything okay, Ellie?' Ben was suddenly standing next to her and more than anything she wanted him to put his arms around her, but his eyes were searching her face and there was no way of knowing how much he'd overheard.

'Ah, just the person I was hoping to see.' Rupert held out his hand. 'We haven't been formally introduced yet, but I'm—'

'I know who you are.' Ben had that look he so rarely wore, as if he was barely holding on to his temper.

'So Ellie's told you then?' Rupert ignored the fact that Ben had rejected his outstretched hand. 'I didn't know if she would, because she wasn't sure how you'd take the news that your senior partners at the practice want to sell the business to become part of a big franchise. Especially as I only found the place on her recommendation.'

'It's not true, Rupert, you know it isn't. Please don't do this!' Ellie repeated her request, but her ex-fiancé was wearing his trademark smirk again, clearly enjoying every moment of it.

'Oh and I suppose all the other businesses you cut off credit for, when you were working at the bank, so my company could buy them up, didn't exist either.'

'Is that true?' Ben looked at her as if he was seeing her for the first time and she shook her head.

'It wasn't like that.'

'It was about making you rich, though, wasn't it, El?' Rupert actually laughed this time. 'You should watch out you know, Ben. She's obsessed with money and kept on and on at me about needing to make more of it. She even had a five-year plan and we had to hit every financial goal before we could get married. But I suppose that's your problem now.'

'That was your plan, not mine! You've got to believe me Ben, I promise this isn't—'

'What's going on?' Alan came marching around the back of the stable block with Karen right behind him, cutting off her attempt to explain. But Ben was still looking at her, then at Rupert, and back again, as if he was trying to follow a conversation in a language he didn't understand.

'Are you okay, love?' Karen caught hold of her elbow and Ellie shook her head, her voice shaking.

'Rupert's just trying to make trouble that's all, because I told him we'll never sell him the farm and now he's making out I put him in touch with the partners at Ben's practice. He just can't bear to lose, that's all.'

'None of us have to lose, if you two just take the sensible option.' Despite the fact his words had every chance of giving him away as a liar, something in Rupert just couldn't seem to give up. 'You could still sell me the farm. Make a profit, get out of this *back end of nowhere* and return to civilisation. They want to build a holiday park here, with static caravans overlooking the sea, a swimming pool and clubhouse – it would be a gold mine, and they'd pay you well for it. There's nothing like it round here, only that little caravan place up the road. My firm bought that, too, years ago, and then sold it on, but holidaymakers want more than that now.'

'That was *your* firm?' Alan had drawn his arm back, and Ellie moved to stop him, but Karen was quicker, slipping in between them.

'He might be pure poison, love, but you can't blame Rupert for what happened to your place. It was before his time.'

'He's cut from the same cloth as them, just after what he can get and I'll not have him turning up here and upsetting Ellie.' Alan's fist was still tightly clenched.

'I know, but I also know he's not worth you getting in trouble for. I need you here, *with me*.' Karen's words had the desired effect, and, slowly, the fingers of Alan's hand unfurled.

'We're never going to sell the farm, Rupert, and I never want to see you again. It doesn't matter what lies you try and tell about me, you can't control me any more.' Ellie spoke slowly, making it perfectly clear she meant what she said. It had gone far enough and her mother was right. Rupert wasn't worth Alan *or* Ben's trouble. He was her mistake and she should be the one to sort it out. 'If you come back here again, I'll call the police.'

'Do that. I'll deny everything and tell them that you threatened me; it's your mother's new boyfriend they'll be locking up then.'

'Just try it. We're a close knit community round here.' Alan's tone was menacing, making Rupert widen his eyes and take a few steps back. 'And we've got a way of meting out our own punishments. Is that a risk you want to take?'

'You're a bunch of bloody in-breds, and I don't want to hang around this backwater any longer than I have to, anyway. I've all but closed the deal to buy the veterinary practice anyway, thanks to the information Ellie gave me, and you won't recognise the place once my company takes it over, that's if they even let you stay on.' Rupert virtually spat the words at Ben. Despite his obvious fear of Alan, he just couldn't seem to help himself. If Karen and Ellie hadn't been there, he'd almost certainly have got what he deserved.

'David and Nigel would never accept an offer from someone like you.' Ben shook his head, but when his gaze met Ellie's, there was so much hurt there. He believed the lies Rupert had told him because at least some of what he'd said about their life together was true and she'd lied to Ben by omission. How could she blame him for not being able to distinguish the truth from the lies when it was all so mixed up together? She had been the person Rupert had described once, and she hadn't been brave enough to tell Ben that. Now he was never going to trust her again.

'Just get out Rupert.' Ellie stared straight at him, holding his gaze until he looked away. She had no way of knowing if Ben would be willing to listen to her when she tried to explain, but she wouldn't even get the chance until Rupert was gone.

'I wouldn't stay here if you paid me.'

Rupert pushed past and the four of them followed him around the stable block. Stopping in his tracks, he grabbed hold of Gerald's mane, but the old donkey jerked his head up in surprise, opened his mouth and sank his teeth straight into Rupert's forearm.

'I should have killed that filthy thing when I had a chance!' Clutching the injury with the other hand, he kicked the stable door hard. 'The whole lot of you deserve each other.'

Rupert was a bully and he'd been given a taste of his own medicine, but Ben wouldn't even look at her and the damage had been done. The sound of his BMW roaring up the lane, from wherever he'd hidden it when he'd snuck on to the farm, should have been like music to her ears, but the silence when it faded out was deafening.

She turned towards the others. 'Thanks, Alan.' Alan nodded, his arm already around Karen, and she glanced at Ben. 'What Rupert said about me giving him information about the practice, it isn't—'

'Look, I'm sorry. I know I said I'd stay and help clean up, but there are clearly some things at the surgery I need to get sorted.' Ben was as still as a statue and she was too scared of being rejected to even try and reach out for him.

'Okay.' Ellie had to make the first move, even if that meant facing the fear of rejection that was paralysing her, because otherwise he was just going to walk away anyway. She held out her hand, but he didn't move towards her and Ellie was more desperate than ever for him to understand. 'Please can we talk later? You've got to believe me when I say I had nothing to do with Rupert trying to buy the practice.'

'I'll call you, if I finish in time. That's if I've even still got a job.' He didn't meet her eyes, and it she had a horrible feeling that Rupert had just achieved what he'd wanted all along after all.

18

Ellie was glad of the distraction that getting the farm back to normal provided. She'd even offered to help pack the marquee tent away, but the hire company had said something about health and safety rules, and so she'd been relegated to making tea again.

Alan had taken Karen out for Sunday lunch, their breakfast having been ruined by Rupert's arrival, and Ellie had been glad to let them go. Being around two people so obviously in love was difficult to take when she didn't know where she stood with Ben. She could understand him being angry. Rupert had done his best to make it sound as though she might still have feelings for him, because she was willing to help him buy Ben's practice. Even worse was the thought that it might have made Ben think she didn't have feelings for either him or Rupert, and that the only thing that mattered to her was money.

It had been the grain of doubt that Ben wouldn't be able to accept who she'd been, back when she was with Rupert, that had stopped her telling him everything, despite trying to convince herself that she just needed to wait until after the wedding. Now that grain was a whole sack full of doubt. She'd promised Ben there were no more secrets and he'd opened up to her about how much he'd been hurt by an ex who'd chosen money over him. Now she looked like exactly the same sort of person as his ex. And, either way, because of Rupert's vindictiveness towards her, there was a danger Ben would have to leave the practice he loved so much.

After Ben had left, and Alan had been the first to give her a hug and tell her he didn't believe a word of what Rupert had said, it had all come tumbling out. The fact that she'd been scared to face up to who she'd been with Rupert. Having money for the first time in her life had seemed so important that she'd ended up pushing all her principles to one side and everything in her life had become a balance sheet. She'd taken a promotion to a new role she hated, where the ethics of the work she did went against everything she believed in, and she'd got engaged to someone she didn't really love and whose ethics had turned out to be far murkier than anything the bank had done. Alan and her mother had reassured her that she'd done nothing wrong, but she felt hollow inside, forcing herself to finally face up to the person she'd been for those three years with Rupert. Now Ben had seen the worst of her too and, given that she didn't like herself much right now, she could hardly expect him to either.

Ellie desperately needed something to do, so she'd decided to empty all of the bedding from the stables and put fresh straw down. Once that was finished, she checked and repaired the perimeter fencing to make sure there was no chance of any other escapes. Working flat out was something to channel her energies into, so she didn't have to think about everything else. At least not for a little while. By the time the men from the Elverham Marquee Co had finally set off, with everything neatly packed up in the back of their lorry, Ellie had completed all of her jobs too and her attempts to distract herself had come to an end. She thought about ringing Ben, or driving down to the practice to speak to him, but he'd said he'd ring her when he was free, and trying to get him talk before he was ready would probably only make things worse. If that was even possible. The truth was, she wasn't even sure what she would say to him when they spoke. A lot of what Rupert had said was a lie, but there was no way of dressing up the bits that were true. Suddenly she missed her best friend more than ever and Olivia was one of the few people she wanted to talk to.

Checking her watch, she realised it would be eleven at night in Brisbane, and so she texted Olivia first not wanting to risk waking her.

Ellie

Are you awake? I've got lots to tell you x

Olivia

Ready and waiting, El. Dying to hear all the news about the wedding :-) xx

Olivia answered the FaceTime call within about two seconds flat.

'So, how did it go, the wedding of the year?' She grinned out from the screen, and, more than ever, Ellie wished they could share a hug and maybe even a large bottle of wine.

'It was brilliant, better than I could ever have hoped for.' Ellie decided not to tell her about the animals' great escape just yet. That was a story for another day.

'So, why do you sound like you've just found out that all your money's been invested in a pyramid scheme?'

'Rupert's been coming to Kelsea Bay and threatening to buy Ben's practice off his senior partners and turn it into the sort of faceless franchise he couldn't stand working for, unless I agree to sell him Seabreeze Farm instead. There are developers interested in it apparently.'

'God that man's an arsehole. Surely he can't do that?'

'If the senior partners accept an offer he can. Worse than all of that, because I worked with Ben for a bit, Rupert told him that it was me who'd put him in contact with Ben's senior partners and made the suggestion about buying the business.'

'Ben can't have believed any of that!'

'I don't know.' Ellie swallowed hard. 'He might not have done, but then Rupert started telling him about the work my department did at the bank and how I had no problem with Rupert's firm buying up businesses that the bank had made vulnerable by withdrawing financial backing. So it made it look like I had form for this.'

'You didn't run the bank for God's sake, you were just doing your job.' Olivia's voice had gone up a level. Her indignation on Ellie's behalf was obvious, but her loyalty was misplaced.

'That's true, but I knew what Rupert did and how ruthless his firm and bank could be. I don't know how I became a person who was okay with living and working in that world. Since I've been at the farm, I can see what I'd become back then. The worst part is that I had the opportunity to tell Ben myself, to explain to him that what drove me was finally having some financial security, after having the house sold out from underneath us, but I kept putting it off. I wanted to be able to take care of Mum and never have to worry about paying the bills that came in. But when Mum and I took on the farm, and risked every penny to keep it afloat, I realised that's what made me happy. Even if we always have to scrape together every spare penny to cover the bills and worry that we might not have enough, it's worth it to be here.'

'Just tell Ben all of that. Okay, so you worked for some corporate arseholes like Rupert, who'd mug their grannies to get their next pound, but it doesn't make you a bad person. You're not a serial killer!'

'I know, but it's the fact I kept those things from him when I had the chance to tell him, especially when I knew his ex-fiancée left him for someone with more money. All of this touches a nerve for him and he might not be able to trust me now. We've only been together a few months. It would be easier for him to just walk away and I can't say I blame him. Even if he can forgive me for not being totally honest, Rupert is out to get him now because of me.'

'It's not just a few months for you, though, is it? You *really* love Ben, I can tell from the way you talk about him.'

'I've never felt like this before and the worst part is that I wasn't even brave enough to tell him that, and now he'll probably never know just how great I think he is.'

'Then m*ake* him understand, El. Finding someone you feel that way about, and who might just feel that way about you, doesn't happen every day.'

'Are you all right, Liv?' Ellie didn't miss the glassy look in best friend's eyes. 'Here I am wallowing in my own drama yet again and I haven't even asked how you are.'

'I'll be fine.' She gave Ellie a watery smile. 'I'm coming home. For good.'

'Oh, my God! Really?' Ellie almost threw the iPad up in excitement. 'What's happened?'

'I'm not telling you until you report back to me and let me know that you've sorted everything out with Ben.' Olivia wagged a finger, and Ellie knew her well enough to know she meant every word.

'You might be in for a long wait.'

'I'm prepared to hold out as long as it takes.'

'Just promise me you're okay?' Ellie looked at her oldest friend, who nodded.

'Better than I have been in a long time. I'm not hanging around here to take the scraps of someone else's life any more. Now just tell me you're going to get things sorted with Ben.'

'I *will* talk to him, even if I have to wrestle him to the ground to get him to listen to me.'

'I always knew life in the country was kinky!' Olivia laughed and blew her a kiss before ending the call.

Her best friend was coming home, the farm looked set to be a popular new venue for weddings and other celebrations, and her mum was happy and settled with a man who adored her. Life was pretty damn perfect, and there was just one more thing to set straight. She only hoped it wouldn't take a wrestling match to persuade Ben to listen to what she had to say.

In her usual style, Ellie needed to get things straight in her head before speaking to Ben, and so she busied herself clearing up the farmhouse whilst she worked through every possible reaction he might have. Spotting the box that contained the silly string and coloured sprays they'd used to decorate the wedding car, Ellie picked it up and headed towards the landing.

Using a wooden pole with a metal hook on it, she pulled the loft hatch and ladder down, balancing the box on her hip as she did. As she reached the hatch itself, she tried to shove it into the loft, not particularly wanting to go up there when she was the only one in the house. Putting her foot through the ceiling wasn't the way she intended to spend the afternoon. The box wouldn't push far enough over to put the ladder back, though, and she was forced to follow it up into the gloom of the loft.

Manoeuvring the box into a space on some old boards, to the left-hand side of the hatch, she dislodged another smaller box, which fell onto its side, sending a bunch of photographs and letters spilling out.

She picked up the first picture, of a young woman. Ellie would never have recognised the face, without a single wrinkle to line it, but the distinctive smile meant it could only be Aunt Hilary. Intrigued, she scooped up the loose letters and photographs, put them back into the box and took them downstairs with her. Looking at old photographs was guaranteed to make the hours slip by unnoticed, and she soon had them spread across the kitchen table.

Hilary and Gerald's love story was played out in those well-handled photos. Even more so in the letters they'd exchanged. Ellie had felt guilty reading them at first, but she quickly became so drawn into them that she couldn't stop once she'd started.

One in particular resonated with her so much that she knew she'd never forget the words that Gerald had written.

My Dearest Hilary,

It's hard being here, so far from my darling girl, but knowing you are waiting for me keeps me going and every day that passes is a day closer to me holding you again.

I can't wait to call you my wife. When it's dark here and I feel alone, I picture the look on your face when I asked you to marry me. Do you remember? I was singing Daisy, Daisy, give me your answer do, as we walked up the hill, and you told me not to keep singing the same line over and over again, because it irritated you so! I almost didn't get down on one knee as I'd planned to, to give you that ring, I was terrified I'd missed my chance. Yet you agreed to marry this irritating fool, who only ever knows one or two lines to a song, and I felt like the luck-

iest man in the world. I still do, despite us being apart for far too long.

Take care, my angel, and know that everything I'm going through is easier because I hold you in my heart. I hope you can say the same of me.

Yours, forever and always, with sincerest love,

Gerald x

That was love, right there in that letter, and Gerald had put it so well. It was about loving someone, despite their faults, and being the support that makes everything in the other person's life better, just because you're there.

Aunt Hilary had had that with Gerald and lost it in the most tragic way. Ellie wasn't going to let someone like Rupert take the chance away from her, too.

The insistent hammering on the front door made Ellie jump, one leg sliding out of the loft hatch and thankfully making contact with the ladder below. Whoever it was at the door was pretty determined and, scrabbling the rest of the way down the ladder, she offered up a silent prayer that it wasn't Rupert, for his sake as much as her own. She had no idea what she might be capable of, if he was standing on her doorstep with that smirk on his face again.

'Ben.' The word was breathless and not just because of her hurry to get to the door.

'Can I come in?' His tone was giving nothing away, but there was something about his body language. It was rigid, just like it had been when he'd been listening to what Rupert had to say about her. Something in him had closed down.

'Of course, can I get you a drink?'

'No thank you.' Ben followed her into the kitchen and her heart hammered in her chest as she looked at him again.

'Do you want to sit down?'

'This won't take long. I just wanted to let you know that David and Nigel aren't selling the practice. When I told them what sort of person Rupert was, they weren't interested.' Ben's words sounded as though they should have been accompanied by a smile, but his mouth was set in a line. 'I'm not sure they would ever really have gone through with it, they just liked the idea of the money when Rupert put some figures to them. But then money appeals to a lot of people, doesn't it?'

'I didn't tell Rupert about the practice, I promise.' Ellie couldn't keep the desperation out of her voice.

'I know. I didn't believe for a moment that you did, but I wish you hadn't kept all that other stuff from me.'

'I'm sorry, I should have told you where I worked and what Rupert did, but I was worried you'd hate me. But you couldn't hate me any more than I hate myself right now.' Ellie wished he'd sit down, just to show some sign that he wasn't going to turn around and walk out without a backward glance.

'I don't hate you. I love you.' He was doing it again, the words he was saying not matching up to the look on his face. 'But that's the problem. If I saw you as someone I could just date for a while, before both of us moved on, then it wouldn't matter to me that you put money first. But I've been there and done that. I'm never going to be the sort of person who can provide a lifestyle like someone in Rupert's line of business could. I can't let myself fall for you any more than I already have, knowing that at any moment you might discover the promise of a much shinier life that would take you away from me.'

'I wouldn't want any other life, because I love you too.' Ellie took a step towards him, but he was already shaking his head.

'We're from such different worlds, El, and I've seen it a hundred times. People moving down here for a new life in the country and finding out that it's not all it's cracked up to be. In the end, they go back to what they've always known. It's what people do, default to type, even when they don't want to. As much as it hurts now, it's going to hurt even more if it happens a year down the line, or maybe later than that. But in the end, one day, I won't be enough for you.'

'You will, Ben. You are.' Even as she called out she knew she was fighting a lost cause, and he was turning away from her.

'I'll see you around.' The words were so final. One step away from 'have a nice life' and there was nothing she could do to stop him going. Rupert had won again and this time he'd taken something from her that money couldn't buy.

19

The two weeks since Ben had ended their relationship had been some of the hardest Ellie could ever remember. Every time she heard a car pull up on the gravel outside of the farmhouse, part of her hoped it would be him. But it never was. Even when Dolly's kids had needed some vaccinations, it was Ben's senior partner, David, who'd arrived to administer them.

Once again, concentrating her energies on the farm had been Ellie's salvation. Although they had taken some bookings for weddings and other events, cash flow was still very tight and Ellie was still picking up some temping work too, after her contract at the veterinary practice had ended and they'd found a new receptionist. It must have been a relief to Ben that it had happened so quickly after things had gone wrong between them. At least he didn't have to try so hard to avoid her at work too. The temping contracts were still a necessary evil to cover the bills and make payments on her credit card. Between that, keeping the farm running and coming up with strategies to raise the profile of the business, she went to bed exhausted every night – grateful for when sleep came and thoughts of Ben retreated to a dream world.

Autumn was well established and the Kelsea Bay half term celebrations were just around the corner, which provided more opportunity for Ellie to spread the word about everything the farm had to offer. If throwing herself into her work was keeping her going, the very least she owed the farm was to do everything she could to keep that going too.

'Why don't you take a day off today?' Karen was brushing Ginger, whose puppies had now all found new homes, outside the back door of the farmhouse. The little dog looked desperate to escape her makeover, as Ellie pulled on a pair of wellies that were already well caked in mud and had been left outside as a result.

'It's already a day off, because I'm here.' Ellie smiled. Farm work days were so different from ones in the office, and it didn't even feel like work.

'So what have you got planned then? I've seen that determined look in your eyes before!' Her mother let go of Ginger, who shot out of arm's reach and immediately started rolling on the damp grass, trying to undo all of Karen's good work.

'Today's job is sheep training.' Ellie couldn't help laughing at the look on her mother's face.

'Okay, you've got me.'

'You've heard about the Sheep Grand National on Saturday?'

'Yes, there are posters all over Kelsea Bay. It says they're donating all the proceeds to the school, so I've volunteered to make some cakes for after the race, to help raise a bit more money.'

'That's brilliant and I thought I should do my part too by entering Holly.' Ellie pulled a face, aware that she might be about to sound just like the person Rupert had painted her as – desperate to cash in on every opportunity to promote her business, by taking advantage of a charity event. 'All the entrants wear little cloth saddles apparently and I thought maybe she could have one with our name on. Holly's such a character and with the funny way she runs, she's bound to get noticed – probably by coming in last! It might be a way of getting Seabreeze Farm out there and reminding people what we do up here. I know bookings are coming in slowly, but we've got to feed the animals all through the winter and I'd feel a bit more secure if I knew the diary was starting to get full.'

'Well it's certainly different from an ad in the local paper!' Karen laughed. 'It's a great idea and it'll be nice to see you having some fun. You've been so down lately and all you seem to do is work.' Her mother furrowed her brow. 'Will Ben be at the race, do you think?'

'I expect so, seeing as it's at Julian and Caroline's place.' Ellie brushed off the question, not wanting to dwell on the prospect of him refusing to talk to her even when she saw him face to face. 'But I need to get on with the training if I'm going to stand any chance of getting Holly to do as she's told.'

'Don't you need a dog to train sheep? Somehow I don't think Ginger is going to be up to it.' Karen laughed again and, grateful for the change of subject, Ellie looked at the little dog. Ginger had now found a patch of dust to lie in, with her belly exposed and her front paws bent over like a meerkat.

'Thankfully it isn't that complicated. Holly just needs to race about a hundred metres and she's run for miles before, when she's escaped. I'm going to put her on a lead rope today, though, and hope to God that for once she's willing to go in the direction I want her to!'

* * *

The Sheep Grand National was held at Coppergate Farm, where Holly had been born, every October half term. According to Alan, the event had been getting bigger over the years, but it wasn't just the number of people watching that was making Ellie feel nervous. She'd caught a glimpse of Ben when she'd unloaded Holly from the trailer, along with Betsy, the only other sheep still living on the farm, who'd also be taking part in the race. Maisie had rushed over to greet them, as soon as she'd spotted Holly, and had told Ellie in no uncertain terms that she expected them to win. Suddenly it seemed there was a lot riding on the event and all of it was outside of Ellie's control.

'You do know that Holly has absolutely no chance of winning this race, don't you?' Ellie looked up at Karen, as she straightened the little cloth saddle her mother had made. This year, the press were coming from all across Kent and there was even a regional news crew coming down to film a small segment. What had started off a few years before as an event for just a few locals in Kelsea Bay was now attracting people from the rest of the county and beyond.

'Well that's sort of the point, isn't it? If Holly does her little comedy trot to come in last place, we should get a mention in the papers and that might drum up a bit more business, like you said.'

'I hope so, because with the cost of traditional advertising we just can't afford to do that much yet. I've spent loads of time posting stuff on social media, but we really need all the help we can get to spread the word about the farm out there. We might make total fools of ourselves today, but I'd do anything to save the farm and I know you would too.'

'Absolutely and it's all going to be okay love, I promise.' Karen squeezed her hand.

'I just hope Holly runs in the right direction, because they won't be on lead ropes today, they'll be running in roped off lanes with just the lure of sheep nuts to get them to the end.'

'Well food is one of Holly's favourite things and I don't think either of them will need a lot of coercing to take part. They haven't actually got to jump over anything, then?'

'No, thank goodness, because that would definitely rule Holly out! I'm not sure why they call it the Grand National rather than the Derby, but I suppose it's just got more of a ring to it. When I first heard about it, I did wonder if it was cruel, but I watched a video and the sheep seem to love it, not to mention the extra food of course! It raises a lot of money for the school, too.'

'With sheep nuts on offer, Holly might surprise us and suddenly turn into the fastest thing on four legs.'

'More like three and three-quarter legs with her gait! Either way we're about to find out whether she's a secret superstar or not.' Heading along the rough track from the makeshift car park towards the much more level field beyond, where the track was set out, Ellie couldn't decide whether she wanted Holly to pull off a total surprise, or not. Sometimes it was easier to expect the worst. Either way, fate – in the form of a very clumsy sheep – would just have to decide.

* * *

By the time they lined up at the start, Ellie was back to feeling strangely nervous. Having people watching her and knowing that Ben was out there somewhere too made her feel hot, despite it being October. Holly and Betsy were wearing little blankets, emblazoned with the words *Seabreeze Farm* that Karen had hand embroidered. It suddenly felt as if the race really mattered and she couldn't put her finger on why. She had an uneasy feeling that this *just-for-the-fun-of-it* race was a make or break moment in more ways than one.

There were twelve sheep racing and there'd already been a fancy dress contest for the best dressed owner, which Julian's daughter had won, in her sheep dog costume that was completely fitting for the event. Then there'd been a best-in-show contest for the non-racing sheep, who'd been brought up to the farm just for that. Ben, along with Nigel and David from the practice, had been asked to judge. Ellie had tried not to keep looking at him, as she'd stood watching, with Holly straining against her lead the whole time, but she hadn't been able to stop herself from turning back towards him. She missed him more than she'd ever have thought possible, for someone she'd known for such a short time.

In the end, Ellie had been desperate for race to start, so she had something else to think about. She wasn't expecting Betsy or Holly to bring the glory home to Seabreeze Farm, but for once she wanted to just have some fun. That was until the moment she was standing on the starting line, ready to let Holly go. If she looked up and saw Ben watching her, from somewhere around the track, Holly might not be the only one in danger of running in completely the wrong direction.

Ellie put Holly into her lane, the sheep blinking and immediately putting her head down to graze, even though the grass was at winter levels and almost bare. It wasn't an auspicious start.

'Go on girl, you can do it.' Ellie couldn't help laughing to herself, forgetting all about who might be watching, as she noticed the other handlers giving their sheep similar encouragement. Anyone would have thought the country air had gone to their heads.

'I'm going to count down from three and then release the rope that's holding them back, so if you give your sheep a pat on the behind at the same time, it should get them moving.' Julian stood on a platform made from bales of hay stacked by the starting line. 'Three, two, one. We're off!'

Heavy rainfall, the night before, sent mud splattering up as the sheep set off, racing towards the sound of children rattling buckets of sheep nuts at the finishing line. All except Holly that was. When the crowd cleared, she was still standing exactly where she'd started, scuffing her lips against the ground, desperately trying to pull up some grass.

'Why isn't she moving?' Julian called across to Ellie, who shrugged her shoulders.

'No idea.'

'Maybe being a bit lopsided isn't her only issue.' Caroline, Julian's wife, walked over to stand next to Ellie. 'She doesn't seem to be reacting to the sound of the sheep nuts in the bucket – that usually has them all running. You really didn't know what you were getting into when you took her in, did you!' As Caroline laughed, a cheer was already going up to signal that the winner had finished the race.

'Maybe I can try to tempt her with some sheep nuts and walk backwards until we get to the finish line.' It didn't matter whether Holly finished, but Ellie wanted her to. Whatever issues Holly might have, and however many problems she caused by escaping and disobeying every command, Ellie would always be glad she'd given her a home and a second chance.

'It's worth a try...' Caroline handed Ellie a bucket of sheep nuts and she ducked under the rope to stand in front of Holly.

'Come on girl.' Shaking the bucket, Holly moved a couple of steps forward, but, when she wasn't given any nuts, she dropped her head again and pulled at the grass. 'And they say sheep are stupid!' Ellie put a few sheep nuts into one hand and rattled the bucket again with the other. Holly took the offered nuts and moved another couple of steps forward, as Ellie began walking backwards. She repeated the process, giving Holly a small handful of nuts each time, all the way to the finish line. Holly got an even bigger cheer than the winner and Ellie wasn't the only one crying with laughter by the time Holly finally made it to the end.

A journalist from the local paper came over to interview them after the race. There were lots of photos taken of Holly and Betsy, who it turned out, much to Ellie's delight, had won the race. Afterwards everyone seemed to want their photograph taken with Holly, and even the local camera crew took some footage, so it was almost half an hour before Ellie had the chance to speak to her mum.

'Well, Holly certainly made her presence felt!' Karen patted the ewe's neck as she spoke. 'Our little superstar delivered the goods after all and that chap from the local paper took down some details about the farm which he said he'd try to mention in his article. You never know, it might even get us a booking or two. Alan wants to take us out to dinner tonight to celebrate.'

'That would be lovely.' Ellie looked down at her jeans, which were covered in flecks of half-chewed sheep nuts. 'Although I might have to change first!'

'Did you get a chance to speak to Ben? We were wondering if he might want to join us for dinner.'

'I've messaged him a couple of times now and he hasn't replied, so I think that ship has sailed. I didn't want to embarrass him, or myself, by trying to talk to him in front of people, if that's not what he wants.'

'Oh love, he'll see sense eventually.' Betsy was tugging on the lead rope that Karen was holding; head down, rewarding herself for winning the race by pulling up whatever she could find. The grass was much thicker off the track and no self-respecting sheep was going to miss the opportunity for a free feed. They didn't care how heartfelt the conversation going on around them might be.

'I was an idiot, but do you know what? It's going to be okay even if Ben decides to ignore me for the rest of my life. I'm not going to pretend I don't miss him and I wish I'd been honest from the start, but I really do love the life I've got here. I've laughed so much today and these animals of ours' – Ellie stroked Holly's ear – 'are making me the happiest I've ever been. I think I must be a chip off Aunt Hilary's old block after all!'

'You were meant for this life sweetheart. I think Hilary realised that long before either of us did.' Karen squeezed her daughter's hand. 'But she wouldn't want you to end up like she did and, if it had been in her power to get her fiancé back in her life, she'd have pulled out all the stops to do it.'

'I've apologised and I've tried to explain, but I think what happened with his ex-fiancée means he finds it hard to trust and now I've broken the trust we'd built up between us.' Ellie sighed. 'But today I finally forgave myself for being the person I was with Rupert. I just want the best for the farm and our little four-legged family and, even back when I was making decisions I'm not proud of, I just wanted the best for our little family then too.'

'I know you did, love, and you've got nothing to forgive your-self for.' Karen gave her hand another squeeze. 'But don't give up on Ben, he's one of the best.'

'None of that matters if he thinks I'm one of the worst though, does it? No, I'm better off on my own. You'd better get used to the idea of our menagerie of animals growing, because I've got a feeling I'm going to beat Aunt Hilary's record.' Ellie smiled, blinking back the tears that were suddenly burning the backs of her eyes. What she'd said to her mum was true – most of the time she was happier than she'd even been – but Ben had been so much a part of her life since she'd moved to Seabreeze Farm and, however much she might pretend otherwise, there'd always be something missing without him.

20

The day after the race, Holly's performance seemed to be all over social media, with the hashtags #SeabreezeFarm and #Hollythe-Sheep even trending on Twitter. Traffic to the farm's website was up by more than a thousand per cent and there'd even been some emails enquiring about bookings, with a whole new side-line of children's parties looking like it might be in the offing.

After Ellie had finished answering all the queries, she wandered down to the bottom paddock, where Gerald's name-sake was scraping his teeth against the almost bald ground of the paddock. Karen and Alan had taken care of all the animals' needs, whilst she'd been busy in the office, so there was nothing to do but think.

Alan had taken them out for dinner as promised the night before, to a lovely cosy pub nestled by the harbour in Kelsea Bay. Every moment she spent with Alan made her even fonder of him, but seeing him and her mother together had brought something home to her too: there was a distinct danger she could become the third wheel. When her mother had talked about coming to the realisation that Ellie had her own life, after she'd got engaged to Rupert, and that, one day, she'd want to move on, Karen had accepted that sometimes three really could be a crowd. Except now it was Karen who'd met someone she wanted to make a life with, and it was Ellie who was going to need to step back and allow room to make that happen.

If Karen decided to move to Crabtree Farm when she married Alan, they'd only be next door, but it would change things forever and Ellie would take another step towards fitting exactly into the space that Aunt Hilary had left behind. It was a lot to take in and she needed some time to work out what to do next, but there was no better place to think than outside on the farm. Sitting on the large flat stone at the edge of Gerald's paddock, the cliffs of France, just visible across the sea, were shrouded in a cloak of mist. The leaves on the trees at the edge of the woods had turned to shades of orange and brown. Autumn had now fully taken hold, after such a wonderful summer, which had been almost perfect. Now it felt as though everything was changing again.

'I thought I might find you here.' The voice behind her almost made Ellie fall off the rock, but she recognised it immediately

'Ben, you nearly made me pass out!'

'I know, and I'm sorry. Sorry about scaring you, and sorry about overreacting so badly to all that stuff with Rupert. Everyone's been telling me I'm a bloody idiot, but stupid pride made me dig my heels in and now I'm terrified I might have blown it.'

'What do you mean *everyone*?' Ellie's cheeks went hot at the thought that her mum might have tried to intervene and persuade Ben to forgive her. If he'd been nagged into finally coming over to see her, then he could turn around and leave again.

'Julian and Caroline, my parents, Daisy, Nathan and Alan to name a few, not to mention everyone at the practice.' Ben looked at her in that gentle way he had and some of the tension in her spine started to relax. 'It wasn't that I ever doubted you, but I just kept thinking that if I wasn't enough for Pippa – who wasn't anywhere near as amazing as you – how could I be enough for you? You're beautiful, funny and clever, and when I thought about trying to recover if you left for someone who could give you the life you deserve, it was like someone had punched me in the stomach. Having some control over when that happened, and kidding myself that it wouldn't hurt so much if I didn't let myself fall any more in love with you, seemed like the best solution.'

'Pippa was the idiot and I bet she regrets it every day, because I know better than anyone that it doesn't matter how much money you've got in the bank if you're with the wrong person. But I also know that a relationship is nothing without trust.' Ellie slid off the rock and stood up to face Ben. 'How do you know that you're not going to stop trusting me again, if I do or say the wrong thing?'

'Because I watched you yesterday.' A smile was tugging at the corners of Ben's mouth as he looked at her, those killer dimples appearing in his cheeks as he gave in to it. 'You and Holly were so funny, and when you threw your head back and laughed, I realised I couldn't possibly love you any more than I did already. It made me see how much the farm means to you too and how being here is exactly where you're meant to be. I can see now that you don't want a different life than the one you've got at Seabreeze, I just don't know if there's still room for me in it?'

'Well, there are always plenty of jobs to do around here. You know, mucking out and that sort of thing.' She was teasing him now and fighting an almost overwhelming urge to kiss him. Somehow he'd found exactly the right words and she was more certain about him than she'd ever been. They'd both been stupid, but they'd been given the sort of second chance that Hilary and her beloved fiancé had never got. 'How does starting with Dolly's stable sound? It turns out that bringing up three kids makes a lot of mess!'

'I'll happily stay on mucking out duty for the rest of my life, if that's what it takes.' Ben was smiling again and she really wasn't going to be able to stop herself from kissing him for much longer.

'*The rest of your life?*'

'If I get the chance. I love you, Ellie, and now I've seen you racing the world's slowest sheep, I know that's never going to change!' Ben smiled again, as she took a step towards him.

'I love you too. I think I have from the moment I saw you taking care of Gerald and ranting at me for not looking after him!'

'Oh God, I really have got a lot of making up to do, haven't I?'

'You can start with this.' Ellie closed the last remaining space between them, finally kissing him and releasing all the pent up passion of wondering for the past two weeks if she'd ever get to kiss him again. It might have been a movie scene moment, except that instead of the soft strains of a love song, Gerald decided to serenade them by braying loudly instead. Laughing, Ellie pulled away. 'Gerald might be doing his best to make sure he stays number one at Seabreeze Farm. But I love everything about my life in Kelsea Bay, and the best part of that is you.'

'Do you think you could put up with me long term? Forever, even? Despite my lack of country dancing prowess and the potential for being a total idiot that I never knew I had?'

'Oh, I think so, but only if you kiss me like that every single day to take my mind off it.' She laughed again as he pulled her back into his arms and Gerald broke into another raucous chorus. It might not be quite the perfect Hollywood movie moment, with a donkey making that sort of racket, but who needed perfect when there was all of this instead?

EPILOGUE

Alan had made good on the vow that his wedding to Karen would be the second one at Seabreeze Farm. It had been intimate, beautiful and exactly the sort of day Karen had wanted. Now, six months after she'd become Mrs Crabtree, it was Ellie's turn to take centre stage.

'Are you nervous?' Karen watched Ellie applying lipstick in the mirror in front of her.

'A bit, but not nearly as much as I thought I would be.' Ellie turned to look at her. 'Because I know marrying Ben is the right thing to do and I can't wait.'

'You'd better get a wiggle on, love, or it's Ben who'll be the one left waiting.'

'Do I look okay?' Ellie looked from Karen to Olivia and back again, and it was impossible to believe she even needed to ask the question. Karen had caught her breath and the tears had come all too easily, when she'd first seen Ellie in her wedding dress, during one of the numerous fittings. But seeing her again now, with her hair and makeup done, she looked even more fantastic.

'Sweetheart, you're the most beautiful bride I've ever seen.'

'Oh El, your mum's right.' Olivia's words seemed to be catching in her throat too. 'You look so beautiful and I suppose I should thank you for not making me wear the mint green ballerina dress you picked out when we first promised to be each other's bridesmaids, when we were about eight!'

'You could have carried it off!'

'Grandma is going to be in bits when she sees you in her dress.' Karen dabbed her eyes. Her parents had flown in from Spain for the wedding and the sense of a family coming together to celebrate one of the most pivotal moments in life filled the air.

'She told me Aunt Hilary paid for the dress and it was part of what made the day so special for her and Granddad, even though losing her fiancé in the war meant Aunt Hilary never got a wedding of her own. Knowing that part of her is here too makes it feel so right.'

'All of this feels like it was meant to be. You being left the farm, meeting Ben, Karen and Alan...' Olivia smiled. 'There's definitely something special about this place.'

'Aunt Hilary always said there was a plan for everything that happens in life and I can't help thinking that Seth arriving in Kelsea Bay at the same time as you came home from Australia was meant to be too.' Ellie winked and Karen didn't miss the smile that had crept onto Olivia's face.

'It's early days, but if I'd known Ben's best friend from uni would turn out to be like Seth, I'd have come back from Oz even sooner.'

'Not just to be with us then?' Karen smiled and put an arm around her daughter's best friend. 'Because we wanted you to come home before you even got on that plane.'

'She's right you know and there's no better place to put down permanent roots than in Kelsea Bay. Take it from me.' Ellie smiled. 'And now that you're back home I've got everything I've ever wanted.'

'Not to mention more animals than Noah!' Karen laughed again. 'Only you could ask for rescued ex-battery hens as wedding presents. You've certainly got over your fear of birds now.'

'I've got over my fear of lots of things.' Ellie took an audible intake of breath, as she looked at her mother. 'Right I suppose we better get this show on the road then, I don't want to keep Ben waiting too long.'

'Alan's downstairs ready for you, but your transportation to the ceremony is already outside.'

'It's less than two hundred metres down to the gazebo.' Ellie looked puzzled. 'Oh don't tell me he's been training Joey to pull a cart, or I'm going to get a leg up onto one of the donkeys!'

'Not quite, just have a look. You can see from the window.' Karen held her breath as her daughter walked over to look out.

'Oh Mum, I can't believe it!' Ellie turned back to face her, tears of the happy kind in danger of undoing her makeup. 'Is it really Barry?'

'It is. Alan started trying to track him down last autumn, because he wanted to surprise you for Christmas. But it took ages to find him and then get him back to the way he should be. Now Barry's as good as when he rolled onto the driveway of Seabreeze Farm for the very first time.'

'I don't think I'm going to make it through this day!' Ellie hugged her mum, as Karen did her absolute best not to dislodge the veil. 'It's too much for anyone to have asked for.'

'No it isn't, it's exactly what you deserve.' Kissing her daughter's cheek, Karen offered up a silent thank you to her wonderful aunt, because Ellie wasn't the only one who'd got everything she wanted. Up until now, Karen's biggest regret in life had been to saddle Ellie with a father who cared more about thinking up scams to make money, so that he could fritter it away again gambling on horses, than he did about his beautiful daughter. But now Karen had finally found someone in Alan who more than filled that gap. Aunt Hilary had probably planned it all out, knowing her. She'd always been the wisest person Karen knew. Her legacy would carry on, and animals in need would always have a home on her land, but it was time to welcome in a whole new era at Seabreeze Farm. And today was just the start.

ACKNOWLEDGMENTS

I hope you have enjoyed the first novel in the Seabreeze Farm series. Although I don't own a donkey sanctuary, I was born a stone's throw from the cliffs that overlook the English Channel. I also grew up on a small holding, where taking in stray animals was a fairly regular event and, by the time I'd left home, I'd done everything from covering the night shift feeds for abandoned lambs to delivering a foal with nothing more than the aid of an Encyclopaedia Britannica – long before the days of Google! So I've drawn upon a lot of personal experiences to write the Seabreeze Farm series and it's very close to my heart as a result.

This book is dedicated to the wonderful Jones family. They are an example of everything a family should be and despite losing their beautiful eldest daughter, Nicky, they continue to demonstrate the love, support and zest for life that everyone should try to emulate.

The support for my books from bloggers and reviewers so far has been incredible and I can't thank them enough. To all the readers who choose to spend their time and money reading my books, and especially those who take the time to get in touch, it means such a lot to me and I feel so privileged to be doing the job I love.

Thanks too to all the subscribers to my newsletter, if you haven't signed up yet you can find the link on my Twitter account and Facebook author page. There are lots of opportunities to enter competitions and contribute to the books by naming a character or, in the case of the Seabreeze Farm series, an animal! You'll also receive exclusive free short stories from time to time too.

My thanks as always go to the team at Boldwood Books for their help, especially my amazing editor, Emily Ruston, for lending me her wisdom to get this book into the best possible shape and set the scene for the next book in the series. Thanks too to my wonderful copy editor and proofreader, Candida, for all her hard work. I'm really grateful to Nia, Claire, Megan and Laura for all the work behind the scenes and especially for marketing the books so brilliantly, and to Amanda for having the vision to set up such a wonderful publisher to work with.

As ever, I can't sign off without thanking my writing tribe, The Write Romantics, and all the other authors who I am lucky enough to call friends.

Finally, as they always will, my biggest thank you goes to my family – Lloyd, Anna and Harry – for their support, patience, love and belief in the years it took to get to this point. I love you all, and baby Arthur, more than you'll ever know.

MORE FROM JO BARTLETT

We hope you enjoyed reading *Welcome to Seabreeze Farm*. If you did, please leave a review.

If you'd like to gift a copy, this book is also available as an ebook, digital audio download and audiobook CD.

Sign up to Jo Bartlett's mailing list for news, competitions and updates on future books.

http://bit.ly/JoBartlettNewsletter

Why not explore the top 10 bestselling The Cornish Midwives series:

ABOUT THE AUTHOR

Jo Bartlett is the bestselling author of nineteen women's fiction titles. She fits her writing in between her two day jobs as an educational consultant and university lecturer and lives with her family and three dogs on the Kent coast.

Visit Jo's Website: www.jobartlettauthor.com

 twitter.com/J_B_Writer

facebook.com/JoBartlettAuthor

instagram.com/jo_bartlett123

ABOUT BOLDWOOD BOOKS

Boldwood Books is a fiction publishing company seeking out the best stories from around the world.

Find out more at www.boldwoodbooks.com

Sign up to the Book and Tonic newsletter for news, offers and competitions from Boldwood Books!

http://www.bit.ly/bookandtonic

We'd love to hear from you, follow us on social media:

facebook.com/BookandTonic

twitter.com/BoldwoodBooks

instagram.com/BookandTonic